WHEN HE WATCHES

A HALLIE MILLER NOVEL

JEN MURPHY

Set in Adobe Garamond Pro

Design and typeset by Matthew Revert

FIRST EDITION, 2022

LILYKAT PRESS, publisher.

ISBN 979-8-9860219-3-5 (Hardback)
ISBN 979-8-9860219-4-2 (Paperback)

For my mother, Patricia Newman,
who is and will always be my hero.

PROLOGUE

Ronald sat in front of the large monitor screen waiting for Veronica to come into view. He leaned back, raising his scrawny and excessively hairy arms above his head to stretch his back while he waited. In the quiet of his apartment, he could hear the twangy, Middle Eastern music from the hookah bar beneath him radiating up through the dusty, wooden floor underneath his socked feet, the bottoms permanently gray. He didn't have much in the one room studio: a secondhand, twin size bed, the mattress stained from its previous bed-wetting occupant; a ratty couch, also second or possibly thirdhand, that smelled of stale cigarettes and dog; a coffee table he bought online for $53.99 that had two deep drawers where he stored his outdated video tapes and CDs; a small dresser where he kept his three pairs of underwear, sweat pants, old concert t-shirts, and two work uniforms; and a large wooden desk, where he ate all of his meals and where his favorite possession resided: his LG UltraFine 5K Display 27-inch monitor that was hooked up to his MacBook Pro. His laptop and monitor were the only two things of any value in the dreary apartment, which sat above the hookah lounge, a tattoo shop, and pizza joint in Ybor City.

Ybor City, located just north of downtown Tampa, dated back to the late 1800's and once served as the cigar-making capital of the world. Its streets still retained much of the original red clay brick and were lined with many of the historic buildings built at the turn of the century but have become home to hip restaurants, bars, retro clothing shops, eclectic stores, and residences, while classic streetcars carry visitors from one end of the city to the other. But these streets also harbor a darker, though not altogether secret, history: for over sixty years it constituted the epicenter of Tampa's organized crime world, where bootleg liquor, prostitution and illegal gambling were a way of life. And with that life came murder and violence at the hands of mobsters battling over control of the illegal but extremely lucrative *bolita* racket, a lottery-like gambling game that originated in Cuba and found its way to Ybor in the 1880's.

Tampa native, Charlie Wall, Tampa's original gangster, controlled Ybor, including the bolita games, for many years until the Italian mobsters moved in and forcefully took over. For a ten-year period in the 1930's, known as the "Era of Blood," Italian mobster Ignacio Antinori battled Wall for control of the "little ball" lottery and other illegal activities, brutally killing each other's associates along the way. Wall eventually relinquished power to the Italians and headed south to Miami after his best friend and associate was gunned down on the front porch of his Ybor home. In 1940, a sawed-off-shotgun wielding thug blew the back of Antinori's head off while he was having lunch in Tampa with a female companion after which the Trafficante crime family took over Ybor. Wall returned to Tampa in 1950 and, in 1955, was found in a bloody heap on the floor of his Ybor home with his head beaten in and his throat slashed. Santos Trafficante Jr. was alleged to have ordered the hit.

This dark, brutal history of Ybor appealed to Ronald. He often wondered what his apartment was used for and who lived in it back in those days. Was it a brothel, inhabited by prostitutes servicing the gangsters, corrupt politicians and law enforcement officers who were on the mafia payroll? Or maybe it was a safe house for one of Wall's or Antinori's or Trafficante's associates who had to hide out after carrying out another hit until the heat wore off. He refused to believe it was just an ordinary apartment, lived in by factory workers or other unremarkable common men, working grueling hours at unrewarding jobs, just like him.

Ronald's cheerless room was devoid of any pictures or personal adornments. The walls were bare, a telling reflection of his lonely life. The sole window in the 550 square foot space overlooked 7th Avenue, the main thoroughfare in the City and the site of block parties, festivals, and parades, the most famous of which was Gasparilla. He especially loved Gasparilla, Tampa's pirate-themed invasion that rivaled Mardi Gras – not that he ever attended. Ronald preferred to watch from his only window, as women in throngs dressed up like pirate wenches, wearing lowcut bustiers and other revealing outfits, walked by on the street below.

After his Mac came to life, Veronica finally appeared on his screen.

"Well, hello, Veronica," he whispered towards the screen, involuntarily blushing as his body responded to the sight of her.

He adjusted the brightness on his screen so he could see the petite, beautiful brunette a little more clearly. As she walked towards her bedroom, she unclasped the front of her bra under her pink silk blouse, pulled her left bra strap down her arm and over her hand, then the right, while in one swift move pulling the bra out of the right side of her blouse.

He clicked a few buttons on his keyboard and the view on the screen changed. Veronica was sitting on her bed, back to the camera, reaching down to undo the straps on her black patent leather heels. His gaze never left the monitor as she got up, unzipped her black skirt, letting it drop to the floor, revealing her perfect ass in a pink lace thong. He watched her as she bent over to pick up the skirt and shoes and then his eyes followed her as she walked towards the master bathroom and closet that were just out of view. He hoped she would return in one of her tight, white t-shirt mini dresses or tank tops and shorty shorts she often wore around the house.

While he waited for Veronica to emerge from the closet, Ronald opened a new tab on the screen in front of him, clicked on the saved link, and logged in, the Mac automatically filling in his password for the often-visited site. The screen before him came to life, and after a few clicks, Sheada came into view, stretching on her yoga mat, in her tight yoga pants and sports bra, her long brown hair tied up in a ponytail. He quickly split the screen so he could have Veronica open on one side and Sheada on the other, side by side. His gratification was interrupted by a knock at the door. He quickly minimized the tabs on his screen and went to the door, unlocked the deadbolt, and cautiously peered out through the narrow crack he allowed.

"Delivery," said the young, tattooed kid standing outside of his door holding his order from the burger place down the street. The kid had dark hair piled into a man-bun, a pierced septum, gages in his ears and never looked up from his phone while holding the white plastic bag imprinted with the words *Thank You* in red lettering out toward him.

Despite his annoyance at the kid's apathy, he managed to mumble a polite "thanks" before he closed and re-deadbolted the door and carried the greasy, indulgence-filled plastic bag to his desk. He reached into the retro olive-colored compact fridge, which was in the tiny kitchenette just to the right of the desk, to retrieve a cold Pabst Blue Ribbon. The only contents of the fridge, besides the PBR, consisted of half and half for his Folgers instant coffee, an expired tub of cream cheese, mustard, and a jar of pickle spears that had probably been in there for at least six months. Adjacent to the small refrigerator in the wall-less kitchenette was a small cabinet with a drawer for his silverware and a neutral-colored Formica countertop, stained from his absolute disregard for anything nice. Next to the cabinet was another cabinet fitted with a small stainless-steel sink, cluttered with his dirty coffee cups and food-caked silverware, which abutted a two-foot wide, two burner gas stove, not that it ever got used. The dreary apartment was small but completely suited most of his needs.

He settled in again at his desk in front of the monitor, sipping on his PBR as he sat down. He pulled up the screens he had been watching before, checking on Veronica first and then Sheada. They were incredibly satisfying to watch. He liked to imagine that he was there in their homes with them, waiting for Veronica to bring him a lovely dinner and waiting for Sheada to finish her exercise to return her attention to him. As he watched the women on his screen, he put his burger down on the wrapper in front of him and wiped the grease onto his gray Motley Crue t-shirt. He clumsily reached into his discolored, frayed sweatpants, took hold of his small, limp penis in his clammy right hand while his intense gaze never left the screen. As he watched Veronica, braless, in a white tank top, preparing dinner in her kitchen and Sheada bending over with her ass to the camera in one of her yoga poses, he felt his carrot-sized manhood finally starting to grow. After he finished, which didn't take long, he picked up his burger with the same hand that had just been down his pants and took a big, satisfying bite. He watched his ladies, as he liked to think of them, until he fell asleep with his hand down his pants, remnants of his greasy burger trapped in the sparse, wiry black hair growing out of his chin, and his head completely tilted back into oblivion.

CHAPTER ONE

Hallie Miller sat in the back of the courtroom as the jury and two alternates – six women and eight men – filed into the jury box. Hallie had agonized over what to wear that morning, changing her outfit multiple times, as if what she wore would make any difference on the proceedings she had come to watch. She finally settled on one of her more conservative suits, which consisted of a short black jacket, matching skirt that fell just above the knee, a cream-colored camisole, and her four-inch black leather platform heels. In the past year, since her divorce, she had struggled to lose the twenty pounds she had gained over the two years she was at her unhappiest. Fitting into her suit that day reminded Hallie how much she had accomplished since divorcing her cheating ex-husband David and how much happier she was now. She had pulled her long, dirty blonde hair into a tight ponytail, leaving a few wisps out to act as long bangs to frame her fair complexioned face. She sat on the hard, wooden bench and watched the last of the spectators hurry into the crowded courtroom to secure one of the remaining seats. Hallie checked her phone, making sure it was on silent, and quickly scanned her emails and texts. She saw she had a text from her daughter, Katie, who was away at college in subrural New York, twelve hundred miles north of their home in Tampa.

"Hey Mom, hope ur doing ok today. ILYSM! Call me later."

Hallie didn't even grimace anymore at Katie's grammatical transgressions. She was just glad to hear from her.

"Hi honey, I'm ok, I love you more. I'll call you tonight. Just got into court now," Hallie typed, hoping to hit send before the bailiff called the court into session.

Just as the text window confirmed delivery of Hallie's text, the bailiff called out, "All rise, the Honorable Andre Washington presiding. Court is now in session."

Hallie slipped her phone into her black Coach purse and watched as the towering judge came in and sat behind the bench. Before going to law school, Judge Washington played defensive end for Florida State University and then for the New York Giants for two years before sustaining a career-ending knee injury. He then returned home to Florida, attended University of Florida law school, and practiced as a commercial litigation attorney in St. Petersburg for twenty years before being elected to the bench in Pinellas County, initially assigned to the family law division before being reassigned to the criminal division a few years ago. Hallie had always liked and respected Judge Washington. He was a tough litigator, but he also had a reputation for being fair and ethical, which is probably why he beat his opponent for the judgeship by a landslide.

As all the sitting judges in Hillsborough County had recused themselves from a criminal trial involving one of their former colleagues, Judge Washington was brought over from across the bridge to preside over the trial of the State of Florida v. William Stephens.

"Is the State ready to begin," Judge Washington asked, looking to his left at the fiery, redheaded prosecutor sitting at the State's table.

Amy Stoll stood up, "The State is ready, Your Honor," and then sat back down.

"Very well," he said, now turning to the defense, "Any last minute motions or housekeeping before we get started?"

"The Defense is ready to proceed as well, Your Honor," answered the tall man rising from the adjacent table as he addressed the court. He was dressed in an expensive-looking navy suit, with a crisp white shirt and a red tie, and had his wavy brown hair pulled into a knot at the nape of his neck. He was clean-shaven apart from the trim goatee that covered his chin.

Carl Adams, referred to as "Creepy Carl" by most female lawyers in town, was a dogged advocate for his clients, even those charged with the most heinous of crimes. Hallie wondered if having to delve into the circumstances of the most horrific and often brutal offenses had jaded Carl, as there was no line he would not cross, especially if he thought it would get him laid or the win. There was no question that he could be charming when he wanted to, self-confident bordering on cockiness, even funny at times. But after spending a few minutes with him, women either wanted to slap him or sleep with him, most often the former. These same characteristics and sharp litigation skills often won over the jury, which is why it was no surprise to Hallie that he was representing the defendant, William Stephens, a former judge in the very same division. The last time Hallie saw Carl at a Hillsborough County Bar Association happy hour about two months after her divorce, he offered his friendship as well as the benefits of that friendship "that would accrue to both of them," he assured her with a wink, should she feel lonely. Hallie steadfastly declined, falling decidedly into the category of women who felt like scouring their souls after being in his presence.

The judge nodded at the prosecutor, her sign to proceed with her opening statement.

Amy rose from her chair, smoothed the back of her classic Donna Karan black dress as she proceeded to the center of the court room, and placed her yellow legal pad and pen down on the lectern. She turned towards the jury, smiling warmly at them as if she had just run into an old friend on the street to disguise the ice that coursed through her veins and contempt she felt towards the current defendant. Amy knew the jury had to like you to believe you.

"Your Honor," she said, nodding deferentially at the bench, "ladies and gentlemen of the jury, good morning. My name is Amy Stoll, and I represent the State of Florida in this case. We are here today because a terrible crime has been committed. My job is to present the evidence to you, to prove to you through that evidence what precisely happened to Naomi Banks on the night she was brutally murdered, and to prove to you, beyond a reasonable doubt, who bears responsibility for this depraved crime, for the brutality Ms. Banks suffered. You will hear testimony from witnesses who saw the young mother out on a jog in her Carrollwood neighborhood on the night she was murdered, never to return home that night. And you will hear evidence that will explain what transpired, from the time she left her home – the home she shared with her loving husband and young child – to the time her battered body, almost unrecognizable due to the severity of her injuries, was discovered a few days later, dumped on the front porch of a dilapidated, abandoned house nearby. Your job will be to evaluate all of the evidence presented to you and, if I've done my job properly, return a verdict of guilty of murder in the first degree against the defendant, Mr. William Stephens." Amy paused and gestured for the first time towards the defendant, forcing the jury to follow her hand to the man sitting at the defense table.

Judge Stephens looked thinner and less confident than he did the last time Hallie saw him. His expensive Italian wool charcoal gray suit hung awkwardly on his gaunt frame and, under the unforgiving courtroom lighting, his ashen face appeared to have aged a lifetime in the past year. The arrogance and power that he once brandished to intimidate his adversaries and conquests were gone, having been replaced by a somber realization that he had been beaten – beaten by the very system over which he used to reign. The time behind bars awaiting trial had not been kind to Judge Stephens, Hallie thought, which offered her meager satisfaction for what he had done to her and many other women.

The prosecutor continued, "Naomi Banks didn't deserve what happened to her that night. You're going to hear testimony about how she came home after a long day at work, excited to see her husband and five-year-old son, and put a chicken in the oven to roast before going for a quick run, as she did on many nights. According to Mr. Banks, Naomi knew the chicken would take about an hour to roast, the seasoned skin turning a crispy brown, which gave her enough time to go for a run and shower before serving her family dinner. She ran along her usual path through her Carrollwood neighborhood, adjacent to the golf course, probably at a rate of just over eight minutes per mile. When she got going, her pace could dip into the sevens. You're going to hear from witnesses who will testify that they saw Naomi run past their homes just after 6:20 on that fateful Tuesday night, and then saw her again at about 6:45 running towards the direction of her house, which was about a mile and a quarter from where she was last seen. But before we get to what happened to her in that short stretch between where she was last spotted and her home, I want to tell you about what you will also learn about the defendant," Amy paused again, returning to the lectern and pretending to glance at her notes, just to let the moment build. She had the jury's full attention.

"The defense is likely going to tell you that the Mr. Stephens, at the time of Naomi's murder, was a well-respected, upstanding criminal court judge in this very courthouse. Well-respected, indeed. But you will also learn that Mr. Stephens knew Naomi, as she was an attorney who also worked in this courthouse, in the very same division as the defendant. More important, you will learn that the defendant lived in the same neighborhood as Naomi; in fact, you will learn that his house is situated in the one mile stretch between the location where Naomi was last seen and where her home is located," she paused again, giving the jury a moment to reflect on the full implication of what she had just said.

"The medical examiner is going to testify about the wounds Naomi suffered that night, and about what ultimately caused her death. He will tell you about the significant head injury Naomi sustained that night, but, as he will explain, that's not what killed her. He also will tell you about the multiple stab wounds found on Naomi's body, but that those aren't what killed her either. You will learn that those were inflicted post-mortem – in other words, after she was already murdered. And you will learn that her body, again post-mortem, was sexually violated."

Amy paused to let the last statement stick in the jury's minds.

She continued, "The medical examiner will testify that Naomi died from being strangled and that the defendant's DNA was found under her fingernails. The testimony and evidence presented in this case will show that Mr. Stephens, and only Mr. Stephens, had the motive, opportunity, and ability to carry out this brutal crime. The defense will try to refute or offer alternative explanations for these crucial pieces of evidence, but ladies and gentlemen of the jury, when this case is over, the evidence will point to only one logical conclusion beyond a reasonable doubt: that the defendant, William Stephens, did willfully and with premeditation kill Naomi Banks, after which he then stabbed and raped her. We will ask you therefore to return a verdict of guilty of murder in the first degree. Thank you," Amy said as she walked back to the prosecution table and calmly sat down, hiding the adrenaline rushing through her body.

"Great job," whispered her co-counsel and second chair, Wyatt Rademacher.

Creepy Carl made his way to the lectern and faced the jury. Hallie half expected him to say, in his best Joe

Pesci impersonation from the movie *My Cousin Vinnie*, "everything she just said is bullshit," but he did not. Instead, he addressed the jury in a more reserved manner than she expected from him, and he did his best to counter some of what the prosecutor said, including planting the seed that there could have been someone else who killed Naomi Banks. The defense had an uphill battle as the evidence against Judge Stephens was damning. But Carl was also very good at smoke and mirrors, so he should not be underestimated, Hallie thought.

Hallie had met Judge Stephens over twenty years ago, before he was a judge, when he was the managing partner of the prestigious firm that hired her out of law school. She was a bright young associate on her way to a promising career and on the fast track to partnership. But that all changed the night she went to a firm function with him and other lawyers from her firm. He slipped a roofie into her drink during dinner and brutally raped and sodomized her that night in her mostly unconscious state. She woke up in bed next to William Stephens bruised, bleeding and with no recollection of the night before.

When she realized what he had done to her, she was ashamed and didn't think anyone would believe her, including her first husband, Kevin Verona, a young prosecutor in the state attorney's office at the time. She remembered fleeing the hotel just before dawn and going straight to her good friend Paige's downtown apartment where Paige begged her to call the police. Paige Rhodes was another associate at the firm, having started at the same time as Hallie. They became instant friends and were still best friends to this day. But at the time, right or wrong, Hallie believed reporting him would ruin her legal career, reputation, and possibly her marriage, because it would be her word against his. It was very much a good old boys' club in the legal community with him one of its more powerful members. She left the firm shortly after the harrowing incident, having confided what happened to her to only two people at the time, Paige and her sister, Trisha. She hadn't even told Kevin; well, at least not back then.

Hallie learned she was pregnant about a month after she was raped but she and Kevin had had sex around the same time so either one of them could have been the biological father of her daughter, Katie. Hallie had convinced herself, and truly believed, that her ex-husband, Kevin, was Katie's biological father for almost eighteen years. But Judge Stephens' DNA was linked to Katie last year when Kevin, his current wife, Jodi, and Katie submitted their DNA to an ancestry genealogy company for a trip to Europe they were planning as a gift for Katie's graduation. The detectives investigating Naomi's murder found a link between the DNA found under Naomi's fingernails and Katie by searching a DNA database that allows law enforcement to upload DNA from a crime scene and search the database to see if it matches anyone (and to what degree) in the genealogy database when a violent crime has been committed.

When Hallie learned of the connection, she knew the awful truth that she had been denying and hiding for all those years: Judge Stephens, the sadistic fuck who raped her, was the biological father of her only daughter and the murderer of Naomi Banks. Hallie believed it would be a type of poetic justice for her if he was convicted of this brutal murder, knowing that it was Katie's DNA that led to his identification as a suspect. She sat in the back of the courtroom hoping that watching the trial would bring her the closure and vindication that had been denied to her for so long.

CHAPTER TWO

Hallie came home after a long day in court, pulling her black BMW into her driveway in Hyde Park, a semi-urban, but upscale neighborhood south of downtown Tampa. It was also walking distance to Bayshore Boulevard, an iconic symbol of affluence running the length of the Tampa Bay from downtown to the edge of the city, ending at Ballast Point, and lined with some of Tampa's premier homes. The four-and-a-half-mile sidewalk, known as the longest continuous sidewalk in the world, runs parallel to the water and is never lacking runners, walkers, bikers, and roller-bladers, many of whom are joined by their dogs. Dolphins and manatees are often seen swimming or chasing fish through the blue-green brackish water right up to the concrete wall separating the Bay from the sidewalk. Hallie imagined that the way she felt when she ran was how dolphins felt when they swam: free and uninhibited.

Hallie thought about the last year of her life and how much had changed as she undressed and tried to shed the tension from watching the first day of Judge Stephens' trial. She slipped out of her suit jacket, carefully hanging it over the back of the dining room chair, unclasped her sling-back heels, kicking them to the side, and perused her wine rack to decide which bottle of wine to select. There was no question she had earned a glass – or more – tonight, not that she needed an excuse to drink. But tonight, certainly, was a momentous occasion that had been long-coming. Today had brought up a lot of memories she hadn't had to think about in a while, and she needed to unwind. She found a nice, Alexander Valley Rodney Strong cabernet, one of her favorites, and opened it with her Williams Sonoma electronic wine opener: one of the few gifts from David that she actually loved and used often. David was her second and most recent ex-husband. Hallie divorced the son-of-a-bitch after it came out last year that he had been sleeping with several of his young high school students, including one whom he had impregnated.

Hallie hadn't realized how broken her marriage was at the time. In the year or two before their marriage ended, David had stopped touching her, stopped making her feel like a woman, and worst of all, stopped loving her. She should have known he was cheating on her, but she ignored his behavioral changes, thinking they were just in a slump, and she could fix it after Katie went away to college, just as she fixed everything else. That was her job, what she did best: fixed problems, overcame obstacles, saved the day. But not this time. When she found out he was living an entirely secret life, she was crushed and angry and heartbroken and all of those things women feel who wake up one day realizing they are sleeping next to a stranger, but knowing that he was sleeping with young girls at the high school where he was principal, Hallie knew he was a monster.

But she was also Hallie: strong, resilient, unbreakable Hallie, and she refused to give him that power, or more accurately, to let him or anyone else see the damage that he had done to her. No one, except maybe her mother, Rebecca, and her best friends, Bridget and Paige, saw her fall apart, saw her at her lowest moments. She may not have fully grieved the failure of her marriage, but she was beyond the sadness phase and well into the angry phase at this point in her life and she hated David, almost as much as she hated William Stephens. Both had betrayed and violated her, but in different ways. In some ways, David's betrayal was worse, more personal: he was a serial cheater and a pathological liar, but even more disgusting to Hallie, she had a daughter the same age as the young girls he manipulated and abused. She was heartbroken for his victims and angry for their parents. What he did was unforgivable.

After Hallie's divorce, Paige asked her to join her firm, Greenlee Remington, previously known as Greenlee, Remington & Stoll before Amy Stoll returned to the State Attorney's office earlier that year, primarily to act as the lead prosecutor in the Judge Stephens' trial. Amy was a board-certified trial lawyer and had started her career in the State Attorney's office before founding Greenlee, Remington &

Stoll with two of her old law school friends. After Judge Stephens was charged, the State Attorney asked Amy to come back to prosecute the case. Missing the thrill of the courtroom, Amy accepted, and the firm became Greenlee Remington.

Hallie had been out on her own for several years with a busy and successful practice but, at Paige's urging, agreed to meet with Elise Batsel, the managing partner of Greenlee Remington to hear her pitch. Hallie had known Elise for years and besides being an excellent real estate and land use lawyer, she was also known as a fierce advocate. Their paths crossed on deals from time to time and Hallie always enjoyed working with Elise, even if they were representing adverse parties. Hallie met Elise at Malio's, Hallie's favorite steakhouse and happy hour bar, to discuss the terms of the partnership.

The original Malio's, owned and operated by Malio Iavarone on a section of Dale Mabry Highway known as the "strip" back in the day, was the go-to steakhouse and lounge patronized by Tampa's mobsters, celebrities, and local elite for over thirty years. Although they were none of the above, whenever someone in Hallie's family had something important to celebrate, such as a birthday, a graduation, or some other notable event, Hallie's father, Charlie, would take them to Malio's. Hallie always thought her father was someone important by the way Malio treated them, but as she got older, she realized that was how Malio treated everyone and one of the reasons he was so successful. But he was good friends with her father and whenever Hallie saw him, he would tell her what a good man her father was. He would allude to some situation that her father helped him out of, although he never expounded on it more than to say, "Boy your father saved my hide one time. He was a good man, Hallie, the best of men." And so it would go, each time she saw him.

Her father, a family law attorney, was believed to have been shot by a client's estranged husband when Hallie was in college. No one was ever arrested or charged with her father's murder because the police said they didn't have enough evidence to investigate further. A few years after Hallie became a lawyer, she tried to obtain copies of the police reports and other records surrounding her father's death but learned the records had been destroyed, which was inconsistent with the department's retention policy on unsolved cases. Hallie desperately wanted to figure out who killed her father but without anything to go on, she believed it would be impossible. And then one hot July day, she learned all was not lost.

Hallie recalled it was a stifling, hot day during a fourth of July holiday weekend. She was still married to Kevin, and Katie was about two years old. Hallie's mother had invited them over, along with some other family and friends, to celebrate the holiday with a barbecue and pool party, but Rebecca had asked Hallie to come earlier than the other guests. When they arrived, she sent Kevin outside with Katie for a dip in the pool before it got too crowded, she suggested, and asked Hallie to stay back to help her retrieve two boxes from the attic. By the time they found the boxes, their faces were red and dripping with sweat as the attic was at least fifty degrees hotter than even the stagnant air outside. Rebecca climbed down the ladder first while Hallie handed her the old, dusty banker boxes, one at time. The boxes had been in the attic for the past ten years and had never been opened or their existence known since Rebecca had put them up there after her husband's death.

After they were both safely out of the attic, her mother went to the kitchen to pour them each a cold glass of her homemade lemonade.

"Jeez, Mom," Hallie complained, somewhat out of breath as she wiped the sweat off her face and neck with a cool, damp towel her mother had handed to her, "what is so important in these old boxes that couldn't wait until this sweltering heat ends? I think I might pass out."

Her mother calmly replied, as she sipped on her lemonade, "I felt it was time."

For the next ten minutes, Rebecca explained that she knew Charlie was dealing with a horrible case around the time of his death, despite the fact that he never talked about his cases or his clients at home, but he wasn't sleeping and he was doing things out of character, such as taking alternative routes home when they were all in the car with him, sometimes passing the house before circling back to park in the garage, deadbolting and chaining the door and obsessively checking to make sure all of the windows were locked, when they had often not bothered to lock the doors at all. When she asked him about it, he would dismiss it and say, "Better to be safe than sorry," kiss her on the cheek, and quickly change the subject. When he was shot and it was obvious the police were not going to investigate it properly, she decided to make copies of all his active case files before handing them over to her husband's friend and colleague who had agreed to take over the open cases and see them to conclusion. Her mother never told anyone about the files, including Hallie, until she learned that Hallie was trying to get copies of the old police reports. And that was when her mother told her what was in the boxes.

On that hot July day, sitting on the floor with the dusty boxes, her mother said, "Hallie, I know your father's killer is named in one of these files, and maybe it's time we find out who that is."

Hallie spent the next few months reading every word in every file but had only been able to narrow it down to a list of ten men who seemed capable of shooting her father, based on their violent histories against their wives or the contentiousness of the divorce proceedings. Based on additional research, including old newspaper articles and conversations with her mother, Hallie was able to eliminate three of the initial ten men from the list. That left seven but

Hallie was unable to narrow it down from there, without interviewing potential witnesses or family members of the men in question, to which both her mother and Kevin strongly objected at the time. They reminded her that she was a lawyer, not a detective, and she had to focus on her career and taking care of Katie. She reluctantly agreed and the boxes were ultimately put in Hallie's attic, moving with her each time she moved. Every once in a while, Hallie thought about her list of seven and would review their old case files, but never came any closer to narrowing down her list. She often vowed to go through the old boxes again, hoping she might see something that she had missed years before, but she never seemed to have the time. She hadn't looked in those old boxes in at least ten years.

But there she was again, months after her divorce, sitting across from Elise in a booth in the bar area at the downtown Malio's, discussing another important decision in her life. When Malio retired, the iconic restaurant on Dale Mabry closed, until Malio's son, Derek, opened a smaller, slightly more upscale version under the same name on the first floor of the distinctive beer can-shaped building that stood out among Tampa's skyline. Even though it was a new location, the vibe was the same and Hallie felt her father was there with her, just as he was when they celebrated the significant milestones in her life when he was alive.

After listening to Elise, Hallie knew it would be nice to work with colleagues again and enjoy all the perks of being with a firm: she would have people to handle her billing, handle her court filings, manage her IT and electronic file management, and do other administrative tasks she previously had to do herself. After two bottles of Faust, one of Hallie's favorite Napa Valley cabs, and three hours of conversation, Hallie accepted Elise's offer to join the firm on the spot. Over the next two weeks, with the help of Greenlee Remington's staff and IT department, Hallie transitioned all her clients and their files to her new firm.

She had been with the firm for eight months now and she loved it. Not only was it great working with Paige again but having the support she did was life changing. She used to spend half her weekends doing all the administrative tasks that now other people in the firm took care of for her. She loved just practicing law again, especially with the badass, powerful women lawyers with whom she had the good fortune to practice.

She walked into her laundry room, a small room adjacent to the kitchen, happy to find a pair of clean sweats and a tank top folded on top of the dryer. She closed the blinds on the back door of her 1920's Hyde Park bungalow, which led into the laundry room off the kitchen, before stripping down to her bra and thong. Then, with a sigh of relief, she removed her bra, which she placed on top of her blouse and skirt she had folded on top of the dryer. She pulled the clean black tank top over her head, but, unfortunately, not before an unseen and unknown camera had captured a number of pictures of her partially naked body, including a close up of her rosy-pink nipples on her large, milky-white breasts. And unbeknownst to Hallie, the photographer, if you could call him that, had just uploaded the images to a server somewhere in the abyss, more commonly known as the cloud.

CHAPTER THREE

Heather McLean was still getting used to the freedom of not always looking over her shoulder or living in constant fear. Her therapist explained to her that she was suffering from PTSD (post-traumatic stress disorder) from the years of abuse inflicted by her ex-husband and the years she spent terrified after her escape from him that he would find and kill her. She tried to remind herself that it would take time, but when she was having a particularly bad day, she would read and re-read the judgments from his murder and rape convictions and find comfort in the fact that he would never get out of prison.

She walked down the deserted downtown Tampa street from the law office where she worked as a paralegal towards the parking lot where she always parked along with the other monthly parkers. At this time of night, the parking lot only had a few cars left in it, including hers, and she was feeling uneasy. She heard footsteps approaching behind her, but when she turned to look, there was no one there. She knew downtown had a way of projecting sounds in between the buildings and the nearby parking garages that could play tricks on your mind, but it still unnerved her.

She pulled her purse up in front of her, hugging it into her body, while retrieving her keys and taking the top off the small can of mace attached to her keychain.

A black Lincoln Town Car with dark tinted windows passed by her, slowly, and turned left at the next block before pulling over into a parking spot on the right side of the road. The driver's side window was cracked open, and Heather could see the burning ember of a freshly lit cigarette and smoke billowing out of the opening. She would have to pass closely by the Town Car to get to the parking lot where her car was parked unless she crossed the street now and approached the lot from the other side. There was no reason to believe that the Town Car was anything other than a hired driver waiting to pick someone up from one of the nearby hotels, but Heather was jumpy and couldn't shake the uneasy feeling that she was being watched.

* * *

It was time to get away. Heather hadn't been back to North Carolina since she escaped her abusive ex-husband twelve years before, but she missed her friend, Julie, who had been her only friend when she lived in the Outerbanks. On that fateful night when she woke up on the beach, having been stabbed and beaten, she ran to her friend's salt-worn but warm and quaint cottage on the edge of the sometimes-unforgiving sea. The wooden ramp leading up to the front door, the rusty nails barely holding the deteriorated and weathered planks in place, warned the old woman inside she had a visitor before anyone reached the once welcoming, now-faded yellow door. There were colorful, glass windchimes hanging from rusty chains hooked into the eaves of the front porch, which provided an incongruent, faint symphony of delicate sounds as the easterly wind blew in from the Atlantic.

Her friend had rescued her on that cool night just as the last hint of darkness was succumbing to the rising orange sun, which was at once beckoning her to follow its warm embrace into the sea as the waves crashed around her and threatening to send her back to her torturer if he found her on the beach. Julie welcomed her that fateful night into her warm home just like the old lighthouse keepers would welcome and guide the wayward and sea-battered vessels into port. She cleaned her up, bandaged the wound on her neck that had missed anything significant by centimeters, and helped her run away. Without Julie, Heather would not be alive today.

Over the years, Heather called Julie from time to time to hear her voice, never speaking, or sent her a postcard with no return address and signed by someone named Margaret, but she knew Julie knew it was her. It was just her way of letting her know she was still safe. But it was always too dangerous to return, not knowing where Bobby was all those years. After he attacked three young women in Tampa the previous year, and confessed to the murder of a young coed, he avoided the death penalty by accepting a life sentence, without the possibility of parole. When he went away for good, Heather finally had her freedom back.

She packed a small suitcase with a few sundresses, her bathing suit, and some shorts and tank tops. Her neighbor, Courtney, had agreed to take care of Oscar, her orange tabby, while she was away for the week. Courtney was a sweet girl, in her late twenties, who worked at one of the high-end seafood restaurants up the street on the water. Heather didn't have many friends, but she and Courtney had become friendly, looking out for each other as they were both single and living alone. She dropped the envelope with the key to her apartment, instructions for Oscar, and a $20 bill in her neighbor's mailbox. She ended the handwritten note with:

Oscar has everything he needs and you know where I keep all his things — the $20 is for you to get yourself a couple of drinks and enjoy yourself! Thanks again!
— Heather

It was time for Heather to visit her old friend and resume her life. She no longer had to be afraid, especially of Bobby, who would live the rest of his life in prison. She longed to walk barefoot on the North Carolina beach under the moonlight, without fear, her feet gritty from walking on the cool, gray sand, while appreciating the beauty of the sand dunes and billowing seagrass and cattails that she had once only viewed as her shield. It was time to live again.

* * *

From inside his prison cell, Robert "Bobby" Johnson retrieved the picture of Heather he had managed to hide from the guards. He had paid the Broker $1,000 for his most prized possession. Actually, it was his only possession other than a few books and toiletries the prison allowed him to keep in his cell. He stared at her honey brown hair, the ringlets cascading around her face and past her shoulders – he always loved her hair long – and hazel eyes set against her ivory skin. He could tell the picture was taken at a distance with a zoom lens when she didn't know she was being photographed. It caught her in a rare, carefree moment, the wind blowing her hair off of her face, her lips almost curved into a smile, her eyes alive and happy, without their usual guardedness and distrust. Staring at her picture, he simultaneously loved her and hated her with the passion only a sociopath could feel. As he studied every feature of her face, every freckle across the bridge of her button nose, and traced the pink jagged scar on her neck in the photo with his finger – the same scar he had inflicted on her so many years before – he started quietly singing *Every Breath You Take* by the Police. He loved to play it for Heather. He always told her it was *their* song. Believing it was a love song, Heather thought it was sweet. But he knew it meant something more sinister. It meant she belonged to him forever.

He stared at the photo, the corners dog-eared from his rough hands holding it every night before going to sleep and every morning after he woke up. As he looked at the woman in the photo, he promised, just as he did every day, "I'll always be watching you, Heather, every single day, now that I've found you. Every breath you take, I'll be watching you until I watch you take your last one. I'll be there. Until your final breath."

He kissed the photo and placed it face down on his chest, while he continued to hum the popular and largely misunderstood song. He was oblivious to the sounds of the prison around him. As he hummed and focused on the picture of Heather, the colors of his eyes turned darker until they were almost indistinguishable from the black pupils in the center of his eyes.

CHAPTER FOUR

Hallie was one of the last attorneys in the office and all of the staff had gone home. The office was eerily quiet, devoid of all of the normal, daily activity of phone calls, printers, people conversing in the hallways. She grabbed a cold water from the mini-fridge she kept in her office and opened her email to see if she had anything else she had to respond to before she called it a day. She had a new notification from the judge's assistant in her upcoming breach of contract dispute.

This case was the absolute worst. Her client, Eden Feldman, a petite, pretty redhead and former professional tennis player turned sports agent had just secured the number seven seeded tennis player in the world. Originally, she had talked about going into business with her friend, Sheryl Gilbert, but Sheryl turned out to be unethical, disloyal, completely unprofessional, and frankly, a bit crazy. Eden figured out early on that Sheryl would be a liability, so she never formalized anything between them. When Eden terminated their business relationship, it terminated their friendship too. Eden took all of the clients with her, including the number seven player, because Sheryl didn't have anything to do with securing them. Nevertheless, Sheryl sued her for breach of an oral contract, claiming damages in the millions for the projected future agency fees she would not share as a result of the termination.

The lawsuit was completely frivolous but, unfortunately, anyone could sue anyone for anything these days and there was usually some bottom-feeding lawyer willing to take on a case like this. That wasn't how Hallie practiced, and she hated that good people like Eden had to pay her to defend these meritless cases. Hallie was doing her best, but the plaintiff's attorney was as unethical as her client. Hallie called Eden to let her know of the latest setback.

"Hi Eden, it's Hallie. So, they're trying to delay our upcoming mediation again. This time, her attorney is saying she has an unavoidable scheduling conflict," Hallie said, as she sighed into the phone, "I know you want this case to end so you can focus on your business but if I file a motion to oppose it, the judge will be pissed, because lawyers should be professional enough to be able to schedule a mediation without the court's involvement. The judge is already annoyed with the lack of movement in this case so I would rather her annoyance be focused on your former partner and her shitty, unethical lawyer rather than you."

"How long of an extension are they asking for?" Eden asked.

"Thirty days."

"Another month isn't going to change anything, I guess. It's just so frustrating. I have interviews with some other players who are unhappy with their current representation, which could be great for me, but I have to tell them about the ongoing litigation, which spooks some of them. Also, if I sign someone new, can she add that to her case to support her damages claim?"

"Well, of course, they'll argue they should be included, but as I've said all along, she doesn't have a case if this goes to court, which is probably why they continue to delay. You were friends and had discussed going into business together, but you never took any steps to formalize that business. The only written agreement you ever contemplated, but did not sign, was a standard operating agreement you pulled off the internet, which I would advise against doing again if you ever decide to go into business with anyone in the future. But fortunately, you never formed the LLC, you never signed the agreement, and, even if they try to argue it is evidence of your oral agreement, it doesn't contain any provisions that would bar you from retaining the clients you obtained and signed independently without her involvement or assistance."

"Don't worry, I've learned my lesson with this situation. I promise you, if I'm ever inclined to take on a partner again, you will be drafting the agreements before I do anything else," Eden sighed. "Okay, don't object to the extension."

She hung up with Eden and finished scanning through the rest of her unread emails. She realized she hadn't checked her junk folder in a few weeks, and every once in a while, a legitimate email was trapped by the filters in place. Thankfully, most were in fact junk or spam emails, but there was one email from a few weeks ago that piqued her interest as the sender's email address was from the Florida Department of Corrections:

To: HMiller@GRLaw.com
From: 1249078@FDOC.com
Subject: Legal Representation

Hello Ms. Miller:
I am an inmate in the Florida State Prison at Stark, wrongly accused and convicted, of course, but that's a story for another day. I have some important information to share with you about a very bad person that has a connection to your family, which you need to hear. Please come and see me when you can.
Yours truly,
Benjamin Young

Hallie read the email a few times. Why would someone from prison be writing her? She wasn't a criminal defense attorney. This had to be a mistake or one of those scams, like when someone calls an elderly person pretending to be their grandchild stranded in a foreign country and demanding them to western union money to them right away. At first, she was just going to delete it but then decided she would save it for the time being and maybe ask her friend Bridget's police officer husband to run the name through the prison system to see if he's actually an inmate. She also thought she might forward it to Peter, the firm's IT guy, to see if it was some type of phishing email or other scam. But she didn't want to think about it right now. She had been at the office all day and wanted to get out of there to go for a run to clear her head. She had a lot on her mind, and it was the only time she could sort things out.

As soon as she got home, Hallie changed into her running outfit and sat at the bottom of the stairs to lace up her running shoes she had left by the front door. She locked her front door, slipped her key into her waistband pocket, and stretched out her calves and thighs before beginning her run. Mrs. Butler, her neighbor, was out on her front porch filling bowls with fresh cat kibble for the neighborhood stray cats she liked to feed. Hallie waved; Mrs. Butler smiled and waved back. Since the murdered body of a young co-ed had been discovered under Mrs. Butler's hydrangea bushes the previous year, Mrs. Butler was more cautious, introverted, and less inclined to sit on her front porch and sip lemonade like she used to. That made Hallie sad, and she wondered how the events of last year had changed her own habits and feelings of security.

She was relieved that she and David had gotten that alarm system installed the previous year after they discovered someone had broken into their house, especially now that she lived alone since her divorce.

She selected her favorite running playlist, turned up her music in her headphones, and began her run towards Bayshore Boulevard. Her legs felt like twenty-pound weights were strapped to each thigh, having not run in a few weeks, but she knew she just needed to power through until she got her rhythm back.

"Where the hell is that so-called muscle memory," Hallie thought to herself, trying to counter all of the voices in her head and the aches in her body telling her to stop running. She kept running. That's what she did. One breath in, two breaths out, one breath in, two breaths out, just keep the rhythm, just keep going, that was all she could do. No matter what else around her failed, this was the constant. This is what she could always rely on, no matter what or who else in life let her down. She could count on herself, and her body, and her strength, and her perseverance, her determination, just like she used to count on her father. But then he was murdered, and she was lost for a few years until she discovered she was more like her father than she realized, but with her mother's softness and love of life. And she found her strength when she needed it most.

Her feet pounded against the concrete running path as she ran along the water, the sun having not yet set, reflecting off the dark, calm Bay waters and warming her face. The sky had been that perfect, cloudless blue that day, and the air lacked its normal humidity, which made Floridians momentarily forget the impending hell of summer that would be fast upon them and also made for an amazing sunset. The ripple in the water told her there was something just beneath the surface, and she slowed her pace to get a closer look. She leaned over the edge and spotted a dolphin close to the wall, chasing a fish.

"Hi there, honey," Hallie cooed to the dolphin as if it was a puppy.

The dolphin flipped back and surfaced, blowing a puff of air out of its blowhole on the top of its head, while looking at Hallie momentarily before resuming its hunt for dinner. Hallie caught her breath and resumed her run, looking out at the water at the dolphin when she could. The music pounded in her ears and she tried to control her pace so she could make the full three miles without stopping. Pink's latest song, *All I know So Far*, played through her headphones, its rhythm helping her maintain her ten minute pace. Pink, one of her favorite artists, belted out the honest and raw lyrics unapologetically, and Hallie could feel them in her bones.

* * *

He parked his car down the block and walked towards the quaint bungalow. The large oak in the front yard would offer much needed shade from the blistering sun on a hot day, he thought, but was glad the sun had already started to set. The front porch, enclosed by a freshly painted white railing, contained two wicker chairs and a wicker coffee table and seemed like the perfect place to share a cold glass of sweet tea with a friend on a lazy summer day. The flowery cushions on the chairs swirled with shades of yellow, blue and orange, complimenting the pretty yellow bungalow with white shutters. The home, like its owner, was warm and welcoming. As he approached the house, he noticed an older woman on the porch of the house next door, eying him suspiciously. He waved and smiled, as if he was exactly where he was supposed to be. Just as he suspected she would do, she quickly retreated into her house. With his blue polo shirt and khaki pants, he looked like a salesman or some type of solicitor, which was enough to send her on her way. He looked down at his clipboard, in case she was watching him from the window, to further confirm the façade. When he was confident that he had lost her attention, he circled around to the back of the house and disarmed the alarm system from his phone. He easily and quickly unlocked the backdoor and slipped in.

He looked up at the camera and smiled before making his way down the hallway and up the stairs into her bedroom. Just as he had the last three times, he gave the yellow lab a few treats and patted her behind the ears before heading up the stairs. Dogs in the past who were not as cooperative didn't fare as well, usually coming down with some unexplained illness before having to be, humanely, put down by their owners. Arsenic-laced treats had a way of doing that to them. But so far, this old girl hadn't given him any trouble, not so much as a bark, so she got the good, safe treats. It's not that he hated dogs, but he didn't particularly like them much either. They were a potential obstacle that had to be dealt with, just as most things in life had to be. And he was very good at dealing with obstacles.

He stopped by the familiar chair in the corner of the bedroom, picked up a blouse draped across the back of it, and inhaled the faint scent of Hallie's perfume, Armani Code. He looked around the room until he found what he was looking for. He knew he only had a few more minutes before she would return from her run, so he had to work quickly. He adjusted the small, hidden camera so that the bed would be in the center of the frame. He went to her closet, opened the second drawer down on the left and retrieved a pair of black silk panties. After stuffing them in his pocket, he went downstairs and quickly left out of the same door he had come in, making sure to lock it before closing it behind him. He reset the alarm and calmly walked down the street to his waiting car down the block.

CHAPTER FIVE

His alarm went off at 7:45 a.m. He was tired from staying up half the night again, but he had to sign into his work app at 8:00 a.m. so he could get his schedule of installations with addresses for the day. He got up, went into his small bathroom that contained a sink, crusted with gobs of toothpaste he never bothered to clean, a shower stall that had mildew accumulating in the crevices, and a toilet that was rimmed with urine and black wiry hairs. After he relieved himself, he brushed his teeth, drying his face on the dingy towel, which rarely got washed, hanging next to the sink, and tried to pat down his unruly hair with a little water. He got dressed into his work clothes, the only clothes he regularly washed, and had enough time remaining to microwave a cup of Folger's instant coffee. Promptly at 8:00 a.m., he signed into work and downloaded his schedule for the day.

His first stop was a home on Davis Islands at 9:00 a.m., which sounded promising. The customer's name was Michele Lowman, and he hoped she was single. Since it would only take about fifteen minutes to get there, he had time to see if anyone had commented on the pictures of

Hallie, including the close up of her tits, he had posted into the private subreddit forum and chat room he shared with other voyeurs on Reddit. He had 23 comments so far, which he quickly read through. Most of the comments were as lewd as he expected and had hoped – bragging about what they were going to deposit onto her full, round breasts or do to her pink nipples – but there was one comment that piqued his interest. It said: "Hmm beautiful face and big blue eyes. dm if u want 2 take it 2 next level" posted by a user named @mrsadist. He was intrigued. What would the next level be, he wondered?

He checked the time, and quickly sent a private message addressed to @mrsadist from @gangster813:

"Interested in what the next level is . . . what did you have in mind?"

He logged out of his Reddit account, unplugged his Mac from the monitor, and secured it in the hidden sleeve he had attached underneath his coffee table, which is where he stored it whenever he wasn't home. The only way someone would find it is if they turned the coffee table upside down. He deadbolted the apartment, armed his Ring door alarm system from his phone, and headed down the back stairway to his car.

He drove through Ybor, down Cass Street, which took him into downtown Tampa. From there, he followed Ashley Drive that ran parallel to the Hillsborough River and Tampa Riverwalk to the Platt Street Bridge, which took him over the river and down onto Bayshore Boulevard where he looped around to drive over the Davis Islands bridge. Five minutes later he was in front of Michele Lowman's renovated, New England style blue-gray bungalow with black shutters, complete with an open front porch and porch swing, which was adorned with colorful potted plants and flowers. He rang the doorbell and was pleased when an attractive, forty-something year old woman answered the door.

He held his clipboard in front of him, looking up at the petite, pretty woman. She had a sweet smile, welcoming brownish eyes, and light brown hair. After he introduced himself, she let him in and told him more information than she should have, but that's what they all did, didn't they? Spewing information out of nervousness or loneliness and he was happy to listen, making mental notes for later when he would set up a file for her on his Mac.

"So, anyway," she continued, "I'm recently divorced and I'm tired of waking up afraid in the middle of the night. If I have an alarm, I think that will help. Don't you think?"

"Yes, ma'am, our alarm system should give you complete security, especially the premium package you ordered, which includes interior and exterior cameras and motion detectors. Also, you can log in right from your phone, even when you're not home, so you will always have total control over your home and your safety."

As soon as he finished his pitch, the cellphone in her hand rang.

"I'm sorry, I need to get this," she said as she walked out of the room where he was starting the installation.

"No problem, I'll get started here," he said, politely.

Michele went into the kitchen and answered her cellphone, "Hey, Margaret, what's going on? . . . . No, I'm still home, I have an alarm system being installed. The guy's here now. . . . This shit is the bomb. I'm never going to feel unsafe in my own home again . . . . No, seriously, it's the mac-daddy system, with cameras, motion detectors, automatic lights, inside, outside, all connected to apps on my phone. . . . Oh my God, yes, it's true, you name it, this system can do it, very high-tech. . . . . Okay let me know if you can meet for dinner later. Love you!" Michele said and clicked "end" on her cellphone.

Michele came back into the front foyer where the scrawny tech was working after she finished her call, "Can I get you a bottle of water?"

"No, I'm okay, thank you."

Since her divorce from Paul, Michele would normally have felt anxious and very nervous having a male serviceman or tech in her house, but, thankfully, this one seemed harmless and more interested in installing her alarm than in her.

"Before a friend of mine recommended your company, I was thinking about getting a dog but then I worried about leaving the dog alone when I go to work and I would always be tied to the dog, so this is better," she rambled on, "what did you say your name was, again?"

"Ronald. My name is Ronald," he said, as he moved into the next room to continue setting up the cameras and motion detectors throughout Michele's house.

* * *

Ronald finished his shift and drove his blue 2014 Ford Fiesta down 7th Avenue on the way to his apartment, admiring the young, attractive happy hour crowd sitting at the outdoor restaurants and the women in their short skirts and tight jeans walking from one bar to the next on the already busy Friday night. He turned off 7th so he could find parking behind his building and was relieved when he found an open spot. His building had three spots reserved for the residents, but it was first come, first served. He opened his car door and an old McDonald's cup fell out onto the ground as he got out of the car. He looked around, making sure no one was watching him, and then kicked it underneath his car rather than pick it up. He grabbed his backpack off the passenger seat and made his way up the back stairwell that stunk from the combination of the Hookah lounge, the pizza place, and the Indian restaurant that all exited out to the same hallway. After entering his apartment, he closed and deadbolted the door, locking out his lonely and insignificant life to enter into the only world that mattered to him.

He took off his uniform, his pits stained from the stagnant ninety-degree heat, revealing his pasty, white bird chest that had not seen the sun in many years, if ever. The black curly hairs sprouting up randomly around his nipples had the same pubic-esque quality as the hairs on his chin. He tossed the foul blue shirt and khaki pants into a pile on the floor. He pulled his ACDC t-shirt over his concave chest and pulled his encrusted, sullied sweatpants, with its failing, stretched out waistband, over his grayish-yellow, rarely washed underwear. He grabbed a PBR out of the fridge and sat down in front of the massive screen while he brought his MacBook to life.

He looked at the time: 4:37 p.m. Too early for Veronica. Sheada too. He hadn't checked in on Laura in a while. Maybe it was time to see what she was up to. But he wanted to see Hallie first. After a few clicks on his keyboard, the downstairs rooms came into view on his screen. He saw the yellow lab lying faithfully by her desk, as she often was. After a few minutes, Hallie came into view, her long blonde hair pulled back in a familiar ponytail, wearing one of her many black tank tops, as she paced the room on her cellphone. Still working, he figured. If he was lucky, she might go for a run when she finished, which would mean she would have to change her clothes. Hopefully he would get a glimpse of her changing in her laundry room, as she often did.

He decided to check in on one of his other ladies while Hallie finished her workday. He grabbed another PBR from the fridge, thinking about who he should check in on next.

"Hmmm I wonder what Laura is up to today," he said aloud as he sat back down, moving Hallie to the left of the screen while opening another window to the right. After a few clicks, another room came to life before him and this time he got what he was looking for. Laura, one of the younger of his ladies, was on her knees in front of the couch in her living room, her long black hair falling easily to one side of her face as she pleasured her boyfriend with the enormous cock. Instinctively, he reached down into his food-stained sweatpants while watching the scene before him, imagining that he was the one sitting on Laura's couch while she kneeled before him, pleasuring him instead of her big-cock real life boyfriend.

Sometimes he liked to follow his ladies in real life: standing behind one of them at the post office, sitting at a nearby table at a café, letting one of them go ahead of him in line at the grocery store – it was all so *normal.* They were so self-assured, comfortable in their space, so fucking oblivious to his presence. They never saw him. But no one ever saw him, did they? He liked to follow closely, just a breath away, or seated at a nearby table – in plain sight but yet completely invisible – listening to their voices, watching them tilt their heads back in laughter and text on their phones with their coy little smiles, all the while pretending to himself that they were laughing, smiling, and texting with him. But, of course, they weren't. None of them were, were they?

* * *

Two days later, he pulled his Ford Fiesta into the parking garage in Hyde Park Village, following two cars behind the black BMW he had been following since it pulled out of the driveway a few blocks away. He knew where all his ladies lived; it was all so easy, and he was confident she never noticed him. As he passed the space where she had backed into, he saw her re-applying her lipstick and checking her appearance in the vanity mirror, oblivious to his presence. But he wasn't worried; he knew it wouldn't be hard to find her on the street below. He parked his car on the next level up and took the stairs down to the street.

He scanned the people walking along the sidewalks that lined the busy restaurants and upscale boutiques. It only took him a few minutes to spot Hallie. She stood out in her sheer white blouse that showcased her generous cleavage and full breasts, her jeans that hugged her round ass just right, and her beige, three-inch platform sandals that exposed her perfectly manicured ruby red toenails. He watched as she gathered her beautiful blonde hair up in one fast motion, automatically pulling the black hair-tie off her wrist while securing it around her hair into a high ponytail on the top of her head while she headed into Forbici, a popular Italian restaurant across the street from where Ronald was standing. By the way she was dressed, and the ponytail, he knew she was probably meeting one of her girlfriends. He didn't think Hallie had been out on many dates since that douchebag husband of hers had left, which pleased him – both the divorce and her infrequent dating habits – but it seemed to Ronald that when she was getting ready for a date, she wore her hair down.

He found an empty bench across the street where he could watch Hallie but not seem like he was watching her. She was seated alone at an outside table with a glass of red wine in front of her, periodically checking her phone. It seemed whoever she was waiting for was late. Ronald looked down at his own phone to check in on his other ladies. It was almost five o'clock when Sheada appeared on his screen. Smiling, he watched the thin brunette put her hair up into a high ponytail and set up her yoga mat. She was a little early tonight, which meant she probably had a date. She always did yoga a little earlier on date nights. He felt his little carrot twitch inside his pants at the sight of her and quickly shifted on the bench, looking around self-consciously.

Ronald put his phone down and returned his attention to pretty Hallie across the street. Watching one of his ladies in person was always more exciting to him. After he finished with Hallie, he thought he might treat himself and drive by Veronica's house. If he was lucky, he would catch her out on one of her nightly walks.

CHAPTER SIX

Hallie needed to get away. Judge Stephens' trial was bringing up painful memories and more emotions than she thought it would. She thought she could handle it and was over the emotional roller coaster it triggered, but she was wrong. She needed a break – from everything – but especially the trial, Judge Stephens, all of it. She waited for Paige at an outside table at Forbici, one of their favorite and approved locales for their regular Thursday night get togethers. A place was "approved" based on the availability of a decent glass of wine and good snacks, which meant they frequented the same spots on a rotating basis, including Malio's, Timpano, Ulele, Cru Cellars, and more recently, Wine and Wood, a hip but charming wine bar, distinct among the usual college crowd drinking establishments on Howard Avenue. Wine and Wood was becoming one of their new favorite go-to's, due in part to the cute owner, Jared, who often served them.

As Hallie waited, she checked emails, Facebook, Instagram and Twitter, occasionally looking up to scan the crowd for her friend. The young waiter brought her a glass of Tua Rita, a red wine from Italy, just as she saw

Paige walking up to the restaurant from the direction of the parking garage.

Hallie waived and Paige noticed her, instantly smiling as she made her way towards Hallie's table.

"Hey, you, sorry I'm late; I got stuck on a call with a client right as I was getting ready to leave," her tall, dark-haired beautiful friend said as she leaned in to hug her.

"No worries," Hallie replied, "it gave me a chance to catch up on all of my social media I have been ignoring lately. You remember Corey McLaughlin, don't you? The banker? Did you see he won big at the Hard Rock Casino? Like, seriously, retirement big."

"No way! Is he still hot? Man, he was hot back in the day."

"Still is," Hallie said, smiling as she thought of her good friend.

"Yeah, I always wanted to . . . well, never mind, bygones. His wife was hot too," Paige said, winking at Hallie while she unwrapped her silverware and placed her cloth napkin on her lap.

Hallie laughed, "Yes, she was and still is, too, at least from what I can tell on Facebook."

Paige settled into her seat, looking down at her phone again before putting it face up on the table to her left so she could see the notifications that came in. Hallie wasn't offended – it was part of the job – lawyers today were tethered to their phones, unable to break away, constantly checking emails, texts, and answering calls from clients. The advancements in technology eliminated the various hurdles clients used to have to overcome before they ever reached their lawyer – the receptionist as the first line of defense followed by the administrative assistant (formerly known as the legal secretary) who not only knew where all the bodies were buried but also knew the code to get into her boss's home and what his wife's favorite perfume was. But those days were, thankfully, over, for the most part.

"So, what is going on with you? How is the trial going?"

"Well," Hallie paused as she sipped her lovely Italian red blend in front of her, "it's rougher than I thought it would be. Sitting there in the same room as him, it makes my skin crawl."

"Oh my God, I can only imagine. You know, you don't need to watch it. Maybe you've seen enough, you know? Sit the rest of this one out," Paige said, as she reached over and patted Hallie's forearm.

Hallie reflexively pulled her arm back, picked up her napkin to avoid the awkwardness of the moment, and wiped her mouth.

"I just can't sit this one out, Paige. He did this to me, and many other girls, and he killed a bright, young lawyer. No, I owe it to all of them to sit there every single day until he gets what he deserves. If I had done the right thing years ago, maybe Naomi Banks would still be alive," Hallie said as her voice cracked a little bit and she reached for her wine.

"Hallie, I'm sorry. I didn't mean to . . . it's okay, you have to do what you have to do but you can't think that way – you were a victim of this mother fucker too, you know? I'm just worried about you, my friend, and I'm here for you, and whatever you want to do. I got your back, no matter what. Ride or die, right?" Paige said, smiling, but with a sadness in her amber eyes, as she reached over, putting her hand on top of her friend's hand again, which Hallie did not pull back this time.

Hallie stayed silent for a moment, looking down into her wine glass in front of her, before lifting it up to her lips to wash down whatever words and tears were caught in her throat.

"Do you ever feel like you're being watched?" Hallie asked.

"What do you mean," Paige asked, while looking around them, "like now?"

"No, not now. I don't know what I'm saying, just forget it."

"What are you talking about, Hallie? Do you think someone is watching you?"

"No, I'm just being silly. It's just a weird feeling I get every once in a while, like someone is watching me but, I look around, and no one is there. Sometimes I feel the same way at home but, of course, all the doors are locked, Juno is there by my side, and obviously there is no one in the house. I think I'm losing my mind," Hallie laughed, trying to make light of it, "I think this trial is getting to me, bringing up a lot of suppressed emotions, and it's manifesting in weird ways, such as my current paranoia."

"Hallie, it makes sense that you're feeling these things after everything you went through, not just last year but all those years ago when he – well, anyway, of course this trial is bringing out all of the feelings you probably never dealt with properly. You're still seeing your therapist, right?"

"Yes, thank God for Dr. Bell, she's been awesome, especially at helping me keep things in perspective."

"So, on the phone you mentioned you're going away for the weekend. Where are you going and are you going with anyone fun?" Paige asked, trying to lighten the mood and change the subject.

"Key West," Hallie responded, clearing her throat and grinning widely, thinking about all of the possibilities, "with an old friend."

"An old friend, huh? And would this old friend happen to be of the male species?"

"Um, do you remember my friend, Tom Egan?" Hallie hesitated.

"Um, would that be the hot Irish-Italian-Cuban, whatever the fuck he was, guy from college? Oh, girl, no good can come of that," Paige responded, smiling and shaking her head in an all-knowing way. "Now I really am going to worry."

"Don't worry," Hallie laughed, "I got this. It will be fine. We're friends."

Paige said, "Mmm hmm, just fine," rolling her eyes, while fanning herself and pretending to be flustered.

* * *

Sitting at the airport bar, Hallie gulped down the rest of her double Kettle One Bloody Mary as she confirmed her gate number and departure time one more time. She paid the $37 tab for her drink, leaving a $10 tip for the friendly bartender, trying hard not to succumb to her nervousness. She gathered her carry-on and black leather backpack, quickly replenishing her Lancôme #283 brownish-red brick lipstick to her dry lips before making her way to her gate. She found her seat on the plane, 7D, always paying extra, if necessary, to secure the aisle seat. She liked to look out the window but never wanted to be trapped in . . . anywhere. She inadvertently reclined the seat, annoying the guy behind her. She threw the Xanax towards the back of her throat and chased it down with a swig out of her water bottle. It would take twenty minutes for it to kick in and mix with the previously consumed vodka before her nerves would settle, which should be timed perfectly with when the jet would be taking off into the air. She needed this trip.

Her friend, Tom, had come back into her life when she needed him most. They had been friends thirty-plus years before, having met as students at the University of South Florida, and had reacquainted on Facebook recently. He, too, was going through the aftermaths of a failed marriage and seemed to need someone to talk to as much as she did. After a few months of texting and talking on the phone late into the night about nothing important to everything that mattered in both of their lives, he asked Hallie to go away with him for the weekend – no expectations, no strings, no obligations. Just go, run away from their responsibilities, just for a moment. Uncharacteristically, Hallie said yes. And here she was, on a plane, heading to Key West for a weekend with a man she knew a lifetime ago. And she was excited for the first time in a long time.

Her phone pinged, signifying she had a text from someone. She looked down at her phone, smiling as she read the text from Paige.

"Hey lovely, have a great trip! Do *everything* I would do LOL!"

"On the plane now, taking off soon, and it's just two old friends getting together in the Keys, nothing more."

"Oh yeah, right, lol, just text me to let me know you're ok in between bouts!"

"OMG, stop, just stop, lol, love you!"

"Love you too! Drinks when you get back – I want all the details!"

"Fine," Hallie typed back, smiling at her friend's playful texts, just as the captain turned on the *Fasten Seatbelt* sign.

CHAPTER SEVEN

The plane flew over swaying palm trees set against the cloudless blue sky and clear, aqua-blue water beneath before landing at the small Key West airport. Hallie gathered her small carry-on from the bin above her and secured her purse strap over her shoulder to exit the plane. Tom was picking her up at the airport. She wondered if he was already there and whether it would be awkward to see him after all these years. But for the Xanax and Bloody Mary, she would probably be more nervous but, luckily, the flight from Tampa was just over an hour so she was still feeling the effects of her ritual flying cocktail.

When she got into the terminal, she checked her phone and saw she had a text from Tom.

"Hey beautiful, I'm right outside, Arriving Flights, black Cadillac."

"Just landed, be right out!" Hallie typed as butterflies fluttered in her stomach.

She stopped in the restroom on the way to check her hair and outfit one last time and reapply her lipstick. Her blonde hair fell easily around her face, just past her shoulders, and had that carefree, Florida beachy look.

When Hallie met with a client or had to go to a professional event, she would flat iron it and try to keep it in place with a lot of hairspray, but in the hot humid months, she mostly pulled it back into a ponytail to avoid it frizzing up and looking too messy. Humidity was lower this time of year in the Keys, and Hallie was able to leave it down. She was pleased with the Key West vibe it gave her. Her legs, toned from running, looked good under her short, black floral sundress and four-inch, wedge sandals. She was ready.

The warm tropical air hit her as soon as she exited through the automatic doors. It only took her a minute to spot Tom, standing in front of a black Cadillac Escalade, in a pair of jeans, an untucked, white button-down collared shirt, the sleeves rolled up mid-forearm, revealing a multitude of colorful tattoos creeping down his left arm. Tom had been living in Miami for the past twenty-plus years and his look had definitely gravitated more towards his Italian-Cuban heritage than his Irish side. His brown hair was short, almost shaved on the sides and back, and peppered with gray at the temples. He had a goatee and mustache, which Hallie normally wasn't into, but on him, it worked. His steel blue-gray eyes against his somewhat weathered, tan skin conveyed a kind soul with a hint of sadness, which disappeared when he saw Hallie and his face lit up into a smile.

"Wow, look at you, beautiful," he said as he walked towards her and picked her up, pulling her into his six-foot frame.

"Hi," Hallie said, smiling and momentarily at a loss for words.

Tom put her down, kissed her cheek, and picked up her bag.

"I can't believe you're actually here. How was your flight?"

"Thankfully uneventful," Hallie laughed, "I can't believe we're both here. You look great, Tom. Miami suits you. It's so good to see you in person."

"Well, life suits you, Hallie, you look amazing. You haven't aged a day since college," he said, before adding, "C'mon, let's go. I have a nice roadie waiting for you in the car – a Cabernet, that's your favorite, right?"

"Oh wow, you're too good to me. Yes, it's my favorite. It should mix nicely with the Bloody Mary and Xanax I've already had," she laughed.

"Why so tense, Hallie? Working too many hours?"

"Well, always," Hallie laughed, "but actually someone I know is on trial for murder."

"Oh my god, I'm sorry, who is it?"

"No one important. He was the managing partner of the first firm I worked for out of law school and he's a horrible man. And he became a judge. I guess his trial is getting to me more than I realized."

"Wait, I've read about this, I think. Is his name Judge William Stephens? He allegedly killed a young lawyer who worked for him, right?"

"Yes, that's him," Hallie said, looking out the window at the aqua water splashing up against the rocks just beyond the roadway leaving the airport.

"Is the trial almost over?"

"It should be soon. I just hope he goes away for the rest of his life."

"From what I've read in the papers, the State has a pretty solid case against him."

"Yeah, they do, but it's just brought up a lot of memories I haven't had to deal with in a long time. And then I got this strange email that unnerved me, too. I think I just need a break from the trial, work, all of it."

"What kind of strange email?"

"It's probably nothing, but it's from a prisoner at Raiford who says he has something important to tell me. It's stupid, probably some type of scam. I'm going to have my IT guy check it out for me when I get back."

"What's the prisoner's name? I still have some connections in law enforcement if you want me to make a few calls for you," Tom offered helpfully.

"Um, let me look, I can't remember," Hallie said, opening her work email on her phone. She quickly scanned the emails, "Ah, here it is, that's right: Benjamin Young. Who knows if that's even his real name, right? It's probably a scam or he mistakenly thinks I can help him in some way. Don't worry about it. Like I said, I think it's mainly the trial that's getting to me. If I wasn't so anxious and emotional about that, I probably would have just deleted the email without giving it another thought."

"Well, my job this weekend is to help you relax and make you forget about all of those things. We're here to have fun."

"Thanks, Tom. And I agree, I don't want to talk about work or the trial or stupid emails for the rest of the weekend. Let the fun begin."

By the time they made it to the Saint Hotel in Key West, a quaint upscale hotel just off Duval Street, Hallie was feeling more relaxed than she had in ages, not to mention a little buzzed. She felt like she was in another world and had truly left everything behind: the trial, her failed marriage, work, her worries . . . everything. And she just wanted to enjoy the moment. A valet brought their bags up to their room, including the case of wine Tom had brought for the weekend. Their room was beautifully decorated in a cobalt blue and white color scheme, accented with blue LED lighting and classic, white sheer drapes, with a private balcony overlooking the pool. After they settled in and unpacked, Tom took her in his arms and kissed her deeply. She didn't resist. It was nice to be held and kissed by a man again.

"Thank you for meeting me this weekend," Tom whispered in her ear.

"Thank you for inviting me," Hallie answered.

"Let's go have some fun," he said, letting go of Hallie, and taking her hand.

They left the hotel and headed towards Duval Street. They spent the day drinking, laughing, and reminiscing about old times. At sunset, they joined the rest of the city at the southernmost tip of the United States to watch the spectacular sunset. Hallie was more than buzzed and feeling genuinely happy for the first time in a long time. As the ball of orange fire appeared to melt into the ocean, the crowd swooned in unison at the spectacular sight before them and Hallie leaned in closer to Tom. As the last of the orange glow disappeared, Tom reached for Hallie's hand. She looked up at him just as he leaned down and kissed her.

"Let's get out of here," he whispered, the sweet smell of whiskey on his breath, and Hallie felt her knees go weak.

By the time they made it back to the hotel, Hallie was more than ready. They had barely made it in the door and Tom was all over her, unbuttoning his shirt with one hand, and trying to pull Hallie's dress off with the other. Hallie helped with both, dropping her cute dress to the floor and trying to unbutton his jeans as he continued to kiss her. He quickly and deftly unclasped her bra, which fastened in the front, but without releasing her large breasts from the cups or touching her in any way. The anticipation was almost more than she could bear, as she stood there in her heels, thong, and unclasped bra, longing for him to touch her anywhere, everywhere. He dropped his jeans to the floor and stepped out of them along with his leather flip flops. Hallie was afraid to look down. He kissed her passionately as he backed her up to the bed, gently forcing her down onto it. He removed her bra as his mouth found her nipples and one of his hands found the throbbing area between her legs. Her body rose up in response, yearning for him to be inside of her.

"Not yet, baby," he whispered.

By the time he gave her what she wanted, what she needed, she was on the edge and it only took minutes for her to reach what she hadn't felt in years, multiple times. Tom finally did the same and they laid there in a sweaty heap, happy, still a little drunk, and beyond content. Hallie hadn't realized how long she had been going without until this night, and she promised herself, she never would again. She drifted off to sleep, happier than she had been in a long time, with her head on Tom's chest.

* * *

As she slept, Tom unplugged her I-phone from the charger on the nightstand, gently picked up her hand and then held Hallie's thumb to the fingerprint unlock button on her phone, the same thumb he had watched her open it with throughout the day. Hallie stirred for a moment until he lightly rubbed her back and her breathing returned to the rhythmic cadence it had before. When he was confident she was asleep, he searched her phone until he found what he was looking for, took a screenshot of it, and airdropped it to his phone. He then permanently deleted the screenshot from her phone, picked up his phone to accept the image, and fell fast asleep, having the most restful night of sleep he had in a long time.

CHAPTER EIGHT

Ronald wired the alarm system and set up the cameras throughout the house. He loved recent divorcees – they were so much more vulnerable than other women, yet trusting because they equated him with safety, and always wanted the works. Michele Lowman was no different. She was adorable, with her light brown bob, cute, perky but small breasts, and petite frame. She would make a nice addition to his other ladies, who all had their own look. Ronald didn't have a type – they were all his type. But, of course, he could never approach any of these women in real life. He knew they wouldn't give him the time of day. He programmed her alarm before she came back downstairs, including adding his own email and special PIN as an administrator, which would be hidden from Michele's view on the panel installed on her wall and on all of her apps. Just like all of the others, she would never know he was there. He couldn't wait to log in and check in on her later.

"All set, Ms. Lowman. Do you have a few minutes to complete the set up and allow me to show you how it works?" he asked.

"Sure, I'll be right down," Michele answered.

Ronald went through the security measures and functions on the panel, explaining each feature in detail. He turned away when he had Michele input her secret PIN, and then helped her download the app onto her phone. He was polite, professional, and very reassuring that her home would be completely secure when armed.

"This is great, thank you so much. I already feel safer," Michele said.

"That's our objective, Ms. Lowman. Also, here is my card, which has the main number on it, so if you have any questions at all or need help with the system, please do not hesitate to call us, 24-7. There is always someone available to help you."

Ronald drove away, pleased that his morning had started out so nicely. He checked his schedule for the rest of the day and saw that his appointments were scheduled by men, so no more distractions for him for the day. He finished his last appointment at 4:30 and headed home, driving through McDonald's on his way. He placed his McDonald's bag containing his Big Mac and large fries on the table in front of his monitor, and then changed out of his uniform and into one of his grungy t-shirts and sweats before sitting down at the table. Before diving into his Big Mac, he immediately logged in to his latest account . . . Michele. She was very different than Veronica and Hallie, who were both professionals and take-charge kind of women; she was also different from Sheada, who was a young, health fanatic. Michele seemed more like the girl next door. He liked her. It took about fifteen seconds for the site to respond, and his screen came to life. And there she was, in all of her natural beauty. He liked to imagine she was thinking about him – that he had made as much of an impression on her as she had on him.

He moved Michele to the left of his screen and opened the Reddit chat room to the right. When he logged in, he saw that he had another message from @mrsadist.

"Next level means live interaction"

Ronald responded, "How?"

Within a few minutes, he received a notification that he had received a message from @mrsadist, who was actively online.

"Set the cameras to record b4 you get there and then you know what to do."

Ronald was intrigued and a little excited about what his new friend was suggesting. He had previously bragged to the group that he had installed cameras in women's homes and could watch them whenever he wanted. He knew that could come back to haunt him if he ever got caught but he couldn't help himself. He wanted to impress the others in the group, which consisted of other voyeurs just like him. And he really wasn't worried about getting caught because he had taken various steps to hide his identity and location by using a rolling VPN (virtual private network), which masked his IP address every fifteen seconds and encrypted his location. No one in the group would be able to find him or figure out who he was, unless he shared personal information via the private message app.

He sent the following message back, "I don't know if I can do that. Do you live in the U.S.?"

"Yeah, southeast, how about u?"

"Same! How far southeast?"

"Land of the most beautiful bitches and beaches in the world."

"Omg, same, you're in Florida, aren't you?"

"Dude, not cool . . ."

"C'mon, you must be using a rolling VPN too, no way to track us."

"Never say never . . ." @mrsadist responded, while looking up at the second floor apartment over the hookah joint in Ybor City.

CHAPTER NINE

Hallie was looking forward to her Friday night with Bridget and her husband, Jay. She had been back from the Keys since early Monday morning, having headed straight to the office from the airport, and was relieved to have finished the grueling week. Even if she had to work that weekend to make up for her jaunt to the Keys, it would be less stressful as she wouldn't have to take calls from clients or opposing counsel. She could catch up on work and other things that needed to get done at home.

On her way to Bridget's, as she usually did, she stopped at Bodega's in Seminole Heights to pick up their favorite Cubans. Hallie's mouth watered as she thought about the slow cooked mojo pork, ham, Swiss cheese, pickles, and mustard layered between the freshest homemade Cuban bread from La Segunda Bakery, hot and pressed with butter on both sides of the bread. She was sad to learn that they were closing their Tampa location, and she would have to travel to St. Petersburg to get her cherished sandwich. But it would be worth the drive, she knew.

She picked up the delicacies from the crowded Cuban place and headed the few blocks from Bodega's to Bridget's

Seminole Heights bungalow. As she expected, Bridget was sitting on her front porch, smoking a cigarette, with a bottle of Windex by her side to chase away the mosquitos. Some things never changed, which made Hallie smile as she picked up her purse, the package of Bodega's, and the bottle of red wine from her passenger seat.

"Hey, bitch," Bridget said as Hallie started up the front steps, Bridget's usual greeting to Hallie.

"Hey, Bridg," Hallie responded, "Mary is looking down on you with pride as you keep up the Windex tradition."

"Oh, Mary knew a thing or two," Bridget said smiling at the memory of her mother as she exhaled the smoke from her Marlboro that had previously filled her lungs, "How else are we gonna keep these damn mosquitos away?"

Hallie sat down on the chair next to her friend.

"No doubt. Mary was quite the woman," Hallie agreed, thinking about her best friend's mother who raised eight children and yet always seemed to have her shit together. She also usually had a glass of wine in her hand, which made perfect sense to Hallie now.

Bridget nodded as she put her cigarette out in the sand pail she kept next to her chair and got up, reaching for the Bodega's bag to help Hallie bring everything into the house. They put the Cubans and wine down on the antique wooden dining room table that used to belong to Mary, and Bridget went out to the kitchen to get a wine opener and glasses.

"Jay's not home yet," Bridget said as she came back in with two wine glasses. "He got called in to help with some home invasion/rape case."

"Oh my God, that's awful. I don't know how he deals with that every day."

"Yeah, some days are worse than others, that's for sure. Don't tell him I told you, but he's still having nightmares about Naomi Banks' murder. To this day, he won't talk about what he saw at that scene. But it fucks up his sleep, that's for sure."

"I can only imagine," Hallie said, shaking her head. "You know his trial is almost done. Closing arguments are tomorrow."

"Yeah, I know. Believe me, Jay tells me about it every day. I can't wait until that son of a bitch gets convicted and maybe that will give Jay some peace."

"A lot of us are hoping for that," Hallie responded.

"Of course, I'm sorry, Hal. I know how important it is to you that this fucker goes down – not just for Naomi Banks but also for what he did to you."

"No need to apologize; he just needs to rot in hell and then we'll all be happy, right?" Hallie asked, not actually waiting for an answer. "Anyway, enough about that; what else is going on with you?"

"Nada, not a damn thing. You know I live a boring life," she laughed. "Now tell me about your trip to the Keys."

"Oh wow, that was a good trip. Tom was, well, Tom, as only he can be," Hallie giggled, "the same live-in-the-moment, fun, carefree guy I went to college with."

"Seriously, that's all you're giving me? I want to know about the sex, Hallie. After all these years, did the two of you finally hook up? And if you leave out any details, I'll never forgive you," Bridget teased.

"Be careful what you wish for, Bridg," Hallie said, blushing as she thought about her weekend in the Keys.

"I ain't scared; give me the goods."

"Fine. Yes, we finally had sex. And it was fucking amazing. What else do you want to know?"

"Hmmm, let me think about what else I want to know, other than the obvious."

"Um, what's the obvious? I'm confused."

"Oh my God, size, Hallie, size. Does he have the package to back up his swagger is all I'm asking," Bridget said, shaking her head.

"Yes," Hallie responded, blushing, thinking about her weekend in the Keys, "he definitely has, well, um, let's just say he is very, very good at what he does, and I'm going to leave it at that, my nosy friend."

"Look, I'm an old married woman. I have to live vicariously through you now. What else am I going to do with my time?" Bridget asked, genuinely happy to see her best friend laughing and happy after the sadness and stress she went through the previous year.

* * *

Sitting at her desk the next morning, looking out her front windows, Hallie watched the resident squirrel gathering acorns at the bottom of the giant oak in her front yard, no longer being stalked by the fat tabby who used to live under her neighbor's front porch. The squirrel looked like he had put on a few pounds since the gray momma cat had been relocated after giving birth to kittens just feet away from where a young, murdered co-ed's battered body had been dumped.

"No judgment, Mr. Squirrel, I feel you," Hallie said.

Hallie thought about her recent weekend in the Keys, smiling involuntarily, even blushing a little, as she thought about Tom. His calloused fingers had worked their magic on her in ways she had long forgotten, awakening things in her that had long been dormant. She started to throb a little just thinking about it and reached for her phone to send him a quick text.

"Hi."

Within a few seconds, her phone pinged with a response.

"Hi beautiful!"

Hallie smiled, and tapped out, "How's your day going?"

"Better now that I've heard from you."

"You need to come up to Tampa soon," Hallie wrote.

"Oh, I definitely do. Will you do that thing you did to me in Key West?" he asked, followed by the little purple devil emoji.

Hallie blushed again, happy no one was around to see her, "Mmmm, yes, I will. Just get here."

"Working on it, babe . . . I'll let you know soon!"

Hallie returned to her computer, trying to focus on the emails she had to send to various clients and opposing counsel. She planned to leave in a few minutes so she could make it to the courthouse in time to hear closing arguments in the Judge Stephens murder case. She finished the last email she had to send and went upstairs to change into her suit. She had showered and done her hair after her run on Bayshore early that morning, but still had to put her makeup on and change out of her sweats. Her run that morning had been as hard as she expected since her weekend of drunkenness and debauchery in the Keys. She was impressed with herself that she ran the first mile and a half without having to stop, although her legs felt like lead. She knew it would get easier and she would get stronger and faster if she could just stick with it, but it was so easy to get distracted or justify not running at all on any given day. Some days she would stay in bed for that extra half hour in the morning and promise herself that she would run after work, but undoubtedly someone would invite her to happy hour, or her horrific day would justify opening a bottle of wine by herself rather than going for her run. She promised herself that she would not quit this time and she would run at least four times a week. Tom was a good motivation for that promise.

* * *

Dressed in her navy suit, white camisole, and four-inch matching blue pumps, Hallie walked up the courthouse steps. She went through security, took the escalator up to the next floor, and waited for the elevator doors to open to take her to the fifth floor where the trial was being held. She was fifteen minutes early and hoped there were still a few seats available in the courtroom. She opened the heavy courtroom doors, entered the foreboding room, and quickly found a seat a few rows from the back on the same side as the jury box. She quietly sat down, silenced her phone, and proceeded to check and respond to a few emails while she waited.

It wasn't long before the bailiff announced, "All rise!" indicating the judge was coming into the courtroom. Next the jury was brought in, and the final day of the trial began. Both sides had called their witnesses, cross examined the other side's witnesses, and it was time for their closing arguments. Amy went first, meticulously summarizing the damning evidence against Judge Stephens, leaving very little doubt, in Hallie's opinion, that he was responsible for Naomi's death. And then Creepy Carl got up and spoke. He was good, too. Hallie had to give him that. If there was any attorney who could taint the facts with enough reasonable doubt, it was Carl.

Hallie watched as the members of the jury listened to the persuasive defense attorney. Had he presented enough to create reasonable doubt in even one juror? The jurors focused intently on Carl as he danced around the evidence, attempting to create an illusion between the facts and circumstantial evidence to suggest there could be another person responsible for the heinous crime. She saw at least two of the jurors – one man and one woman – nod slightly in agreement as Carl spun his alternative tale. That was not a good sign, Hallie knew. All it would take was one outlier to hang the jury, meaning they couldn't reach a unanimous verdict, or worse, convince the others that Stephens wasn't guilty. Creepy Carl finished and sat down, seemingly pleased with his performance. Judge Washington read a number of instructions to the jury, the wording of which had been agreed upon in advance by both sides, and excused them to deliberate. And now they would wait.

CHAPTER TEN

He rang the doorbell. No answer. He had his spiel ready to go should someone answer, or he be questioned by a nosy neighbor. He even had his uniform on, just in case. But he knew no one was home. He quickly deactivated the alarm through the app on his phone, walked around to the back of the house, and expertly unlocked the door in a matter of seconds. He entered the small contemporary home, admiring the pristine kitchen with its black granite countertops set against the white cabinets and stainless-steel appliances. In the middle of the kitchen was a built-in counter with four bar stools tucked neatly underneath, with a magenta-colored orchid centered perfectly in the middle of the counter.

He made his way out of the kitchen, traveling down the familiar hallway to the living room and two bedrooms off to the right. The rest of the home was as orderly and free of clutter as the kitchen, with modern furniture that also looked warm and welcoming. In the bedroom, he went straight to the dresser and opened the top drawer. He admired the contents until he selected two pairs of Veronica's lace thongs, one red, one black, which he stuffed into his front pocket.

He picked up her pillow, the one he knew she slept on, and inhaled deeply, picking up notes of lavender and vanilla, momentarily feeling dizzy from the scent of her. Next, he went into her bathroom, found her hairbrush and took from it a number of her perfect, brown strands of hair and placed them in the plastic bag he retrieved from his back pocket. Moments later, just beyond the walls of the bedroom, he heard the sound of a car door being shut.

* * *

Veronica pulled into her driveway, exhausted from battling with the City of Tampa permitting department on the downtown project she was overseeing. Veronica was an architect with a large firm who specialized in commercial buildings. The latest trend, however, was to have commercial retail and office space on the lower floors of a building with high-end residential apartments on the upper floors. Since the Tampa Riverwalk – a two- and half-mile continuous path that ran along the Hillsborough River from downtown to Tampa Heights – was completed, the demand for residential apartments in the downtown area skyrocketed. The Riverwalk was lined with restaurants, outdoor bars, museums, hotels, and offices, all connected by the pedestrian/bike path running along the beautiful river that emptied into the Tampa Bay, and eventually into the Gulf of Mexico.

She gathered her purse and large black bag that contained her laptop and the latest designs she had printed out before leaving the office and got out of her car, slamming her car door with her hip a little stronger than she had intended. She unlocked her front door, the cool air from inside her home contrasting sharply with the warm, humid air outside. Habitually, she went to the alarm monitor on the wall to turn it off when she noticed it was not armed.

"That's strange," she said aloud, shaking her head and wondering if she forgot to set it that morning in her rush to get out.

Veronica looked around her living room and down the hallway towards the kitchen. Nothing seemed out of place. She walked into the kitchen and checked the back door, relieved to find that it was locked. She headed into the bedroom and then into her closet. Something seemed off in the back of her mind, but she couldn't quite place it, nor did she really try. She had obviously forgotten to set the alarm that morning in her haste to make it to the meeting with the city attorney in time. She slipped out of her slacks and put them in the dry-cleaning bag that was hanging on the hook her handyman installed when she had her closet redone. She took off her jacket and hung it up. Dry-cleaning was expensive and she had worn the jacket less than an hour, collectively, the whole day as most of the time it was draped over the back of her office chair. She slipped out of her black silk blouse, placing it in her hamper, before walking back into her bedroom to grab a tank top and shorts out of her dresser.

That's when she noticed it. Her pillows had been moved. She made her bed the same way every day and today was no exception: she would place the two king-size pillows up against the headboard and then lean the thinner, regular sized pillows in the pretty shams up against them. One of her pillows, the one she slept on, was lying flat on the bed with the pillow in the sham leaning up against it, neither one of them against the headboard. There was no question someone had been in her bedroom.

A chill ran up her spine and she fought the urge to immediately run out of the house in just her bra and thong. She grabbed the top pair of shorts and tank top from her dresser and quickly put them on, trying to steady her breathing in case someone was still inside of her house, listening to her, watching her. She just had to get out into the living room, grab her purse off the table by the front door and run out to her car. She was ten feet from the front door when she heard the wood floor creaking behind her, and she started to run. She reached the door, struggling clumsily with the lock in her panic to get out, when she felt someone grab her by the back of her long hair and yank her backwards causing her head to slam onto the hard wood floor as she landed.

CHAPTER ELEVEN

The cement walls around his cot reminded him of his dire situation. He had a life sentence, no possibility of parole, and, unless he escaped, he would die and rot in there. At this point, the prospects of escaping were slim, so he had to make the best of his life on the inside. And the only way to do that was with money and power. Money bought him drugs, protection, and other contraband, which gave him power. He had the connections on the outside to get whatever someone on the inside needed or wanted. The Broker was the guy to go to, but it would cost you. And because of that, no one fucked with the Broker.

"Hey, Broker, I need another favor," Bobby said, slipping the Broker a twenty as a showing of good faith, just to make the request.

"Oh yeah? Wore your dick off already with that last pic, huh, bro? Need another?" the Broker said, chuckling.

Bobby repressed his urge to throat punch him, pretending to laugh, "Well, that was just the appetizer. I want a video now," and then in hushed tones, "but not just any video."

"Oh yeah, bro? What kind of video you lookin for?"

"So, let's just say the subject of the picture you previously got for me – I would like a video of her, natural, you know, without her knowing. I don't want her to know she's on camera."

"Well, well, that's quite the jump from the picture, bro. Someone will have to follow her around and be discreet. That's gonna cost you a lot. Don't fuck with me, bro, you got that kinda change?"

"I got it. Just make it happen."

"A'right bro, I got you," the Broker responded.

* * *

Hallie looked through her desk until she found the business card she was looking for: Detective Marcelo Garcia. She wondered whether she should email him or call him and decided to try his cellphone listed on the card. She hadn't talked to the detective in almost a year, not since the arrest of Judge William Stephens and Robert "Bobby" Johnson, the teacher at her ex-husband's school who confessed to raping and killing multiple women in Tampa. The six-foot-two, good-looking detective had dark, curly hair, a chiseled and serious face, which contradicted his kind brown eyes that sparkled when they looked at you, and a slight Spanish accent that reminded Hallie of Andy Garcia in the movie *When a Man Loves a Woman*. Andy Garcia's character loved his wife, played by Meg Ryan, without hesitation, despite her alcoholism and other demons. That was all Hallie ever wanted, someone to love her the way Andy Garcia loved Meg Ryan in that movie: unconditionally. The way her father had loved her mother and her. So far, she was 0 and 2 in that department, she thought sadly.

A lot had happened in the past year since the arrests of Judge Stephens and Bobby Johnson, at least in her life. She had divorced, merged her practice into a larger firm, and saw her only daughter off to college. Bobby Johnson had spared his victims and their families from the trauma and stress of a trial, not out of any benevolence towards them, but in exchange for avoiding the death penalty he surely would have received. She hoped the detective would remember her. He picked up on the third ring.

"Detective Garcia," he answered, very curtly.

"Hi, Detective, this is Hallie Miller, um, we met about a year ago on the Judge Stephens' case?"

"Yes, of course, Hallie, how are you? To what do I owe the pleasure? No more dead bodies turning up in your yard, I hope," he joked.

"Oh my God, no, thank God, nothing like that," Hallie laughed nervously.

"I'm sorry, I shouldn't make jokes about that. I know that had to be very traumatic for you. Forgive me – chalk it up to a dark sense of humor due to occupational hazard. Please, what can I do for you?" he asked, with a softer tone, sounding more like Andy Garcia again.

"Is this a bad time?" Hallie asked, beginning to wonder why she had called.

"No, it's fine, really, what can I do for you?"

"I don't know if you can help me, but I got a strange email from someone incarcerated at Raiford. I don't do criminal defense or appellate work so I'm confused why he contacted me, but I was hoping you could run his name and let me know what you know about him, his charges, conviction and anything else you might be able to tell me about him. I don't get emails from convicts so this makes me a little nervous after what happened last year," Hallie said, finally taking a breath.

"You don't recognize his name?"

"No, not at all."

"Well, I wouldn't worry about it. Maybe he just emailed a bunch of attorneys, hoping someone would take his case. You know, they have that capability now in the prisons. There are literally kiosks where they can email attorneys or family members. Some inmates are rewarded for good behavior with tablets where they can download educational material, watch movies, and play games."

"Really? Well, I guess it could be just a random phishing email, but he didn't ask for my help as an attorney. He said he has something important to tell me about a very bad person that is connected to my family or something like that. After everything that happened last year, I can't shake things off if my gut is telling me otherwise. Would you mind just running the name for me? I just want to know who this guy is and what I'm dealing with."

"Okay, no problem, Hallie. Give me the name. I'll see what I can find out for you. How are you doing, by the way?"

"I'm good, thank you. My divorce was finalized last month, and my daughter is doing amazing in her first year of college. So overall, things are good. How about you?"

"It's been an interesting year for me too. A lot of personal changes, some good, some not so good, but for the most part, I can't complain. I'm glad to hear you're doing better. So, what's this guy's name?"

"Benjamin Young."

"Okay, Hallie, I'll let you know what I find out about your pen-pal. Am I aging myself with that term?" the Detective chuckled.

"Well, not to me, because I knew exactly what you meant, so we must be in the same age group," Hallie responded.

"Good, glad to hear it," he said, "I'll be in touch in a few days with what I find out."

"Thanks, Detective, I really appreciate it."

"Marcelo, Hallie. Call me Marcelo."

Hallie clicked the end button on her phone while the butterflies began figure eights in her stomach. She was asking herself why she called him when she could have called her friend, Bridget, whose husband, Jay, was also a police officer and probably could have easily gotten the information for her. Bridget was her best friend since 4th grade. No question Jay would have helped her out. She felt a connection to the detective with the warm, brownish-hazel eyes and she had no idea why. She would have to bring this up with her therapist, Dr. Jill Bell, at her session the following week.

CHAPTER TWELVE

Veronica woke up, her head pounding, as she fought to remember what happened to her. The fog on her mind started to lift, the same way the sun slowly burnt off the morning dreariness. She remembered being grabbed from behind by someone she couldn't see and being slammed backwards onto the floor. From the darkness of the room and her throbbing skull, she had no idea how long she had been unconscious. She recognized she was in her bedroom but quickly realized she couldn't move. Each hand was tied to an opposite corner of her headboard while her long, now bare, legs were spread apart, her ankles bound to opposite ends of the footboard. Her eyes began to focus, and she could make out the large silhouette of a man – wearing a ski mask and dark clothes – in the corner of her bedroom, sitting there, watching her. Her screams, muffled by the thick duct tape covering her mouth, were heard by no one.

"Hello, Veronica," the man whispered as he came towards her, looking down over her naked body.

He knelt down next to the bed, stroking her long, brunette hair, gently at first but then gripping it aggressively and yanking her head back to force her to look directly up at him. He picked up a sharp butcher knife that was on the floor next to him and began tracing an imaginary circle around her left nipple with the tip of the blade, slightly cutting the delicate skin. Veronica's ample chest heaved at the touch of the cold steel against her bare skin and her already labored breathing became more frantic. She tried desperately to calm down to avoid hyperventilating but it was almost impossible at the sight and feel of the knife. Her eyes, wide with terror, focused on the man's cold, dark eyes and rough bare hands and she tried to memorize any distinguishing features in case she survived this nightmare. The light of a passing car momentarily filled the room, and she noticed the sliver of a tattoo peeking out from under the edge of his shirtsleeve. The image of the purple and black dragon tail, winding down and encircling his wrist, would be etched in her mind forever.

When he spoke again, he was louder than before, and she could hear his breathing was getting more excited.

"Are you afraid, Veronica?" he asked, mockingly, while he held up the knife as if to admire it.

Veronica didn't move – not that she could move with her wrists and ankles tied securely to the bed – and closed her eyes. She didn't want to give him the satisfaction of seeing the fear in her eyes and began to recite the Hail Mary prayer silently in her head.

The first cut was so sudden she barely felt it. She only realized she was cut when she felt the warm liquid pouring out of the fresh gash down her ribcage and accumulating down her side onto the bed beside her. She saw him raise the knife again and again and could feel pressure each time the knife landed on her body like she was being punched, and yet she could not comprehend that the blood splattering against the wall and dripping off the end of the sharp blade was her own.

> *Hail Mary, full of grace,*
> *The Lord is with thee,*
> *Blessed are thou amongst women*
> *Blessed is the fruit of thy womb, Jesus.*
> *Holy Mary, Mother of God,*
> *Pray for us sinners now*
> *And at the hour of our death . . . .*

As she faded into unconsciousness, reciting the prayer over and over again, she was strangely comforted by the warmth that was continuing to envelop her naked body and she was no longer afraid.

* * *

Ronald paced in front of his large monitor, excited by what he had just watched but revolted at the same time. His Veronica. His Veronica. What had he done? He looked back at the screen again.

"Oh my God, oh my God," he mumbled, "why is there so much blood?"

He started pacing again, trying to figure out what to do next. He walked to the window, looking down onto 7th Avenue, all of a sudden quite paranoid. Was anyone watching him? He noticed a guy in a blue and black flannel shirt and jeans in the alcove of the vacant building across the street smoking a cigarette. He noticed the man looking up at him. Ronald quickly ducked out of sight. He looked again and the guy was gone. Maybe he wasn't watching him. He was starting to become unraveled.

"Oh my God, maybe I should call 911!" he almost shouted, quickly lowering his voice, trying to think about the implications of that decision. He had a headache from all the adrenaline and the stress this was causing him, not to mention the six PBRs he had consumed in the last hour. No, he could not call 911, he quickly realized, without having to explain how he knew a woman across town had been stabbed in her home. In his drunken, panicked haze, he decided he should secure the recordings from the system before they were erased in case he ever needed them.

He sat down at his monitor and shakily moved his mouse to bring the monitor back to life. Veronica's bedroom came to life. It was dark; the bloody scene from before seemed to have disappeared; Veronica was gone. What was happening?

Was he losing his mind? He knew what he saw. He started clicking away on his keyboard and frantically moving the mouse, looking in the history, the deleted files, everywhere he knew to look, to recover the video files. He sat back in his chair, the gravity of the situation weighing on him like a heavy cloud. The files were gone. And so was Veronica.

CHAPTER THIRTEEN

Sheada logged into her yoga class registration platform to see how many students had registered. She had recently started teaching on Zoom, the online virtual platform, where she could teach out of her house via a camera on her laptop. After each student would Venmo or PayPal her the $25 fee, she would send them the Zoom link a few minutes before the class would begin. She was averaging about ten students per class, which she taught usually twice a week after work and another class on Saturday mornings. She loved teaching virtually from her own home, although she missed the interaction and physical assistance she could offer her students who needed the extra guidance. But she couldn't make that kind of money at the yoga studio because the studio took half of the registration fees. Sheada also started offering one on one sessions in people's homes where she would charge $100 per session, and she was starting to build up a nice set of personal clients too. It was a nice supplement to the 9-5 job she had as a receptionist for a local architectural firm where she made $30,000 per year plus benefits.

Most of the architects at the small firm were very nice to her, especially the owners and senior architects. The firm's clients, who mostly consisted of commercial real estate developers, were usually polite and professional too. She felt she could deal with the ones who were not and didn't let them get to her. But one of the junior designers, Harrison, a trust fund baby whose father had gotten him the job as a good friend of one of the owners, was always asking her out or stopping by her desk to chat with her. At first, she was polite, pretending not to notice his blatant advances and embarrassing come-ons, until she finally had enough and realized subtlety was not going to work with him. She very nicely told him she was flattered but that she had a boyfriend and that she also had a rule about not dating co-workers, neither of which were true. Unfortunately, Harrison the Third, as he always introduced himself, was not dissuaded. Her favorite person at the firm, by far, was Justin, the intern. He was still in graduate school, and the closest to her age of anyone in the firm, although she was about two years older than him at all of twenty-six years old. One thing Justin had going for him that Harrison the Third did not, besides a decent personality, was a wicked sense of humor. And he started rescuing Sheada whenever Harrison was lurking around her desk.

"Hey Lawson, you up for a drink after work or do you have plans with Thurston Howell the Third?" Justin asked her that Thursday afternoon.

Thurston Howell, the wealthy, elitist character from *Gilligan's Island*, which truthfully, Sheada had only watched on Roku after Justin explained the source of his nickname for Harrison, made Sheada laugh every time.

"Oh my God, no, of course I don't have plans with him," Sheada said, rolling her eyes.

"Good, then I'll meet you at Bar Taco in twenty minutes. I'll get us seats at the bar."

Their office was around the corner from Hyde Park Village in a refurbished old bungalow off Swann Avenue that had been converted into an office. The outside looked quaint, like most residential homes in the mixed-use area, but the inside was completely modernized with an industrial setting, charcoal-hued faux hard wood floors, exposed brick walls, and a lot of steel lighting fixtures. Sheada greeted people from her desk on the first floor where there were also two conference rooms, a small kitchenette, a bathroom, and a small bedroom that was converted into a copy and storage room. The architects' offices were on the second floor, including Justin's desk, which was in the open loft area at the top of the stairs overlooking Sheada's area down below. Every once in a while, a paper airplane would glide down from above with a funny note in it.

Sheada walked into Bar Taco and saw Justin sitting alone at the bar. It was still early, so it was not crowded yet, but the place would be packed by 8 p.m. His dirty blonde hair was cut short except for the top, which consisted of longish, uneven wisps that he would swipe out of his eyes periodically, especially after looking down at his phone. He was still dressed in his work clothes, a pale blue button-down, collared shirt, which he wore untucked over his straight leg, blue jeans, that fit him perfectly. He looked like the quintessential singer in a boyband, the one who got all the girls.

"Hey, this seat taken?" Sheada asked as she walked up to Justin at the mostly empty bar.

"Only by you, if you don't mind inappropriate conversation and weird references to 1970's TV shows from before either of us were even born," he answered.

"Oh, that's my favorite kind of conversation," Sheada cooed, batting her eyelashes in an exaggerated way, as she climbed onto the bar stool next to Justin.

Justin ordered her a gold IPA from one of the local breweries, the same that he was drinking, without pausing to ask her. Normally that would annoy her but for some reason, it was charming when he did it.

"Why do you know about all of those old TV shows, by the way?"

"When I was younger, my mom and I would watch TV together. My mom loved all the old shows she grew up watching with her mom, and there was a cable station that aired them exclusively. Don't even get me started on *I Dream of Jeanie* or the *Dick Van Dyke Show*," he laughed easily, "you're not ready to hear about those yet."

Sheada liked the way his blue eyes lit up when he laughed while a slight dimple appeared in his left cheek.

They drank their beers, telling each other about their childhoods, families, and other random information you talk about when getting to know someone. Being around him was just easy but she still didn't know if they were stuck in the perpetual friend zone or if he liked her at all. After the third beer, she was starting to feel buzzed and her confidence, or rather courage from the alcohol, was starting to build.

"So, Justin, I'm just curious, is this a date or are we just friends? I'm a little buzzed and confused so if we're just friends, that's totally cool, but I also don't want to misinterpret anything, and if it's a date, well that's fine, but I'm just trying to figure things—"

Justin leaned over and kissed her, mid-sentence. She could smell his cologne, which had a clean, fresh smell, and could taste his beer on her lips as he pulled back after kissing her. For a moment she was speechless and could feel the heat in her face rising. She hoped he wouldn't notice her blushing, the thought of which only made her blush more.

"I hope that clears things up for you and we can resume our discussion of how we became the amazing yet fucked up people we are today," he said as he casually reached over and held her hand. She expected his hands to be smooth but they weren't. His hands were rough and calloused, the hands of someone who worked outside or with wood or some other material, but definitely not the hands of a graduate student trying to become an architect. There were many things about Justin she did not know but wanted to find out.

Sheada cleared her throat, "Well, that was presumptuous of you. What if I didn't want to kiss you?"

"Did you?"

"Well, that's not the point," she stuttered, trying to hold her ground.

"It's exactly the point. Did you want me to kiss you or not? Because I thought you did and so I kissed you. But if I was wrong, then I must apologize because I must have misread the situation."

"Wait, you only kissed me because you thought I wanted you to? You are so cocky," Sheada replied, beginning to get annoyed, although she wasn't sure why or how the conversation had turned sideways. She probably shouldn't have said yes to that third beer. She wasn't a big drinker and they were going straight to her head.

"No, absolutely not. I kissed you because I've been dying to kiss you from the first day I met you and realized you were smart and funny and beautiful. And then we became friends and then I really wanted to kiss you. But I didn't think you wanted to kiss me until today. And here we are and I want to kiss you again."

His honesty and confidence unnerved Sheada, while exciting her at the same time. How was this guy only twenty-four years old? He was definitely someone who had an old soul. She took a sip of her beer as she tried to think of how to respond.

"May I kiss you again, Sheada?" he asked, almost in a whisper as he was already leaning in towards her.

She tried to sound nonchalant but inside she was melting, "Fine, yes, you can kiss me again."

He smiled at her response and leaned in further and kissed her more intensely than before. By now, the bar was starting to fill up and Sheada realized they were literally making out at the bar, which is something she never did. She always made fun of people who hooked up in public, like what were they thinking? And yet, here she was, and she couldn't seem to stop herself.

She gathered her thoughts, unlocked her lips from Justin and gently pushed him back, "We need to get out of here. I'm not saying anything more than kissing you is going to happen, but I can't be doing this sitting at a bar in the middle of Hyde Park. My place is around the corner. Do you want to come over?"

"I thought you would never ask," he replied, smiling that boyish grin again and throwing cash on the bar to cover their drinks.

CHAPTER FOURTEEN

Veronica woke up in what she slowly realized was her bathtub. Her head was pounding, and her sides and chest stung sharply every time she moved. She was bandaged from the waist up, all the way across her breasts. She tried to move but the pain was excruciating. Blood had soaked through her bandages, and she felt weak and nauseous. Her head pulsated every time her heart pumped. Her cellphone was resting on the edge of the tub, plugged into the charger nearby. The memories started to flood her consciousness and her body trembled uncontrollably, the tears streaming down her face, as she tried to suppress her cries just as the duct tape had suppressed them before. She greedily inhaled the air, her lungs thankful they were no longer limited to the fretful gasps she was able to intake through her nostrils. Other than her bandages, she was naked and her once white tub was stained with her own blood. She was terrified he was still in the house. Had he put her cellphone next to her as some type of game? Nothing made sense. She lifted her hand, fighting through the resulting pain, and picked up her phone: 1:37 a.m. She dialed 9-1-1 and waited for someone to pick up, praying he was gone or at least wouldn't hear her.

"9-1-1, what's your emergency?"

Veronica said nothing, paralyzed with fear, feeling like she was going to throw up, terrified any noise would bring him into her bathroom to resume the torture.

"9-1-1, what is your emergency? Hello? Is anyone there?"

Again, Veronica said nothing. Her breathing becoming more erratic, and she desperately wanted to scream into the phone. But she was afraid it was all part of his game and as soon as she spoke, he would be back to hurt her again.

She brought the phone close to her mouth and whispered, "Help."

"Hello? Do you need help? Who am I speaking with?" the dispatcher asked in a monotone voice, much too calm for the circumstances, Veronica thought.

Veronica focused on the bathroom door and waited, saying nothing.

The dispatcher asked again, "Hello? Is there someone there? Can you tell me your name?"

"Veronica," she barely managed to squeak out, her raw throat cracking as she said her name.

"Okay, Veronica, good, stay with me. What's going on? Are you hurt? Do you need medical attention?"

Veronica whispered again, "Help me, please," praying only the dispatcher on the other end of the cellphone heard her and that they would get to her in time. She didn't feel she had much time left and she so badly wanted to go back to sleep.

"Have you been in an accident?"

No response.

By now the dispatcher had traced Veronica's cellphone. "Veronica, honey, stay with me, I've got help on the way," was all Veronica heard before she drifted off into that warm unconscious haze once again while sirens wailed somewhere in the distance.

CHAPTER FIFTEEN

He enjoyed scaring women. He especially enjoyed hurting them. He discovered early on that killing his victims was not as satisfying to him because once they were dead, they were no longer terrified. As he honed his craft, he realized he loved – no, *craved*, viscerally – the power of bringing them to the edge of death and then reviving them. He got off on their suffering and their fear, reveling in the fact that he had the ultimate power and control over whether his victims lived or died. They would live the rest of their lives always looking over their shoulders, wondering if he would be back, afraid to sleep with the lights off, powerless. And he thrived on all of it.

Oh, but now to have someone watching him while he exerted that power? That was a whole new level of excitement. Veronica, oh Veronica, how he had enjoyed his date with her, especially knowing that Ronald was watching him. He almost took it too far, but he purposely used a very short, thin blade so that he wouldn't hit any vital organs or arteries. He had become very skilled with a knife, precise, like a surgeon. Veronica had bled more than he expected but the steri-strips he applied to her wounds and covered hat the fuck have I done?" he said aloud as he started

* * *

a Rico settled back into the alcove across the street the hookah lounge on 7th Avenue. The aroma of the cooking in the brick ovens wafted across the street m and he realized he was hungry. He was hidden in arkness but had a clear view into the windows across street including the windows of the second-floor ments above. He lit a cigarette and watched the smoke out over the deserted Ybor sidewalk in front of him, y that it was a slow night in the city with most of the crawlers at the opposite end of 7th Avenue. He could by the whitish-bluish light emanating from inside the nd story apartment that its occupant was still awake on his computer. As he often was at this time of night, o noticed.

The phone in his pocket vibrated, signifying he had eived a text. He took the phone out of his pocket and d the text. He quickly tapped out a response, "yes, firmed," hit send, and slipped the phone back into back pocket. His phone told him it was 1:46 a.m. He uld watch for another fifteen minutes until the pizza nt and hookah lounge closed. As in the past, his subject uld call it a night at about that time, so there was no

with bandages should have been more than enough to keep her from bleeding out until the medics got there.

Right before he moved Veronica to the bathtub, he logged into the app on his phone and looped in the feed he had recorded earlier of Veronica's bedroom so that all Ronald would see now was her pristine bedroom, just the way it always looked. He cleaned up her bedroom, first wrapping the bloody comforter into the heavy-duty tarp that he had placed under her comforter when he first arrived and then placing both the tarp and red-stained comforter carefully into the large, black plastic lawn bag he had brought with him. Next, he placed the blood-spattered throw pillows into the bag and made her bed with the new, identical comforter and pillows that he had picked up from a Bed Bath and Beyond in Clearwater, paying cash for them, of course. He retrieved his rechargeable hand-held vacuum from his black leather backpack, and vacuumed everywhere he had been in the room, expending extra effort near Veronica's bed and the chair in the corner. He hadn't touched anything in the house, including Veronica, without his gloves on, so he was confident he had not left any fingerprints. Hopefully when he vacuumed, he collected any DNA or hair follicles he could have left behind.

He went back into the bathroom and confirmed Veronica was still breathing. Her bleeding appeared to have stopped or at least significantly slowed down. He plugged her cellphone into the nearby outlet and rested the cellphone on the side of the tub within reaching distance so she could call for help when she regained consciousness. He packed everything, including his hand-vac, into his backpack, picked up the large black garbage bag and left the house, casually walking down the street to his silver Audi Q7. After he was a safe enough distance away from the house, he pulled over and deleted the video loop so the cameras would once again be filming Veronica's bedroom in real time. He hacked into the security system, adjusted the times so that there was no interruption, and deleted the videos of his attack on her, which he had already saved and transferred to an encrypted file. It was time for him to visit Ronald to let him know who was running the show. And it was almost time for him to visit Hallie. But not just yet.

* * *

Ronald was enraged but also scared and horrified at what he had just witnessed. He logged into the Reddit chatroom. There were no recent posts from Mr. Sadist. He opened the private message app inside Reddit and typed,

"WTF? Where is she? What did you do to her? You better fucking get back to me asap and tell me what the fuck is going on!"

Within moments he received a notification that he had a private message.

"Or what? Be careful, Ronnie. F
my slice of pizza tonight, I thought,
make this night better? Maybe a lit
which I was delighted to find right
place. Ybor is so nice this time of yea

Ronald stood in front of his c
message, sweating more than he us
window unit air conditioner cranked
He instinctively looked at the door to
was in place. He quickly shut his blin
from the windows before sliding the
dresser in front of his deadbolted front c
fridge and retrieved a somewhat still w
been sitting in his car most of the day
around his small, 550 square foot apartm
another ping notifying him that he had a

"Are we done with the drama now,
stop moving your furniture around – yc
a muscle. From now on, I call the shot
to do it my way. I have enough video sa
to your actual IP address to incriminate y
have connects you to the girls, including o
and nothing to me. So, let's settle down an
fun. Let me know when you're ready."

Ronald read and re-read the message,
unless you counted the involuntary shakin
doing.

reason to stick around any later. He was curious what this guy had done to earn the attention of the man for whom he worked. He didn't ask – he never asked – but it couldn't be good, he thought, chuckling to himself as he took the last drag of his cigarette and flicked the butt out onto the redbrick street. Ten minutes later, the apartment went dark, the places downstairs closed, and there was nothing more for him to see.

CHAPTER SIXTEEN

Hallie had texted Tom a few times since their trip to the Keys. He would eventually respond, but he was always busy. She longed for his texts or communication from him the way restless dogs waited for their owners to return home. She craved his words like an addict craved his next fix. Why did he have this effect on her? She had never been a needy person before, but now, if he didn't text her or respond to her text, it would affect her mood for the entire day until she finally heard from him. "What is wrong with me?" she questioned herself.

She looked at the time on her computer: 3:57 p.m. She had been there since 8:15 that morning, had skipped lunch, and had only billed 4.30 hours. Where had the other three-plus hours gone, she wondered. Unable to concentrate on work, she walked down the hall to Paige's office, dropping the latest contracts she had finally finished reviewing on her assistant's desk on the way.

"Hey, wanna grab an early dinner, and by dinner, I actually mean, happy hour?" Hallie asked, walking into her friend's office and sitting down in one of the two leather chairs facing her desk, the standard law office set up.

Paige looked up from whatever she was doing on her computer, smiling at the interruption, "Yes, that would be great. Let me finish this email and we can go. Where do you want to go?" she asked as she continued typing.

"Somewhere that serves good wine."

"Ooh, that kind of a day, is it?" Paige asked, as she looked up from her computer.

"Yes, something like that."

Paige finished typing, opened her desk drawer to retrieve her very expensive Louis Vuitton handbag, took out and applied her lipstick as she got up from her desk, and grabbed her keys, "Let's go. I know just the place."

They walked the few blocks from their office to Malio's where Dina, the manager, greeted them warmly, as she always did.

"How are my two favorite attorneys doing today?" she asked, as she hugged and kissed each of them on the cheek.

"Oh Dina, it's been a helluva week already, and it's only Tuesday," Paige replied dramatically, "I know we don't have a reservation, but can you hook us up with one of our favorite booths?"

"For you two? Absolutely, my dears," their beautiful and always endearing friend replied. Scanning the reservation book, she looked up smiling, "The Britton booth is available."

The booths in the bar area had gold plates affixed to them, each one bearing the name of a VIP who came often enough to be deemed worthy of the recognition. The Britton booth, the first booth as you entered the dark lounge, referred to Brett Britton, a popular intellectual property lawyer in town, known for his tattoos, white spikey hair, and love of music. Besides being a pretty decent lawyer, from his Facebook posts, he appeared to be an exceptional piano player too.

"Any chance you can join us?" Hallie asked Dina.

"We've got a stacked book tonight so probably not, but if I can steal away for a glass, I will for sure. I just got a case of Faust in this afternoon, so hopefully a bottle of that will cure what ails you."

"You know the way to my heart, for sure, my friend," Hallie said as they followed the spunky Italian, who looked like a young Elizabeth Taylor, to one of the coveted booths in the bar area.

After ordering their wine, Hallie told Paige about the closing arguments in the Stephens trial.

"Don't worry, Hallie, Carl can try to spin it anyway he wants but Amy is the best. And bottom line, the facts, which are supported by the evidence, are what they are, no matter what theories Carl throws out there."

"I'm sure you're right. I'll just be glad when this is over. The jury's been deliberating for three days now. That makes me nervous."

"Well, just try to forget about it for now. As my mother always said, 'Don't borrow trouble,' meaning you don't know what's going to happen and you can't do anything about it anyway. What else is going on with you? Have you heard from Tom?" Paige asked, changing the subject.

"Yes, here and there, but, truthfully, not as much as I would have liked. Before the Keys, he blew up my phone with texts every morning and late at night. Then we go to the Keys, have an amazing weekend, and it's practically crickets since I've been back," Hallie said, shaking her head.

"Maybe he's just really busy," Paige offered.

"No, it's something else. I can't put my finger on it, but he was different even our last day there. More distant or distracted, I don't know, but definitely different."

"Well, how was he different? Give me an example."

"Okay, so we have this amazing, drunken day in the sun followed by hot sex that night. The next morning, he seemed different, less attentive, like he was ready to go back to Miami, and on his phone constantly. Not exactly great for the ego, ya know? But then that night he was back to the Tom of the night before, so maybe I'm just paranoid and distrustful because of David living his double life. I guess I need to talk about this with Jill at my next appointment," Hallie said with a nervous laugh, trying to make light of the situation.

"Jill?"

"Oh, Dr. Bell. I like to refer to her as Jill now rather than Dr. Bell because it's less embarrassing than admitting you're seeing a shrink. Jill says lots of her patients do that."

"Well, he's the first guy you've been with since David, so it's got to be a little weird and, after what you've been through, anyone would be guarded about his motives. Did he do or say anything else that made you uncomfortable?"

"No, not really," Hallie hesitated.

"Not exactly reassuring, counselor. Please explain."

"I'm sure it's nothing. I think, wait, no, I know, I was quite bombed. I had started drinking at the airport at 8:30 that morning, followed by a Xanax, you know, because of my fear of flying. Anyway, he picked me up at the airport with a roadie of red wine and then we had more wine at the hotel, not to mention what we drank up and down Duval Street that day."

"Okay, so you weren't feeling any pain and your judgment was probably a little skewed, but what's bothering you, Hallie?"

"You're going to think I'm crazy, and I might be, but I swear I woke up at one point that first night and he was holding my hand, which in the moment I thought was sweet, but then I realized he was holding my hand so he could use my thumb to get into my phone."

"Hallie, that's crazy. Why would he want to get into your phone?" Paige asked.

"I agree, it's crazy. I kept going over it in my head the next morning. Before he woke up, I walked over to a quaint little coffee shop named after one of Hemingway's many island cats. As I drank my coffee and ate my toasted bagel, trying desperately to soak up the remaining alcohol still in my system, I asked myself the same question. But as much as I tried to dismiss it as a dream or some drunken confusion, I know what I felt and I know what I saw. For whatever reason, he opened my phone," Hallie said, relieved to have finally acknowledged that she hadn't imagined it.

"That's weird, Hallie. Did you confront him about it?"

"No. As I mentioned, at the time I wasn't positive that I hadn't dreamt it. By the time I finished breakfast, I had convinced myself that there would be absolutely no reason for him to go into my phone. I mean, really, we met up in the Keys, drank incessantly for ten hours straight, went back to the room, had sex, and went to sleep. We had a great time. My head was more than a little foggy when I woke up, and I wanted to believe that I had imagined it. But the more I've thought about it since then, I don't think I did. So, then the question is, why? What was he looking for?"

"I can't imagine, but I think you ought to just ask him and see what he says. Maybe he's the jealous type and wanted to see if you were texting anyone else," Paige offered.

"Yeah, I thought of that too. You're probably right. The next time I see him, if I see him again, I'm going to ask him. But for now, I'm just going to forget about it and forget about him. I think he ghosted me anyway."

The women finished their wine and spent the rest of the evening talking about Paige's wedding plans, which was a nice distraction for Hallie from everything she had on her mind.

CHAPTER SEVENTEEN

The Broker pulled his burner phone out from the slit inside his mattress where he kept it hidden. It wasn't as if the guards didn't know it was there, but he paid them their cut whenever he scored so they didn't fuck with him. Inside the joint, the system worked very much the same as outside: those with the money or the goods were at the top and those with the power always had their price. And the guards at Raiford definitely had their price.

The Broker texted the familiar number: "yo, u got my video bro?"

"Working on it, our subject is MIA."

"What do you mean, MIA?"

"Gone bro, hasn't been back to her place in a few days. We're watching. It'll happen"

"Get that shit. The green is riding on it"

The Broker had his reputation to protect; he didn't need this creepy as fuck teacher fucking with his rep because he didn't get the video he wanted yet. He had to turn the tables so that it wouldn't spook the other customers. He entered the common recreation area and looked around. He had two of his protectors by his side, as he often did.

He spotted Bobby and signaled to his enforcers to bring him over to his table. He sat down and waited.

Bobby came over, "You got my shit?"

"No motherfucker, I don't got your shit. You wanna tell me what you didn't tell me before?" the Broker asked, never taking his eyes off Bobby.

"I don't know what the fuck you're talking about. Want to elaborate?" the former chemistry teacher asked.

"Motherfucker, are you taking an attitude with me?" the Broker yelled as he jumped up, shoving the trays that were on the table crashing to the floor.

The guards instantly surrounded them. The Broker quickly sat down, holding up his hands in a show of surrender to the corrupt guards, "My apologies for my outburst, gentlemen, just a little misunderstanding, we're good," the Broker said calmly, hoping the guards would move on and not investigate further.

"I'm sorry, no attitude intended," Bobby quickly offered after the guards walked away, "I just want to see my wife, as we discussed."

"I got you, boy, but these things take time. Now get the fuck away from me and don't you ever come at me like that again or I'll fucking kill you, you got that?"

"Yeah, I got it. Just get me the video and I'll get you the cash."

CHAPTER EIGHTEEN

It had been about a week since Ronald last heard from Mr. Sadist. He was hoping he wouldn't contact him again, but he knew he probably wasn't that lucky. He grabbed a cold PBR from his fridge and sat down in front of his large monitor. He hadn't logged into any of the accounts of his ladies for the last week either, terrified as to what he might see. But he felt it was time, especially since Mr. Sadist had gone dark. He wasn't ready to log into Veronica's account yet, so he started with Laura. Not only was she home but she appeared to be alone, which pleased him. She looked so pretty, her long black hair the color of onyx, falling loosely off her shoulders and down her back, while she sat on her couch reading a book called *Find Me*, by Alafair Burke. He watched her for about ten minutes, but she never picked her head up from her book. He was becoming bored.

He clicked on the link for Hallie. Good old Juno was there, in her familiar spot on her bed next to Hallie's desk. Hallie wasn't home. He always knew whether Hallie was home or not based on Juno. If Hallie wasn't home, the sweet dog would lie patiently on her little bed until Hallie got home from work or back from her run. Juno would also lie there when Hallie was working at her desk, but he could see Hallie wasn't at her desk so that meant she wasn't home. Ronald liked dogs. He imagined Juno curled up at his feet in the living room as he cuddled next to Hallie on the couch, watching her favorite TV shows, either the *Bosch* series on Amazon or *Criminal Minds* on Netflix. He looked at the time on his monitor: 6:23 p.m. Hallie was probably out having drinks or something. She did that a lot. Ronald often wondered if she would go out as much if he was her boyfriend. He hoped not.

Sheada and Veronica were the last two he had to check in on. He decided to save Sheada for last. It was Tuesday and he knew Sheada would be teaching one of her yoga classes from her living room at 7, so he still had time. She could wait. He needed to check on Veronica, but he was petrified at what he might see, or frankly, not see. He wanted to believe he had imagined the whole attack on her, but he didn't think so. Her crimson blood, spilling and spattering onto her white down comforter, and pouring out of the slits in her beautiful, olive skin, was like a surreal Dali painting, except Ronald knew it wasn't a painting and she was really hurt. His heart ached knowing he was responsible for bringing this monster into her life. He loved her. He loved all of his women. He never meant for any of them to get hurt, especially Veronica, his first. He took a big sip of his PBR, fighting back the tears that were welling up in his eyes, while he choked down the cheap, shitty beer, which was all he could do to drown his feelings of shame, regret, and helplessness.

He opened the familiar link on his computer. But before logging in, he activated the rolling VPN, which meant that every fifteen seconds the IP addresses would expire, so that his actual IP address and location were virtually untraceable. His screen opened on the interior of Veronica's house, and the first room he saw was the kitchen, which was the default. Nothing in the kitchen looked out of place. He tapped on his keyboard and her living room came to life. Like the kitchen, nothing out of place. He manipulated the camera so he could see down the hallway, towards the front door. It was quiet, nothing seemed out of place, except the large fake plant that used to sit in the foyer was gone. How long had it been gone, he wondered? Was it still there the night she was attacked? He just couldn't remember. His hand started to shake as he moved the mouse to switch to the bedroom camera.

And there she was. As alive and beautiful as she'd ever been but he could tell something was different about her. He took a long swig of his PBR, trying to settle his nerves, as he watched her, relieved she was still alive.

CHAPTER NINETEEN

"Has the jury reached a verdict" Judge Washington asked the foreman of the jury.

"We have, Your Honor," replied the jury foreman, a soft-spoken, older gentlemen with wire rimmed glasses, wearing a white, long-sleeved, button-down dress shirt and gray slacks.

"And is that verdict unanimous?"

"Yes, sir, it is."

Judge Washington nodded to the clerk to retrieve the written verdict form the foreman.

"Mr. Stephens, please rise as the clerk reads the verdict."

The galley was still and quiet, as if everyone in it was holding their collective breath, and Hallie felt her heart pounding inside her chest. The air handler in the old building jolted on with a wheeze as the defendant and his attorney rose, their chairs scraping against the courtroom floor.

"What says the jury as to Count One?" the judge asked the clerk.

"As to Count One, we, the jury, find the defendant, William Stephens, guilty of second-degree murder," the clerk read.

There was an audible gasp of relief in the room while whispering resonated throughout the room. Hallie sat frozen, unaware that she was still holding her breath.

Judge Washington banged his gavel on the bench to quiet the courtroom before he spoke again, "And as to Count Two, abuse of a dead body?"

"As to Count Two, we, the jury, find the defendant, William Stephens, guilty," read the clerk.

The galley erupted again, but quickly quieted down as the foreboding judge looked down upon its occupants.

Directing his attention to the jury, the judge asked, "As to both counts, are the verdicts unanimous?"

"Yes, they are, Your Honor," the foreman replied.

Hallie slowly exhaled, relieved that this ugly chapter of her life was almost over. She hoped she would never have to lay eyes on Judge Stephens again, but more importantly, she prayed that Katie would never see or hear from him ever.

Creepy Carl sprang to his feet, "Your Honor, the defense requests the Court to poll the jury."

"Very well, counselor," Judge Washington said before addressing the jury, "Defense counsel has asked me to poll the jury, which means that I will ask each one of you individually to confirm your verdict of guilt. We will start with Count One, and then we will go through the same process as to Count Two."

The judge began by calling juror number one of the twelve-person jury, and asked, "Juror number one, as to

Count One, murder in the second degree, how do you find?" to which juror number one answered, "Guilty," and so it went for the next five jurors.

"Juror number seven, as to Count One, murder in the second degree, how to you find?"

A stout, blonde woman in her mid-to-late forties, looked down at her clasped hands and, unlike the six jurors before her, nervously said, "I don't think he did it."

"Juror number seven, please speak up," the judge's voice boomed. "I am asking you to confirm that you voted in favor of finding the defendant, William Stephens, guilty of second-degree murder. Is that your verdict?"

"No, I mean, yes," the rosy-cheeked woman stuttered, "th-th-that's what I voted back there, but I don't think he killed that young lady."

The courtroom erupted and the judge slammed his gavel on the bench to quiet the room. "Bailiff, please remove the jury to the deliberation room immediately. Counsel, in my chambers, now!" the obviously angry judge barked into the courtroom.

As she got up to follow the judge into chambers, Amy whispered to her associate and second chair, Wyatt, "Find my notes from the voir dire of the jury and figure out what the fuck happened with juror number seven. I want to know who the fuck this woman is and why we didn't strike her."

Amy picked up her legal pad and pen and headed into chambers fearing the judge was about to declare a mistrial and wondering if there was any way to salvage this trial. The attorneys walked back into Judge Washington's chambers to find him furiously flipping through the latest edition of the Florida Rules of Criminal Procedure on his desk. Before either attorney could speak, the judge held up one of his baseball mitt-sized hands, wordlessly securing their silence, and motioned for them to sit in the two, uncomfortable wooden chairs that faced the large, oak desk. The attorneys dutifully followed his command, experiencing the same feeling as having been called to the principal's office as children.

After a few minutes, the judge read aloud, "Florida Rules of Criminal Procedure, Rule 3.450, and I quote, '*On the motion of either the state or the defendant or on its own motion, the court shall cause the jurors to be asked severally if the verdict rendered is their verdict. If a juror dissents, the court must direct that the jury be sent back for further consideration. If there is no dissent the verdict shall be entered of record and the jurors discharged. However, no motion to poll the jury shall be entertained after the jury is discharged or the verdict recorded.*' As you can see, counselors, the rule is clear: I must direct the jury back for further consideration, but, frankly, I don't see how this doesn't end in a mistrial."

Creepy Carl spoke first, "Your Honor, we have a juror who has declared in open court that she does not believe the defendant is guilty. Even if the jury comes back and she's changed her verdict back to guilty, how can this verdict stand?"

Amy responded quickly, but calmly, "Your Honor, I am very concerned with this juror's veracity and the obvious change of heart from the deliberation room to open court. The foreman said the verdict was unanimous. Had defense counsel not moved to poll the jury, a unanimous guilty verdict would have been recorded and the jury discharged. As was proved in this trial, this defendant used his position as a criminal court judge to bribe, intimidate, and make deals with criminal defendants who came before him. How do we know he didn't get to juror number seven?"

"Your Honor, this is outrageous! I object to any suggestion that my client had anything to do with juror number seven's alleged change of position from the jury deliberation room to open court," Carl exclaimed.

"Oh really, Carl? You jumped up almost instantly to poll the jury. I would love to know how often you have polled the jury in other cases," Amy said, her arms crossed over her chest while she rolled her eyes.

"Exactly what are you accusing me of, counselor? You better have facts to back up what you're implying, or I'll file a motion for sanctions against you," Carl retorted, his voice rising and his face turning redder by the second.

"That's enough," the judge growled, "I've heard your positions and I'm inclined to declare a mistrial, but I believe I need to send the jury back to deliberate first. We are going back in there now and neither of you will speak – no motions, no statements in open court, no statements to the media, nothing. I will recess these proceedings for lunch and will render my decision when court resumes this afternoon. Do I make myself clear?"

"Yes, Your Honor," the attorneys said in unison, after which they all filed back into the stunned courtroom.

CHAPTER TWENTY

Juror number seven felt the other jurors staring at her as they all resumed their seats around the large conference table. No one spoke for the first five minutes, and the awkward silence caused her to start sweating more profusely than she normally did. She could feel her black polka dot dress sticking to her damp back while the sweat trickled down her thick, girthy legs until it absorbed into the top of the leather straps of her sensible sandals. Linda Morgan sat there, wringing her chubby hands while she looked down at her lap, afraid to make eye contact with anyone in the room. She knew the other jurors were mad at her, but she didn't care. She saw how the defendant, William Stephens, had been looking at her throughout the trial. She could feel their connection deep in her soul. And she believed the nice young attorney who wore his hair in a bun on top of his head when he explained – very convincingly, in Linda's opinion – how someone else could have committed this terrible crime.

Her eyes locked with William Stephens briefly during the closing arguments. His eyes told her, "*Thank you for believing in me*" and she knew. She knew in that instant that he didn't do it. Her Billy, as she started referring to him in her private conversations with herself, could not have done what they accused him of. She had written on a napkin *Linda Mary Stephens* and *Mrs. William Stephens*. She had folded and unfolded the napkin to peek at it so many times, the flimsy paper was starting to fray. She folded it up once again and placed it inside her 40-DD bra – close to her heart, she liked to think. She couldn't wait until they could be together after this silly trial was over.

* * *

Amy and Wyatt didn't speak until they returned to their office on the 4th floor of the Courthouse Annex building, which was across the street from the courthouse. Amy dropped her stuff on her cluttered desk and picked up her phone to advise the State Attorney, her boss, Craig Behrenfeld, about what had just happened in court. News agencies were already beginning to report on the events of the morning, scrambling to find legal analysts to explain what it all meant.

"I have to go up to the fifth floor to meet with Craig. While I'm gone, I need you to find a case that says the court does not have to call a mistrial if the jury comes back unanimous after further deliberations. Got it?"

"Got it. I'm on it," the young attorney said as he got up and quickly left her office, his barely used leather trial bag over his shoulder.

Amy hadn't smoked in over a year, but she was about to break. She rummaged through her bottom desk drawer to see if she had an old pack of Marlboro Lights stashed away where she used to keep an emergency pack or two. She knew she should not, but she needed something to settle her nerves.

"Just this one time," she promised herself.

She found a half empty pack towards the back of the drawer with a Bic lighter stored safely inside the cardboard box next to the remaining, likely stale, cigarettes. She didn't care. There was no question she would need one after her meeting with Craig. She threw the old pack in her purse and stored her purse securely under her desk before heading upstairs to explain what went down after the verdict was read.

"So, what happened in there today?" Craig asked, his eyes looking more tired than usual.

Amy knew Craig had a lot of pressure on him, especially with the scrutiny he was under from the media as well as the Governor's office. The Governor was likely going to make a run for the presidency and didn't give a shit about the State of Florida, but he had to appear that he did and he was running on a "tough on crime" platform, vowing to clean up Florida's cities. This put extra pressure on the State Attorneys in Florida's biggest cities because the Governor loved headlines.

"I honestly don't know, Craig, but we're going to find out. Juror #7 changed her mind from the deliberation room to the time the judge polled the jury. There was nothing in voir dire that set off any red flags for us. I've got Wyatt scouring her social media posts and looking up case law as to whether a mistrial can be avoided. As soon as I have answers, I'll report back."

"Okay, do it fast and keep me posted. This is going to be a shit storm."

"I know. Maybe someone got to her? It just doesn't make any sense. We put on a solid case and the guilty verdict should stand. I'll report back after I check in with Wyatt."

Amy returned to her office to grab her purse, badly craving the nicotine fix that was awaiting her. Her nerves were shot. Before she had a chance to run downstairs, Wyatt came into Amy's office, excited with what he had found.

"If the jury deliberates and returns with a unanimous verdict, there is no mistrial. *Bouie v. State*, case out of the Third District Court of Appeal, citing a Florida Supreme Court case from 1966. Almost identical facts to our case: one of the jurors stands up during polling and says, 'No, that's not my verdict, I don't think he's guilty.' Judge sends the jury back for more deliberations, jury comes back, verdict is unanimous. Defense moves for mistrial, judge denies the motion, and verdict stands on appeal. Judge Washington did it exactly right by immediately sending the jury out of the courtroom when he did."

"That's awesome, Wyatt. Print me that case and the Florida Supreme Court case it relied on with extra copies for the judge and defense counsel."

"Already did. Got 'em all right here," the eager attorney replied, tapping three separate stacks of clipped papers in his hand.

"Now all we need is for juror number seven to change her verdict back to guilty, right? What do we know about her, by the way? Did you have a chance to review our notes from voir dire?"

"I have those copied for you, too," he said, handing over a separate set of papers to Amy. Reading from the notes in front of him, he continued, "She didn't raise any red flags during voir dire. Linda Morgan, divorced, no children, two cats, lives alone, works at an insurance company as an intake claims agent. She works remotely from her home in Town and Country. We didn't have any reservations about her, figuring she would be more sympathetic to Naomi Banks and her family than to the defendant."

"Does she have social media? Let's do a deeper dive on her and see what we can find. We've got forty-five minutes before we have to be back in court. I'll have Jenny order us some sandwiches from downstairs."

"You got it. I'll see what I can find."

Amy took the stack of cases Wyatt had handed her, a yellow highlighter, her legal pad, and her purse and walked out of her office towards the elevator. On her way, she asked her assistant, Jenny, to order a couple of Cubans from the downstairs sandwich shop. They were no Bodega's but they would have to do. And then she went downstairs to smoke, hoping the nicotine would settle her frayed nerves.

CHAPTER TWENTY-ONE

Hallie pulled the old, musty boxes down from her attic, praying there were no roaches in the boxes. She wasn't afraid of anyone or anything except the infamous Florida palmetto bug, also commonly referred to as the American cockroach, the most terrifying creature alive, in Hallie's opinion. What made these horrific creatures stand out was their size and ability to fly. Fortunately, they preferred the outdoors, especially palmetto bushes and oak trees, but in the hot summer months they would come in to find water or avoid the rain, sometimes taking up residence in damp, dusty attics. Hallie swore she suffered from PTSD from the time a flock of them, as then fourteen-year-old Hallie had called them, invaded the family living room from the fireplace after the damper had been mistakenly left open from the previous winter. Hallie screamed and fled to her upstairs bedroom, leaving the living room in complete disarray: the TV on, her snacks and empty dishes on the coffee table, and couch pillows thrown around the room, which is what she used to defend herself from the invading species. When her parents returned home that evening, they thought there had been a break-in and the house ransacked. But, true to form, her father saved the day by setting off a bomb, closing the damper, and assuring Hallie that all intruders had been eliminated. The memory gave Hallie the chills to this day, and she always had to look around to make sure there were none flying towards her.

Before opening either box, Hallie poured herself a glass of wine to calm her nerves. After she had drunk about a half a glass, feeling a little less rattled, she armed herself with her twenty-foot wasp spray and proceeded to open the first of the two boxes. That was the only thing she missed about David: he was the resident roach killer on the few occasions one would venture into their house. She would scream, David would come running, kill the dreadful intruder, and they would both expound on his bravery, only partly with tongue in cheek. Now if she saw one, she still screamed but then she had no choice but to kill it herself, because, of course, she had to know it was dead. There was no way she could sleep in the same house if she saw one and it happened to get away. She took another sip of her wine and placed the top of the first box to her left on the living room floor where she sat, Juno faithfully by her side.

The first box contained the seven files she had previously identified and grouped together as "files of interest," as she liked to refer to them. She hadn't read the case names in over ten years, yet she knew them by heart. She decided to review each of the seven files again, from start to finish. She read the names on the label affixed to the outside of the fifth

Redweld file she pulled out of the box: In Re: The Marriage of Nina Martino and Gaetano Martino. The names were not unfamiliar to her, as she had read their file many times before, but this time they triggered an unrelated memory, something more recent. She had to think. What was it, she asked herself? She couldn't think of anything and decided that it was just one of those déjà vu moments. She opened the file and read her father's notes on the case, seeing his familiar handwriting on the aging and fraying yellow legal pad paper, which is how most attorneys took notes back in the day. Hallie still often took notes on a yellow legal pad, but those notes would eventually be scanned in by her assistant and the hard pages shredded. Hallie missed her father terribly and seeing his handwritten notes made her both happy and sad.

In this case, her father was representing the wife, Nina Martino. Her father often represented the wives in their divorce cases, because he felt they deserved a lawyer who wasn't afraid to go up against Tampa's prominent and powerful men in town. He always told Hallie, "I like the underdog. They need someone who can bite back for them."

She continued reading through her father's notes. The Martinos had one daughter, Monica Martino, who was about eighteen or nineteen when her parents were going through their divorce and was away at college at the University of Florida at the time, hopefully avoiding the worst of their tumultuous relationship. There were no other children born during the marriage, so custody was obviously not an issue. It would have been a fight over alimony and assets, which was often less contentious and emotional than a custody battle, but not always. She flipped the pages as she continued reading her father's notes when she saw something she didn't remember reading in the past. The case was about three months in after filing the petition for dissolution on behalf of the wife. Her father always dated his entries.

8/28/90, t/c Nina, more issues. "Family" getting involved. RO? Withdraw? F/up next week to discuss next steps.

The entry was one week before her father's murder and was the last entry in his notes. When she first reviewed the file, she was a young lawyer and probably did not understand or appreciate the implications of the note. Now, reading it as a more experienced lawyer, she saw it in a completely different light. Her father was considering withdrawing from the case or withdrawing the divorce petition, both of which were significant to the situation. Her father was not one to withdraw from a case. If his client ran out of money, the most common reason attorneys withdrew from ongoing cases, he would simply finish the case pro bono, meaning without charge. He said it didn't happen often and it was important to give back when he could, so her father's note about withdrawing was very suspicious. "RO" which she had mistakenly assumed meant "reach out" so many years ago likely stood for "restraining order." And why was "family" in quotes? This file just moved to the top of her list. She needed to find out more about the Martino family, including what happened in their divorce and what they've been up to for the last thirty years.

A google search of the Martino family revealed that Gaetano "Tommy" Martino was the son of Nico Martino, allegedly a soldier in the Trafficante crime family. This certainly put a different spin on the word "family" in her father's notes. Hallie went down a rabbit hole of research, reading everything she could find about the Martino family. Most of what she found, however, was about Nico Martino, once known as Tampa's premier bookie and gambling man, getting his start in Ybor City as one of Santos Trafficante Jr.'s most trusted men. He was a "made man" in the Trafficante crime family, meaning he had been inducted into the family and had sworn to uphold the codes of silence and honor. During the sixties and seventies, he had been arrested multiple times for assault and battery and various weapons charges, but allegedly had retired from illegal activities in the eighties after a stint in prison for manslaughter.

His son, Tommy Martino appeared to be a law-abiding businessman, a successful real estate developer, but as the son of one of Tampa's most notorious mobsters, anything was possible. Tommy died in early 1991 at the age of 51, about six months after Hallie's father had been shot.

According to his obituary, he was still married to Nina when he died: *"Gaetano "Tommy" Martino was survived by his loving wife, Nina, his daughter, Monica "Moni," his brother, Nicolas, his sister, Gianina, and many beloved cousins, nieces and nephews."* If Tommy had killed Hallie's father before the divorce could be finalized, that could have been enough to scare Nina into a reconciliation if that's what Tommy had wanted. His mafia connections would also explain why the police never investigated and why the case files were destroyed, especially after his death only a short time after her father's death. Hallie decided she had to talk to Nina Martino. Hallie felt like she was onto something for the first time since her father's murder. She needed to do this for him. For her mother too. And, if she was being honest, for herself. They all needed closure.

CHAPTER TWENTY-TWO

Sheada wasn't sure what woke her, other than she had to pee and wanted some water. She looked at her phone and saw that it was 3:37 a.m. She got up, half asleep, and headed towards the bathroom. As she was wiping the sleep and the previous day's mascara out of her eye lashes, she was suddenly slammed backwards into her bedroom door, landing on her back on the floor unable to catch her breath. Instantly dazed, she had no idea what hit her. After she was able to breathe again, she started whimpering, terrified that the sounds she was emitting would bring her further punishment and pain. She was agonizingly aware that something horrific was happening to her, yet she couldn't comprehend the scope of it and didn't understand why it was happening.

She managed to curl up into the fetal position, hugging her knees and praying that she was having another one of her nightmares. This just couldn't be real. And then she saw him, or at least the outline of a burly silhouette in the darkness of the hallway. As her eyes adjusted, she could see his shadow on the wall behind him, reflecting from the moon peeking in through her half open miniblinds. She tried to scream but just like in her nightmares, her vocal cords were paralyzed, and no sound came out.

"Hello Sheada," she heard whispered in the darkness just before her world went black.

* * *

Sheada's head was throbbing and her back hurt as she shifted uncomfortably on the mattress beneath her. She had no recollection of going from the floor to the bed. She opened her eyes. She was in complete darkness. Did she just have a bad nightmare? She was trying to unscramble her brain, but the disjointed images of the dark figure and the attack replayed through her mind like reels from an old black and white movie. She needed to text Justin. She couldn't see anything in the darkness and her eyes had not yet adjusted. She instinctively reached over to her nightstand where she placed her cellphone each night before she went to sleep. Her hand found only air: no nightstand and no cellphone. She was confused and she sat up, leaning against the wall behind her. As she tried to shake the heavy fog out of her aching head, her body started to shake as she realized she was not in her own bedroom. She leaned over the edge of the bed and threw up, which intensified the excruciating pain in her head.

Her coughing and clearing of her throat alerted her captor that she was awake. She heard heavy footsteps echoing off the floor outside of the room, making their way closer to her. She tried to regain her composure but continued to dry heave due to the ever-present waves of nausea likely caused by her head injury. As the door opened, a sliver of light streamed into the room from the hallway and Sheada backed away to the farthest corner of the bed, trying to shield her sensitive eyes to the intruding light. Through the slits she allowed between her fingers, Sheada could see that there was no other furniture in the room, just the mattress she was on, and nothing else, unless you counted the dark streaks she could make out on the walls.

"Well, hello again," the voice said, "I'm so pleased that you're awake. Now the fun can begin."

CHAPTER TWENTY-THREE

Moni Martino took a long drag from her cigarette, blowing the smoke out of her red, creased lips, stained from years of wearing her signature bright red lipstick. The deep lines around her mouth revealed her lifelong smoking habit and aged her beyond her fifty years. Her once striking features, her thick, black hair set against her olive skin and hazel eyes and her curvy, sexy body, and infectious personality would captivate her targets before she would inevitably use them up and run them off, much like the black widow devouring her mate after sex. But the years had not been kind to Moni, largely due to her penchant for whiskey, cigarettes, and the wrong men. Always the wrong men. Her flimsy nighty hung off her now-small frame, exposing her cleavage from the perfect size DD breasts one of her lovers had paid for many years ago. She put her cigarette out in the overflowing ashtray on the nightstand next to the empty whiskey glass from the night before and looked over at the man still sleeping next to her, the tattoo of a tiger emblazoned on his back. For the life of her she could not remember his name.

She got up and found her way to the small bathroom in the one-bedroom Gulfport garage apartment she had been renting for the past year. She enjoyed living in the small, fishing village-turned-artsy-Bohemian beach town, where all the locals knew each other but that attracted enough visitors to keep her from getting bored, such as her recent jaunt with Tiger-man snoring loudly in the bed next to her. The entire city consisted of less than three square miles, which ended at the Boca Ciega Bay. From her apartment, she could walk to the bars, restaurants, and the beach, which is where she spent most of her days and nights, not necessarily in any particular order.

She casually swiped a Twenty and an American Express Black credit card from Tiger-man's wallet, a/k/a Alex D. Birch according to his Florida driver's license, before returning the wallet to the dresser where he had left it the night before next to his Tag Heuer vintage watch. She went out to her tiny kitchenette and made herself a caffè, using her favorite Italian coffee, LaVazza Classico, which she ordered by the case on Amazon. Many mornings she would add a shot of Irish whiskey or bourbon to her coffee but not today. She checked the time: 9:34 a.m. She had just over an hour before she had to leave to meet Nina. She took her caffè and her pack of smokes and went out to her small balcony overlooking the alleyway behind her apartment to enjoy both. The humidity had already arrived but the salty air coming off the Gulf made it bearable, almost pleasant. In another hour, the balmy breeze would disappear leaving behind it a stagnant stifling heat, tolerable only to the natives. Moni never minded the heat. It was the loneliness that got her.

She took a sip of the bitter espresso followed by a drag on her cigarette. Looking down, she spotted a familiar black and white feral cat scouring for its breakfast among the metal trashcans lining the alley.

"We're always searching for our next score, aren't we, kitty?" she rasped towards the cat, smoke billowing out of her mouth as she laughed, "I see you," she said, gesturing with her two fingers from her eyes down at the oblivious feral cat in the alley.

She checked the time on her phone again: 9:53 a.m. Time to wake up Tiger-man and send him on his way. She had to shower, wash the sins of the night before off of her body, and put on her most demure dress. Today, the last Friday of the month, Nina would be expecting her at the usual place, the Columbia, at the usual time, 11:45. Moni knew better than to be late, drunk, or dressed like a whore, as her mother had admonished her on prior occasions. And with Nina in control of the money since Daddy had died, Nina controlled Moni. Just as she always had. She often wondered how things would have turned out if Daddy hadn't died.

She stubbed out her last cigarette of the morning in the brimming ashtray and went into her apartment to kick out Tiger-man and begin her transformation.

CHAPTER TWENTY-FOUR

As he watched Veronica, Ronald realized she was not alone in the house. There were two women in the bedroom with her as Veronica sat on her bed, her back against the headboard. Veronica directed the women who were busy emptying drawers into suitcases and retrieving items from her closet. Was Veronica moving out? He couldn't blame her after what she had been through. He felt terrible that he had somehow brought Mr. Sadist into her life, but he didn't know how that monster had found her. All he did was share pictures and videos of his ladies with the group in the chatroom, but he had never told anyone, including in his private messages with Mr. Sadist, where any of the women lived. He wouldn't do that. But he *had* found her. That awful night, he saw him in Veronica's house. And he hurt her. He hurt her really bad.

The women continued to gather Veronica's belongings from her dresser and closet into suitcases and boxes with a sense of urgency. Veronica seemed so frail compared to her previous commanding presence. Her noticeably thinner frame was lost under her baggy sweatshirt and sweatpants the way a child would play dress up in her mother's clothes.

Her long hair was pulled tight into a ponytail on top of her head, seemingly devoid of its normal shiny luster, while her pale face conveyed a hopelessness that no amount of makeup would be able to conceal. As she reached up to rub her temples, he saw the bandages wrapped around her wrists peeking out under her sleeves. Ronald's eyes teared up, his guilt overwhelmed only by his helplessness.

"I'm so sorry, Veronica, I'm so, so sorry," Ronald said sincerely to the screen in front of him, wiping his eyes with the back of his hand. He heard a siren approaching from the east, quickly passing by his front window with the siren getting quieter the farther the cruiser headed west, likely into the last remnants of the projects that had not been extinguished by gentrification. He went to the small fridge and retrieved a PBR, his second of the night, and noticed his hand was shaking when he went to pop the tab.

When he sat back down again, he couldn't bear to watch Veronica any longer, so he decided to check on Sheada. He logged into her system, his Mac automatically filling in his password for her account and waited as the cameras came to life. He tapped on his keyboard and clicked his mouse until he had viewed each room in her house. She wasn't home, which was strange because this was one of her normal yoga nights. She hadn't missed one of her Thursday night yoga sessions in at least two months. She was probably on vacation, he told himself, maybe with that young blonde guy she had started bringing back to her place. Ronald didn't like him. He was good looking, very confident, and too comfortable with Sheada, which was everything Ronald was not. He could tell Sheada liked him. She would giggle at whatever he said and sit close to him when they would watch a movie on the couch. She was probably out with him, which made Ronald angry. A few more clicks on the keyboard and he was viewing the most recent history from her cameras from earlier that evening.

"Noooo!" Ronald cried when he saw the grotesque, looming figure in one of the video clips. He jumped up and started pacing, covering the length of the small room in a few strides. He could see it wasn't the skinny blonde kid. No, he knew exactly who it was. Evil had found Sheada and he feared for what he was about to witness. He grabbed another PBR from the fridge, this time trying to steady his hand as he opened it. He guzzled half of it before he had the courage to look back at the monitor screen to watch the rest of the video history. He let out a large burp as he sat down, regurgitating a little of the sour beer into his mouth at the same time.

A few more clicks and the last clip that was recorded came into view: a large man carrying Sheada out the front door to Sheada's car parked in the driveway, just out of view but the camera captured the front corner of the car, and Ronald knew it was Sheada's car. The security device recorded the thud of the passenger door being closed followed by the figure returning briefly into sight before the sound of a second car door closing was heard. Ronald sat there motionless as he listened to the sound of the car's ignition and tires on the asphalt as it backed up and drove away outside of the camera's view. His Sheada, his beloved Sheada, gone, into the darkness. The bitter PBR mixed with stomach acid travelled up his esophagus, burning as it made its way to his throat, forcing Ronald to race to the bathroom and heave the contents into the grimy toilet.

CHAPTER TWENTY-FIVE

Hallie was pent up from her stressful week at work and the bizarre court proceedings that had occurred in the William Stephens trial. Judge Washington had sent the jury back for further deliberations after Juror #7, the plump, middle-aged juror Hallie had seen nodding during Carl's closing argument, recanted her guilty verdict during the polling of the jury. As of that evening, the jury was still deliberating. She and Paige had missed their usual Thursday night dinner the night before, so Hallie had invited Paige over for dinner. Cooking was a different kind of therapy for Hallie than running, which released her endorphins and energized her, whereas cooking calmed her down and relaxed her. Being in the kitchen reminded her of her childhood, her mother cooking for the holidays, the smells, the amazing food, family coming together, the joy of it all. And after the week she had, she needed to cook.

She decided to make Paige's favorite, chicken piccata with a side of linguine. She took out her large pan and poured olive oil into the pan. She chopped a few cloves of garlic and put them in the pan to sauté while she coated the chicken cutlets in flour mixed with garlic powder, salt, pepper, and paprika. When the oil and garlic were heated, she cooked the chicken perfectly, squeezing a lemon over it and adding a little white wine to the pan. When the chicken was mostly done, she transferred it to a Pyrex square cooking dish and placed it in the preheated oven while she made the piccata sauce and pasta.

Just as she finished everything, her cellphone rang. She expected it to be Paige, telling her she was running late, when she looked down at her phone and saw it was Detective Garcia.

She tried to conceal her excitement when she answered, which made her voice sound unnatural and like someone she didn't know, "Detective Marcelo, I mean, Garcia, I mean Marcelo," she stammered.

Marcelo laughed, "Hi Hallie, bad time?"

"No, it's actually perfect timing. I just finished making dinner," Hallie responded, somewhat recovering her voice and composure.

"How are you doing?"

"Good, how are you?"

"I'm good, thank you. Were you at the courthouse yesterday?"

"Yes, it was insane. I don't know what happened with that juror. Were you there?"

"No, but I heard about it. Sounded crazy."

"It was. Have you heard anything yet? Last I heard, jury was still deliberating."

"Yeah, that's what I heard too. I'm sure we'll hear something soon. So anyway, about the email you received," Marcelo continued, redirecting the conversation.

"Right," Hallie said, "what did you find out?"

"Benjamin Young, Prisoner #1249078, convicted in 2014 of fraud and other crimes related to his corrupt real estate development business, including attempted murder for hiring a hit man to kill his business partner. He was 61 years old when he was convicted and was sentenced to fifteen years at Raiford. With gain-time credit for good behavior, he'll probably be out in about four or five years."

"So why did this guy contact me? It doesn't make any sense," Hallie said. "Who did he try to kill?"

"Hmm, let me see, I think that's in this file, give me a minute . . . . okay, here it is, the intended victim was his business partner, Vincent Martino. Do you recognize that name?"

"Is he related to Tommy Martino? Do you know who he is?"

"No, but there was a large Martino family here in Tampa, some of whom were connected to the Trafficante crime family back in the day, but I think they've all pretty much died or retired as the cartels and younger gangs took over. Who's Tommy Martino?"

"My father was a family law attorney, often representing the wives of Tampa's powerful men. At the time of his murder, he had several active divorce cases, one of which was representing Nina Martino against her husband Gaetano, aka Tommy, Martino. A note in the Martino file dated about a week before my father's death suggested he was considering withdrawing from the case or possibly withdrawing the divorce petition, I'm not sure which. But Nina and Tommy never got divorced, although Tommy died less than a year after my father did. I wonder if this Vincent Martino is related," Hallie wondered aloud.

"Wait, your father was murdered? When? What happened?"

"About thirty years ago. My father had a reputation for representing women who wanted to leave their powerful and often abusive husbands. He said he liked to represent the underdog. Anyway, he was shot in the back leaving his office one night and his murder was never solved. According to my mother, the police didn't seem to care or investigate it too thoroughly. But we always suspected it was the estranged husband of one of his clients. My father was a good and kind man and didn't have any enemies, other than potentially one of these angry husbands," Hallie said matter-of-factly, having told the story so many times before.

"Wow, I'm sorry, Hallie. That must have been really hard on you."

"It was but it was worse on my mother at the time. He was her life. But we're both good now; that was a long time ago. But I would still like to figure out who did this, get some closure, you know?"

"Yeah, that makes sense. If there's anything I can do to help, let me know."

"Thank you, you already have. I'm going to see what I can find out about this Vincent Martino guy before I jump to any conclusions. He may not even be related to Tommy and Nina Martino, right? And even if he is, it doesn't mean there is any connection to my father's murder. My father had a number of other active cases at the time, so it could be anyone."

"You're right, but it seems like a good angle to explore. In the meantime, would you be interested in meeting me for a drink?"

Hallie was caught off guard and instantly responded, "Won't your girlfriend be upset?"

"I don't have a girlfriend anymore. As I mentioned on our previous call, I've been through some changes in my life this past year too. My ex-girlfriend, who was also a police officer, shot a suspect in the line of duty and the guy died. He was a pedophile, and the world is a better place because of it but she couldn't reconcile it, even though he drew a gun on her first. She would have been killed if she hadn't shot him. She was fully cleared after Internal Affairs determined it was a clean shot, but she quit the force anyway and moved back home to her family in Georgia. She's happy now, managing a bakery with her sister in a small town just outside of Atlanta."

"I'm sorry, I didn't mean to pry."

"No, you didn't, it's okay. So, when can you meet me for that drink?"

"How about Monday or Tuesday night?" Hallie responded, surprised by her own assertiveness.

"Monday will be perfect. I'll meet you at Hooch & Hive on Cass Street at 5:30. Do you know it?"

"Yes, I do. I'll see you then, Detective."

"Looking forward to it, Counselor."

Hallie hung up, unable to suppress the butterflies fluttering through her stomach, just as her doorbell rang to let her know that Paige had arrived for dinner.

* * *

The next morning, Hallie got up early, took Juno out for her morning walk, which was shorter than usual so she could get back to see what she could find on Vincent Martino. Juno didn't seem to mind the shorter walk with the heat and humidity starting earlier each day. Juno also knew she got her breakfast as soon as they returned, which was the highlight of her lazy dog day.

"There you go, baby, eat your breakfast," Hallie said as she placed the dish down in front of the old lab waiting anxiously in her usual place in the kitchen.

As Juno dove in, Hallie made herself a cup of French Vanilla coffee, brought it with her into her office and sat down at her desk. Most mornings she liked to enjoy her coffee on her front porch. Her big oak tree in the front yard was usually enough to keep the sweltering heat at bay for a couple of hours. But today, for the first time in a long time, she was excited about what she had learned that might be connected to her father's murder and was eager to learn more. She heard Juno in the kitchen slopping up her water, knowing half of it was splashing onto the red tile floor. At least she didn't play in it and knock her bowl over like she did when she was a puppy. Hallie shook her head, smiling at the memory, and flipped open her laptop to begin her research.

She read everything she could find about Vincent Martino and the Martino family. Vincent was Nico Martino's nephew, which made him Tommy Martino's cousin. Vincent's father, Salvatore, was Nico's younger brother and also a soldier in the Trafficante family. Sal Martino was involved in the same illegal activities as Nico had been and was arrested for various crimes in the early fifties. But in 1957, when Vincent was about seven years old, Sal was gunned down on 7th Avenue in Ybor City allegedly by a group out of Chicago trying to take over the area from the Trafficantes. Nico took Vincent and his mother, Catalina, Sal's wife, into his home after his brother was murdered and raised Vincent like his own son, Tommy. Vincent was ten years younger than him, but, like Tommy, became a successful real estate developer. Hallie found a number of articles about Tommy's various developments and one article about his death:

Real Estate Developer Falls to Death in Tragic Accident
By: The Associated Press
March 24, 1991

A fifty-one year old real estate developer, Tommy Martino, fell to his death in a tragic accident on Friday morning. According to witnesses, he had gone up to the tenth floor of a new high rise he was developing in South Tampa when he must have lost his footing and fell ten stories to the ground below. He was pronounced dead at the scene. Police are still investigating but at this time no foul play is suspected. Martino is survived by his wife and daughter.

Hallie couldn't find anything linking Tommy and Vincent together, outside of the family connection, but it was clear Ben Young and Vincent were in business together since the eighties. There were articles about them successfully developing and renovating buildings in blighted areas of Tampa and developing high-end hotels along the beautiful shores of the Pinellas County beaches.

Unfortunately, the 2008 real estate crash brought Vincent and Ben's success to a screeching halt. According to a *Tampa Bay Times* article about Ben's trial and conviction, the two had a falling out after their loans were called, sending them into financial ruin, and each accused the other of wrongdoing. It was rumored that some of their loans were from nefarious sources out of New York, putting additional strain on the business relationship. The only assets with any value remaining in their corporation, Catalina Development, named after Vincent's mother, were two life insurance policies insuring the two owners' lives. During the trial, the prosecutors argued that Ben's motive for hiring a hitman to kill Vincent was the life insurance policy on him. Vincent also testified against Ben on the fraud charges.

After Ben went to prison, Catalina Development went bankrupt, and Vincent lost everything. The last thing Hallie found about Vincent was a 2018 article about a raid on a popular strip club on Dale Mabry Boulevard following an investigation of the club hiring underage girls and running a human trafficking operation. The manager, Vincent Martino, was quoted as saying, "*We run a legitimate business here. Every one of our girls gives us their ID to show they're legal before we hire them. If one of these girls gives us a phony ID, how is that our fault?*" The case against the club, which was owned by a company called Yamamoto Enterprises, was dropped when the company produced copies of the dancers' drivers licenses they kept on file, and the D.A. couldn't prove the club knew any of them were fake.

Finding the connection between the Martinos and Ben Young intrigued Hallie. Could he have information related to her father's murder? There was only one way to find out: she would go visit Mr. Young to see what he wanted to tell her.

CHAPTER TWENTY-SIX

Linda Morgan stood her ground with the other jurors, trying to convince them of William's innocence. They just wouldn't listen. It made her so angry. Why couldn't they see what she saw in him? Every time one of them tried to tell her about the supposed evidence against him, Linda would pretend she was listening, but she would go "la la la la la" inside her head over and over again until they finished. And then she would remind them about what his attorney said about who else could have killed the young woman. You know it's always the husband, she tried to convince them but none of them wanted to listen to her. They were so upset with her. She didn't care. It wasn't the first time someone was upset with her for the wrong reason. Her husband used to get upset with her all the time, especially about what she ate. They had met on one of those online dating sites and had a long-distance relationship for a year before Toby was able to move to Florida to be with her.

When Toby arrived from Oklahoma, he accused Linda of lying to him about her weight and said something about cat-fishing him. She didn't even know what that meant but she explained that she had a thyroid condition that, admittedly, may have caused her to gain some weight since the pictures she had posted on her dating profile. But when two people were in love, weight should not matter. Toby disagreed. So, she promised to go on a strict diet, and they got married two weeks later at the Hillsborough County courthouse. It was the happiest day of Linda's life. Six months later, Toby emptied her bank account to which she had added his name at his insistence shortly after the wedding – as the man of the house, he had said – and took off in the truck she had bought for him. Before that, they were the most glorious six months Linda had ever experienced and she was sure, at the time, that he would be back. But that was seven years ago, and she hadn't heard from him since. Even she had to admit that it was time to accept the fact that Toby was never coming back.

She was ready to welcome William, "Billy" as she liked to call him, into her life and there was no way she was going to let these other jurors get in the way of her happiness, no matter how mad they got at her.

"Oh fiddle-dee-dee, no siree," she sang in her mind.

She looked at the wrinkled napkin, on which she had written *Linda Mary Stephens and Mrs. William Stephens*, in her clammy hand one more time before stuffing it back into her bra, next to her pounding heart. One day soon they would be together, she hoped.

* * *

By the end of the second day of further jury deliberations, the foreman sent a note to the judge, informing him that Juror #7 would not change her vote. The jury remained deadlocked and could not reach a unanimous verdict, 11-1 in favor of guilt. At 5:30 on Friday night, Judge Washington's judicial assistant sent word to the attorneys that court would resume on Monday morning promptly at 9:00 a.m.

Amy texted her old partner, "Hey Elise, just got word that the jury in the Stephens case is back Monday morning, probably not a good sign. Can you meet for a drink?"

"Of course, was just wrapping up anyway. Our usual place? 15 minutes?"

"Perfect! See you there. You're the best!"

Amy drove the few blocks from her office in the Courthouse Annex to Malio's in case a summer thunderstorm erupted, which was the norm for this time of year. As the lightning capital of the United States, according to the National Weather Service based on the number of people who died from lightning strikes each year, Amy didn't like to take any chances. As the engine started, her car instantly filled with the sound of Alicia Keys singing *Underdog*. The irony was not lost on Amy as she made her way out of the parking garage and headed to Malio's.

* * *

The Broker settled onto his cot grateful the day was over. Keeping up his badass persona was exhausting at times, but it was the only way to survive in the joint. After the guards locked everyone in their cells and did their final headcount for the night, the Broker retrieved the burner phone from the slit in his flimsy mattress. He had three new messages from his outside contact who had been following the chemistry teacher's wife.

"Bro, subject is back."

"Still on?"

"Waiting 4 go"

The Broker read the messages and replied, "Good to go."

The teacher was going to pay him $5,000 for a five-minute video of his wife living her life on the outside without him. What a pathetic fuck, the Broker thought. Whatever, he didn't care. He would net $2,500 after paying the guards their cut and his outside guy to get the video. Not a bad day's work, he thought.

He drifted off to sleep, ignoring the sounds coming from the nearby cells – the crying, the moaning, and the occasional scream – and had the same recurring dream he often had, always about *her*. He dreamt about her long, dark hair, cascading onto his chest when she was on top of him, riding him, her flawless olive skin glistening from their sweat, the sound she made when they both climaxed. He could feel her strong legs tightening around him, a feeling he never wanted to end. His dream elated him and depressed him at the same time: elated because it felt so real, but sad when he woke up to the realization it was only a dream, knowing he would never have her again, never see her again. That was his only real punishment, not having Moni in his life. Maybe he was the pathetic fuck.

* * *

The morning sun shone into the windows of the small cottage with such promise and warmth, it was impossible to feel anything but optimism for what the day would bring. Heather had just returned from her trip to North Carolina and her visit with Julie, the warm glow peeking through reminding her of her mornings spent with her old friend. Each armed with a strong cup of coffee in hand, they would saunter down to the beach in the early hours when the sun was just a hint on the horizon. Navigating their way down the sandy paths lined with sea oats and past the dunes, they would arrive at the water's edge where they would sit down on the cool gray sand, listen to the waves crash against the shore, and patiently wait for the orange and yellow beams to cut through the clouds in the distance and light the way for the early morning fishing vessels. She suspected Julie started each day that way long before Heather had arrived and would continue to long after she had left, probably thinking about her husband who had spent a lifetime on those unforgiving seas before his death many years before. She already missed Julie, who had become like a mother to her, but she had promised her she would return at Thanksgiving. She had been hiding from Bobby for so long, she had forgotten what it was like to plan for upcoming holidays or be a part of a family. Julie was the closest thing she had to a family. It was liberating to know she never had to fear or run from him again.

She walked into her small kitchenette to pour herself another cup of tea. She decided to pour it into her Yeti cup and walk the few blocks over to the beach. She was glad that she had returned on Friday night so that she would have the weekend before she had to return to work on Monday morning. Oscar, afraid she might leave again, wouldn't leave her side, following her into the kitchen and rubbing up against her legs.

"Don't worry, old boy, I'm back and I'm not going anywhere for a while," she said, as she bent down to scratch the orange tabby's head. He leaned into her caresses, purring, and meowing at her touch.

* * *

A few blocks away, a black Lincoln Town Car pulled over and parked in front of a small bagel shop on the corner. The man inside the car checked his phone again for further instructions.

He read the text on his phone and responded, "Confirmed. Target is home."

Within a minute he received, "Just get the video."

* * *

Heather walked down the street towards the beach access path a few blocks away, noticing the white sand accumulating along the curb on Gulf Boulevard. Smiling, she remembered her father always telling her as a child, "Darlin', there are three ways you can tell you're getting close to the beach: 1) the closer you get, the sand starts collecting along the curb; 2) you smell the salt in the air, practically tasting it on your lips; and 3) you hear the seagulls squawking above about one thing or another, likely just before they steal someone's lunch," he would laugh. She cherished the memories of her father who had been gone for too many years now.

She walked along Gulf Boulevard the few blocks towards the beach access path, smiling at the sound of the seagulls flying and squawking above her. She was so at ease for the first time in years, she never noticed the black Lincoln Town Car driving slowly by while a man in the passenger seat took video of her every move. The car turned left at the next block, circled back, and took one more round as Heather reached the path to the beach and headed out of sight.

The Broker reluctantly sat down, leaned back in the black plastic chair and crossed his thick, tattooed arms over his broad chest. He stared at the man, refusing to let him intimidate him, while the man looked at him with a mixture of contempt and amusement.

"Mr. Kane, I will get right to the point. I work with someone who has learned of the unique services you offer in here. What is it that they call you? The Broker, is it? We would like to hire you for a special assignment, and, unfortunately, declining isn't an option."

* * *

Thirty-one years ago, Christian Kane, formerly known as CK on the street and now the Broker, was convicted of murdering two soldiers of La Familia Michoacána, a Mexican drug cartel responsible for smuggling thousands of kilograms of cocaine into the Tampa Bay area from Mexico. Before his conviction, his job wasn't much different than his job in prison: he was the middleman, the broker if you will. He connected the Mexican drug cartel players to the local players and, as a security officer at the Port of Tampa, would coordinate the influx of cargo coming in through the Port. He knew in advance when illegal shipments were coming in and would pay the other security officers on duty to avoid thorough inspections of the cargo.

* * *

Twelve hours later, when the Broker was back in bed, he retrieved the phone from the slit in his cot. Within moments he was able to upload and view the short video sent to him by his outside contact. He now understood why that Johnson guy wanted it – the woman was stunning, in a natural, girl-next-door way, smiling, having no idea she was being filmed. For a moment he contemplated keeping it for himself and never sharing it with that sick fuck. But he wanted the money – needed the money – to keep his status in the prison intact. But that wouldn't stop him from keeping a version for himself and possibly selling it to others at a hefty markup, which made him realize there was an untapped market out there where he could make a killing.

"Hmmm, videos, now that is something I hadn't considered before," he thought. "The possibilities and potential revenue stream are endless, especially in a place like this."

He smiled to himself as he watched the video of Heather McLean one more time.

CHAPTER TWENTY-SEVEN

After breakfast Saturday morning, the Broker was surprised to learn that he had a visitor. Visiting hours occurred every Saturday and Sunday from 9:00 a.m. to 3:00 p.m., although the Broker hadn't had a visitor in seven years. He was escorted to the visitor area together with the other inmates who had visitors and waited in the holding area to be admitted into the visiting area. The Broker was anxious. Who would be visiting him? His parents had died years ago, he had no children, and his only sister had disowned him when he went to prison for murder. And there was no way *she* would be visiting him. He couldn't even remember who he had put on his visitor list other than his lawyer.

The loud alarms buzzed, signifying the guards could open the steel door to bring the four inmates, including the Broker, into the holding area. The door automatically locked behind them. No one spoke. No one smiled. Each prisoner, cuffed at the wrists, walked in single file at the pace and as directed by the guards. After the next alarm sounded, the guard in the front opened the locks to the door that would afford the prisoners a brief moment with those who visited them from the outside world. The Broker

had no idea who that would be. As each prisoner reached the door, the guard unlocked his cuffs, and allowed him to enter the visitor's room.

The Broker entered the noisy room and spotted a man in an expensive black suit with his hands clasped together casually resting on top of the table. The man had salt pepper hair, a wide, somewhat crooked nose that looked like it had been broken a time or two, and a long and brooding face. The man's goatee, which was almost all just about hid the two-inch scar that ran from his just underneath his jawline. He had piercing blue eyes were devoid of any emotion, but commanded respect, fear or both. The Broker felt the man's eyes on him as he made his way past the crying wives or girlfriends with their imprisoned men over to the small, cold table bolted to the floor. He stood in front of him did not sit down.

The Broker, not wasting any time, spoke, looking down at the well-dressed stranger, "Who are you and what do you want with me?"

"Mr. Kane, please, take a seat."

"Why don't you tell me who the fuck you are," the Broker replied, not moving, his Boston accent pronounced whenever he was mad or had been provoked.

The man frowned and, while motioning to the seat in front of him, said very quietly, "I insist," with a coldness that made the Broker's adrenaline surge.

On that rainy night thirty-one years ago, CK was on the dock at the Port of Tampa, waiting for the incoming cargo ship. It was going to be his biggest payoff yet, which made him more nervous than usual. When one of his buddies and fellow security officers called in sick just before shift began that night, he didn't have a good feeling about it. As the ship approached, he saw the blinking red light on the bow of the ship cutting through the choppy water towards the dock in the darkness and he knew it was too late to stop it. He lit another cigarette and pulled the hood of his government-issued rain slicker up over his head.

The crew would have to offload twenty-two crates containing plastic resin pellets from the ship and into a waiting truck that, according to the paperwork CK had received, would be on its way to a plastic manufacturing plant in Riverview, Florida. What was not contained in the paperwork was that hidden underneath the resin pellets were packages of cocaine and fentanyl having a street value of approximately two million dollars. Somewhere between the dock and the plant in Riverview, the truck would stop, and the valuable contraband would be moved to another truck. But CK didn't care or need to worry about that. Once the truck left the Port, CK's job was done, and his fee was earned.

When the last crates were offloaded from the ship, one of the soldiers on the ship started speaking to his partner rapidly in Spanish while eying CK. The wind carried the words "el canalla" and "rato" across through the rain to CK and he knew something bad was about to go down. He casually reached behind him underneath his slicker to unsnap the strap keeping his loaded Glock 19 secured behind his back. The one who spoke English spoke next. He asked CK if the Port had many rats as his partner didn't like rats. CK remained calm, responding that the Port had no rats just as he saw the other soldier pulling out a gun from an open bag hanging off his right shoulder. CK pulled his Glock from his back and gunfire erupted as he took cover behind a nearby dumpster.

CK shot and killed the two soldiers, while the rest of the crew scattered, including the driver of the truck, leaving the truck and drug-filled crates behind. CK took two bullets in his shoulder but survived. After he was cleared to be released from the hospital, he was promptly arrested and charged with two counts of first degree, felony murder (murder committed during the course of committing another felony), and three counts of conspiracy to distribute and possession with the intent to distribute five or more kilograms of cocaine and 400 grams or more of fentanyl. His buddy, the officer who called in sick, testified against him. CK refused to name any other names, knowing that if he did, he would be dead before the jury could reach a verdict. As a result, he was convicted on all counts and received a sentence of life in prison without the possibility of parole.

And now here he was, sitting across from a stranger with cold eyes and a disarming demeanor, his first visitor in many years.

"Who do you work for?" the Broker asked.

"I'm not at liberty to share that information with you. However, I can assure you that the person requesting this favor is a very powerful person and will pay you very well for your services."

"What's the job?" the Broker asked, almost in a whisper while shielding his mouth with his meaty hand to avoid the video camera in the visitation room capturing the words coming out of his mouth.

"We'll be in touch when we're ready. For now, consider this our polite introduction," the man said as he got up, turned, and headed towards the exit door without looking back or saying another word.

CHAPTER TWENTY-EIGHT

Justin got to the office about fifteen minutes earlier than usual on Monday morning. He wanted to make sure he was already at his desk upstairs before Sheada arrived. He hadn't heard from her since Thursday night, which was unusual, except that they had gotten into their first fight that night and the office was closed on Friday. In retrospect, their fight was so stupid, but they were both so stubborn, it did not end well. Justin felt bad but not bad enough to text her over the weekend. She obviously didn't either. He stopped at Starbucks on his way into the office, picked up her favorite – a venti caramel macchiato – and left it on her desk as a peace offering. To be funny, he grabbed a sharpie off her desk and wrote "call me" with a heart and his number under his name already written on the cup, which he copied from a scene from her favorite movie, *The Proposal* with Sandra Bullock and Ryan Reynolds, which she had forced him to watch one night. He had enjoyed the movie more than he let on.

By 9:30 that morning, almost everyone had arrived. But not Sheada. She was never late, always in by 9:00, but she had still not arrived. He looked over the ledge of the upstairs balcony railing down at her empty desk, the caramel macchiato in the same exact place he had left it forty-five minutes before. Had she called in sick, he wondered? He thought about their stupid fight. She got mad at him because he didn't answer her call earlier that night when he was out with his friends, but, in his defense, he did text her saying he would call her later, which, of course, he forgot to do. She called him again right after he got home, drunk. He accused her of being jealous and needy. She said it was just a matter of respect. Not answering her call, when he obviously could have since he took the time to text her, was a sign of disrespect in front of his friends. All he had to do was apologize and tell her he would answer his phone the next time she called, and the fight would have been over. But instead, because he was buzzed and annoyed, he dug in, and they didn't talk all weekend. He hated it. What a stupid fight, he thought.

His thoughts were interrupted by a voice behind him that said, "Justin, do you know where Sheada is this morning?"

"Um, no, didn't she call in?" Justin asked, turning to look at the office manager behind him.

"No, she didn't. I called her cellphone, but it went straight to voicemail. I know you guys are friends; did you see her this weekend?"

"No, actually, I didn't. This isn't like her," Justin said, the worry creeping into his voice.

"When's the last time you spoke to her?" the manager asked.

"Thursday night," Justin said, looking down at his shoes, ashamed for not reaching out to her all weekend. "I'm going to run over to her house. She lives like ten minutes from here. Maybe she overslept and forgot to charge her phone," Justin said, more optimistic than his heart felt.

"You really think that's necessary? I'm sure she'll come in or call in when she wakes up."

"I do. I really feel like I need to go check on her."

"Justin, I know you guys are friends, and rumor has it, maybe more than that, but this isn't the first time an employee overdid it over the weekend and didn't come into work on Monday morning. Why don't we give it a few hours to see if she calls in?"

"No, Sheada isn't like that. She's super responsible. She wouldn't do that. I need to go check on her."

"Okay, Romeo, give me a call when you get to her place and confirm she's sleeping her Sunday Funday off," the manager chuckled, amused at the young kid's naivete.

* * *

Justin arrived at Sheada's house, immediately noticing her black Honda Civic was not parked in the driveway where it normally was when she was home. He went to the door and rang the doorbell. No answer. He tried the door handle and his stomach dropped. It was unlocked. Sheada had an alarm, but she always locked her door, always, no matter what. He pushed open the door expecting to hear the alarm go off but heard nothing. He called her name. Still nothing. He walked into the familiar home, darkened from all of the blinds being uncharacteristically closed, with the only light coming from the bathroom light across the hall from her bedroom. He was feeling sick to his stomach. He proceeded anyway, calling out her name again.

* * *

Across town, Ronald got an alert that Sheada's front door had been opened. He pulled up her system from his phone and watched, hoping to see his beautiful Sheada on the screen. He was not completely surprised to instead see the tall lanky blonde kid making his way through her small one-bedroom home, the concern evident in his expression. He wondered what he would find, feeling the now familiar pit in his stomach return as he watched the boyfriend explore the home.

CHAPTER TWENTY-NINE

Sheada jolted awake, realizing that she must have passed out again. This time when she woke, she was alone in the hot, dark room. Like before, she could smell her own vomit. Her head was pounding, and her naked body was shivering despite the crippling heat. He was no longer in the room. She felt wetness between her legs and underneath her bottom and wondered if she had wet the bed when she passed out. Or was it something worse? The thought of him on top of her repulsed her. She reached down, gently wiping her hand across her labia and immediately cried out from the excruciating pain. She brought her palm, now wet with a warm substance that felt thicker than urine, up to her nose. She recognized the tinny and all too familiar smell of iron, causing her to retch and her head to spin like she was on a dizzying and never-ending tilt-a-whirl.

She forced herself to take a few deep breaths and to focus on the sliver of light peeking in from underneath the door across the room. As she lay there in a pool of her own blood, she remembered her last conscious memory was of him slicing and stabbing her repeatedly until she passed out. She was terrified that the burning, throbbing pain he had inflicted was only the beginning of what he intended to do to her. And then she started to scream, her vocal cords no longer paralyzed, and prayed that someone, anyone, would hear her before it was too late.

Someone did . . .

CHAPTER THIRTY

"Detective Garcia, the Chief needs you back here. There's an interview she wants you to sit in on," the dispatcher reported over the radio.

"On my way back now, be there in fifteen."

"Copy that. I'll let the Chief know."

Marcelo drove down Howard Avenue, turned right onto Kennedy Boulevard, and headed towards downtown. As he passed the University of Tampa's stainless-steel minarets – the iconic backdrop to Tampa's skyline – and crossed over the Kennedy Street bridge, he was filled with the same sense of nostalgia that the Sulphur Springs Water Tower evoked in him whenever he drove down Florida Avenue. The long-abandoned tower, built in 1927, was situated on the Hillsborough River and looked more like a watchtower or lighthouse from the civil war era than what it was. Born and raised in Tampa, these were the images that came to mind whenever he thought about his city.

He pulled into the parking garage behind the police headquarters. As he got out of his car, he heard someone call his name.

"Hey Garcia, long time no see, bro."

"That you, Hargett?" Marcelo asked as his eyes adjusted in the dimly lit garage.

"Yeah, bro, just got switched back downtown. Wanna grab a beer after work?"

"I can't today but tomorrow should work. Hit me up if you're around," Marcelo said as he thought about seeing Hallie after work.

"For sure. Good to see you, man."

"You, too. Gotta run, the Chief is waiting for me."

Marcelo dropped his keys and backpack off at his desk before making his way to the Chief's office. Chief Mastandrea was finishing a call and motioned for him to come in.

"Of course, I'm putting my best detective on this right away. . . . Yes, I understand. . . . I will let you know as soon as we have anything solid. . . . I'll be in touch," the Chief said as she hung up the phone and rubbed her temples.

"Detective, have a seat. Thank you for coming in so quickly."

"What's up, Chief?"

"About two weeks ago, a 911 operator received a call from a female victim after she was attacked in her home. Luckily, we located her, and she was taken to the hospital where she received stitches for her stab wounds and medical care for her other injuries. The victim came in today to give a statement about the brutal attack. The initial details of the attack based on the medical records she provided are horrific. Officer McCrink is in with her right now taking her full statement."

"Did she know the perp?"

"She doesn't think so, but he was wearing a ski mask. When McCrink finishes with her statement, I want you to talk to her. See if you can find out anything else. Her name is Veronica Hill, thirty-seven years old."

"Okay, I'll head back there now."

"Wait, not yet. We also have a twenty-six-year-old female reported missing by her boyfriend, last seen or heard from late Thursday night. He's in interview room #3 and appears to be pretty shaken up. We're trying to reach the girl's family in New Jersey but haven't been able to reach anyone yet. I want you to talk to the boyfriend to see what you think. I've already sent a team over to her place to check it out."

"Do you think the cases are related, Chief?"

"No, not at all. It's possible the girlfriend took off out of town after her fight with the boyfriend. That's why I want you on the boyfriend; see what you can find out about their fight and whether you think there's any reason to suspect he did something to her."

"Okay, I'll be in with the boyfriend and let you know when I'm done. Then I'll talk to Ms. Hill."

* * *

"Officer Campbell, what is your current location?" the dispatcher asked over the radio.

"Heading south on Tampa Street, just crossed over Columbus."

"We've received several calls from residents in the Tampa Heights area, around the 500 block of E. Frances Street, reporting that they heard a woman screaming. Can you go check it out?"

"Yup, I'm on it."

Jay Campbell turned left on Palm Avenue and left again on Central. He was very familiar with Tampa Heights, which was just south of his Seminole Heights neighborhood. He and Bridget loved to go to Lee's Grocery, a quaint little craft beer and pizza place tucked into the back of the neighborhood on Central Avenue. Lee's only sold pizza and baked wings, both of which were delicious, but their favorite pizza was the one called "Don't Stand So Close to Me," which had olive oil, garlic, red onions, black olives, artichokes, mushrooms, ricotta and mozzarella cheese. His mouth watered just thinking about it. After he finished responding to this call, he decided he would pick up their favorite pie to surprise Bridget before heading home.

Jay turned right onto E. Frances, opened the windows of his police cruiser, and slowly drove the length of the short street until it dead-ended at the interstate. He turned the cruiser around and headed back towards Central. The tree-lined street had only about seven houses on it, some in better shape than others. There were also a few vacant lots in various states of overgrown weeds and upkeep. Without deed restrictions or an HOA, the eclectic neighborhood housed five hundred-thousand-dollar homes situated next to eighty-five-thousand-dollar homes, further evidence of the gentrification taking over some of the old, historic neighborhoods. Some homes had been built at the turn of the century while others were newer, having replaced their knocked-down predecessors.

He sat and listened for a few minutes but heard nothing out of the ordinary, a dog barking a few streets away and the hum of the cars passing by on I-275.

"Dispatch, this is Officer Campbell, come in."

"Dispatch, what have you got?"

"I don't hear or see anything unusual. Do you have addresses for the callers? Maybe I'll knock on a few doors, make sure it's not a DV situation."

When police received calls reporting someone screaming, they were usually the result of a domestic situation in the neighborhood. But even when there were clear signs of domestic violence, the victims often did not want their partner arrested and would say anything to protect them. Jay had heard it all before and felt sorry for the women who were too afraid to seek help. If he found the source of the scream today, he expected it was probably a domestic squabble that had de-escalated by now. But it was important for him to check.

"Okay, we got a call from a man named Harry Teichman at 505 E. Frances and a call from someone who didn't leave her name at 508 E. Frances. The woman at 508 called twice."

"Alright, let me knock on some doors. I'll report back when I'm done."

He was parked on the street near the two houses, which were across the street from each other. Jay rolled up the windows on the cruiser and turned off the ignition. He walked down the sidewalk, portions lifted and uneven from the large oak tree roots growing underneath for the past hundred years, to 505 E. Frances and knocked on the door. No answer. Jay waited a minute and knocked again.

"Who is it?" came a frail voice from the other side of the door.

"Mr. Teichman? I'm Officer Campbell from the Tampa Police Department. I want to ask you a few questions about what you heard."

Harry Teichman opened the door, looking nothing like what Jay had expected from the sound of his voice. Instead of a frail, older man, Harry was a tall, albeit thin, dark-haired man in his early fifties, with a tightly trimmed salt and pepper beard. He was wearing a casual knit sweater over freshly pressed khaki pants, tortoise shell rimmed glasses and had a book in his hand. A small black dog sat at his feet, wagging his tail in excitement over the unexpected visitor. As the air from inside the home wafted out, Jay smelled the aroma of a sweet cigar and could hear John Coltrane playing softly in the background.

"Thank you for coming, officer," Harry said, extending his free hand, in a deeper voice that did not match the original voice behind the door, "what can I do for you?"

"Thank you, Mr. Teichman," Jay began.

"Please, call me Harry. Would you like to come in, get out of that heat?"

"Thanks, Harry, this should only take a few minutes," Jay responded as Harry backed up to welcome Officer Campbell into his home. Harry placed a leather bookmark into the book he held in his hand, closed it and placed it on the end table next to the ashtray that contained the stub of the recently smoked cigar.

The sweet dog had now jumped up onto his back legs, placing his front paws on Jay's shins.

"Nico, get down," Harry admonished.

"It's okay, I love dogs," Jay replied as he scratched the friendly dog on the head. He glanced over and read the title of the book on the end table: *Never Far Away*, by Michael Koryta.

"Do you read?" Harry asked the officer, gesturing towards the book, as he saw him looking at it.

"No, not really, but my wife does. She loves those murder mysteries. Always has her nose in a book."

"Well, if she hasn't read Michael Koryta, she should. He's excellent."

"I'll let her know, thanks. As I mentioned, I'm here because you called in a report of a woman screaming. Can you explain to me what you heard and as much about it as you remember?"

"Of course. I had just finished lunch and was sitting down, enjoying my cigar before diving back into my book. When I was married, my callous bitch of a wife absolutely abhorred me smoking in the house, so I had to smoke outside, no matter how relentless the Florida heat was. But now that the overbearing whore is out of my life, I can do whatever I want."

Jay was struck by the abrupt change in the man's demeanor when he brought up his ex-wife.

Harry's voice returned to a pleasant cadence that matched the still intact smile and continued, "When it's cooler, I do like to smoke on my front porch, but it is way too hot for that this time of year. But I open this window next to my recliner so that I can blow most of the smoke out the window, and that's when I heard her."

"What time was this, approximately, do you recall?"

"Yes, as I mentioned, I had just finished lunch, so it would have been about 1:30. I sat down, opened the window, and lit my cigar."

The window and the recliner were on the left side of the house, which was about thirty feet from the house next door, immediately to its left.

"Go on," Jay prodded.

"I had only taken a few puffs when I heard the most God-awful scream coming from somewhere outside the window. Whoever screamed seemed terrified or in a tremendous amount of pain, or both, frankly. For a minute I thought it could be a couple of cats fighting. We have a lot of feral cats in the neighborhood and when they fight, they can make horrific sounds, but I just don't think it was the cats this time. The scream sounded like someone was being tortured."

"Which direction did it come from?"

"It was coming from somewhere down this street, in that direction," Harry said as he pointed out his window towards the house next door to him. "I don't know how far. From my open window, I couldn't tell if it was coming from inside a house or somewhere outside, but it was just so agonizing. I went outside onto my front porch and listened, but I didn't hear it again. After waiting a few minutes and not hearing anything else, I came back inside and called the police to report it."

Jay took notes while Harry continued to talk.

Tapping the thriller on the end table, he said, "You probably think I'm reading too many of these but I'm telling you, the sheer terror in that scream will haunt me. I've never heard anything like it."

"Is there anything else you remember that you think will be helpful?"

"I can't think of anything. As I said, I only heard the scream once, but it lasted for what seemed like forever. It was probably only like ten seconds but that's actually a long time if you're screaming."

Jay closed his notebook and headed towards the door, retrieving one of his cards out of his wallet on the way, "Thank you for your help, Harry. Here's my card with my direct line on it; if you think of anything else or see or hear anything else, please call me. One more question, who lives next door to you?" Jay asked, pointing to the house to the left.

"No one. There were renters in there until about two weeks ago, but they moved out. Not sorry to see them go either. Always had their music blasting, which would have been fine except they had horrible taste in music. Always blasting rap music, but not classic rap like Snoop Dog or Dr. Dre. I could have handled that, even respected it, but no, they listened to this new shit where every verse is about sex or killing someone, sometimes at the same time. It was all just too much."

"Okay, thank you for your help," Jay said, as he bent down to scratch Nico's head one last time before he walked out the door.

Jay looked at the house next door to Harry's. The mailbox reflected the address was 507 E. Frances. The blue-gray house had a wraparound front porch, white trim, and looked well maintained. He jotted down in his notes that 507 was vacant according to the neighbor.

He walked across the street and rang the doorbell of 508 E. Frances. The home, which was one of the newly constructed homes built in the same style as the old Victorians in the neighborhood, was twice the size of Harry's. Like the houses across the street, it also had a wraparound porch, but was furnished with a white wood porch swing and matching white wicker furniture adorned with colorful floral-printed cushions and pillows.

A petite, blonde woman opened the door, after looking out of one of the glass panes that abutted each side of the heavy wooden door.

"Hello, officer, is this about my calls earlier?"

"Yes, you called to report that you heard a woman screaming?" Jay asked.

"Yes, it was the most horrifying thing I've ever heard. Thank you for coming. My name is Valerie, Valerie Yost," the pretty blonde said as she extended her hand to Jay.

"Please tell me everything about what you heard."

Valerie relayed a very similar story as her neighbor Harry had. She had just returned from grocery shopping and was bringing in groceries from her car when she heard a woman's bloodcurdling scream. Like Harry, she said that if she had not been outside, she probably would not have heard it because it sounded like it was coming from inside a house. She pointed towards the three houses across the street from her house, including Harry's, when Jay inquired as to the direction of the scream.

"What do you know about your neighbor, Harry Teichman?"

"Harry?" Valerie questioned, looking across the street, "A little weird but harmless, I think, unless you don't bring your empty garbage cans up from the curb on a timely basis. That infraction will warrant an angry post on the neighborhood Facebook page," she laughed nervously.

Jay wrote himself a note to check into Harry's background, asked Valerie a few more questions, jotted down some additional notes, and thanked her for her time. He handed her his card, giving the regular spiel about calling him if she remembered anything else, and walked back to his patrol car. He was sitting in his patrol car, writing up his notes from both interviews when he noticed that the front door of the allegedly vacant rental house next door to Harry's was slightly ajar.

CHAPTER THIRTY-ONE

"Has the jury reached a verdict?" Judge Washington's resounding voice echoed throughout the silent courtroom.

The exhausted foreman stood up to address the judge. As he spoke, his head automatically tipped downward, as if ashamed that he had let the court down, "No, Your Honor, we were unable to reach a unanimous verdict."

"Do you think that with additional time, you might be able to?" the judge asked as a formality and to preserve the record but knowing the answer before he asked the question.

"No, Your Honor, I'm sorry to report that I do not think additional time will help."

The stunned courtroom remained silent, and the prosecutor looked down, scribbling something on her yellow legal pad before passing it to her second chair.

"Very well. Before I excuse the jury, I would like to thank each one of you for taking the time out of your busy lives to serve on this jury. With our rights and freedoms as citizens of this great country and this state also comes a civic obligation, which each of you answered by sitting on this jury. The bailiff will now escort you to the deliberation room to retrieve your personal belongings and then you are free to go. Thank you again for your service," Judge Washington said before turning to address the courtroom.

He waited until the jurors were out of the room and then he addressed the attorneys and the defendant, "Counselors, Defendant Stephens. As the jury was unable to reach a unanimous verdict, I must declare a mistrial in this case. Are there any last-minute motions that I need to hear before we adjourn?"

Creepy Carl jumped up first, "Your Honor, I would like to move for an emergency bond hearing. The defendant has been held without bail for the past thirteen months. In light of the mistrial, and to assist with his defense should the State decide to re-try this case, he should be let out on bail."

Amy jumped up, "The State objects, Your Honor. The State is definitely re-trying this case, and the same reasons the Court did not grant bail originally still exist: he is a flight risk, he has the means to do so, and he is a danger to the witnesses who testified against him, witnesses he now knows by name, by the way. Those risks that existed before the mistrial are even greater now, justifying that the defendant remain in jail until this case is retried. Therefore, the State requests that bail be denied, and the defendant be remanded until a new trial date is set."

Creepy Carl, still on his feet, started to speak but was cut off by the judge, "Your Honor, this is an abuse –"

"Counselor, save your breath. For now, the defendant will remain in custody. But I am scheduling a hearing for," the judge paused, turned to his judicial assistant, who quickly looked up the schedule for the rest of the week, and whispered a day and time to the judge, "this Friday at 9:00 a.m. to hear your arguments about whether bail should be set for the defendant pending a retrial. Until then, this Court is adjourned." The judge slammed the gavel once and got up and retreated to his chambers before anyone else could say a word.

After Carl talked briefly to his client, he was led away. Amy gathered the documents and cases she had brought with her to present to the court and placed them in her Coach Italian leather briefcase that her wife, also named Amy, had given to her on their last anniversary. Having the same name as her spouse confused people who were not in their inner circle, so everyone referred to her wife as Amy B., using the initial of her last name. The women, both very successful and well respected in their fields, had each retained their own surname after their marriage. She met Amy B. at a benefit for an animal rescue organization two years after her divorce from her husband, and they quickly realized they had all the same interests. Before long, they were spending every weekend together until they eventually decided to combine their households, which included three rescue pups, two cats, and a bird named Keith. When Amy B. moved into Amy's 3,600 square foot house on St. Pete

Beach, she bought monogrammed bowls for all the pets and a name plate for the bird cage that read: "Mr. Keith Byrd." Amy and Amy B. got married three years ago in the Keys surrounded by their closest friends.

As fierce and direct as Amy the prosecutor was, Amy B. was the opposite. She was smart like Amy, but she was laid back, nonconfrontational, and the only person who could reason with Amy and calm her down. She had long, naturally curly blonde hair, fair skin, with delicate features, and was the perfect ying to Amy's yang. As Amy packed up her stuff, she was thinking about getting home, sitting in the hot tub with her lovely wife, each with a tumbler of scotch, Sting playing on their Bose player in the background, and telling her about the mistrial and her horrific day. Amy B. always had a way of soothing her and making her feel better.

Carl approached Amy just as she finished packing up her stuff, "So, what do you want, counselor?"

"What do I want, Carl? I want justice for Naomi Banks and all the other women Stephens has hurt over the years. How about you, what do you want?" the fiery redhead shot at him.

Carl rolled his eyes, "C'mon Stoll, what's it going to take? You really want to re-try this case?"

"If I have to, absolutely. But for Juror #7, who inexplicably changed her mind, we had this locked up. So, you tell me, Carl, you want to bank on another Juror #7 when we do this again? I like my odds," Amy said, staring at Carl with her arms crossed over her chest. Her associate, Wyatt, stood behind her, pretending to organize the files in the banker's box he brought to court each day during the trial.

"How about second degree, no less than ten but no more than fifteen years?"

"No way. Naomi had a five-year-old son! This poor kid is going to grow up without a mother. First degree murder, mandatory minimum."

"That's bullshit. Stephens is in his late fifties. Twenty-five years means he probably dies in prison."

"And that's a problem? At least the women in this city will be safe from him."

"Alright, second degree, at least sixteen but no more than twenty years with a mandatory 85% of his sentence to be served, which is more than fair given his age. And it spares the family from having to go through another trial. What do you say?" Carl asked, ready with the alternative offer knowing the first offer would have been summarily rejected.

"Maybe. I'll need to clear it with Behrenfeld first. I'll let you know by the end of the day."

"You going to let me take you for that drink when this case is over, Stoll?"

"I don't think my wife would like that, Carl."

"I was hoping you would bring your hot wife, too. We can make a party of it," he chuckled as Amy walked away from him.

"Don't you ever get tired of that lame routine of yours?" she asked, shaking her head, "I'll let you know before the end of the day whether we have a deal."

CHAPTER THIRTY-TWO

Sheada lay in the dark, waiting for her captor to come in to punish her again. She was still dizzy and weak, getting weaker with each minute or hour that passed. She had no concept of time. The dark room smelled of vomit, blood, sweat, and now urine as she could not hold it in any longer. She regained consciousness when she pissed herself and the urine burned her open gashes. The pain was excruciating. She cried out in pain, and she prayed he would not come back into the room. And then she heard the footsteps coming down the hall and she started to cry. She wrapped her arms tightly around her naked body, knowing at the same time it was futile, and curled up into the fetal position, ready to accept her fate.

At her darkest moment, when she was ready to give up, she had a vision of her Aunt Claire, her mother's sister and her favorite aunt. Aunt Claire's smile always lit up a room and no matter what you might be upset about, Aunt Claire's smile made it all better, even if it was only for the glorious moments you got to be in her presence. Aunt Claire had faced her own hardships, including battling and surviving breast cancer and the death of her beloved

Frank, but through it all, she smiled, always trying to lessen the burden on those around her, extending her love and warmth to them. Sheada needed her now more than ever.

The footsteps down the hall got closer. She heard the door handle jiggle and the door open. She hugged herself tighter and tried not to sob. The light from the hallway streamed in, revealing a dark silhouette in the doorframe, followed by a blinding, brighter light being flashed directly into her sensitive eyes. She closed them tightly, wishing she was dead.

"Holy shit, oh my God," Jay yelled, unable to stop the words from escaping his mouth at the sight of her, despite his experience. "It's going to be okay miss, hang on, I'm here to help," Jay said, while picking up his handheld radio, which went directly to headquarters, "Hello, this is Officer Jay Campbell. I need an ambulance at 507 E. Frances, stat! Female victim in need of medical help. I also need back up. And notify the Chief, we need forensics," as his flashlight scanned and lit up the blood-stained mattress underneath the battered girl.

Sheada heard the words from the unfamiliar voice but didn't understand them. She thought about Aunt Claire, focusing on her beautiful smile, her warmth, and all the love she had bestowed upon her since Sheada's mother had died two years before. She drifted in and out of consciousness thinking about her beloved mother and kind aunt, dreaming that she was with them, as things were happening around her that she couldn't comprehend.

CHAPTER THIRTY-THREE

Amy gathered her file, notes, and a fresh legal pad and walked down the hallway to the State Attorney's office. Behrenfeld was on the phone but motioned her to come in. She sat in one of the two leather chairs facing his desk, noticing the new picture of his family from their recent ski trip to Park City on the credenza behind him. She admired how Behrenfeld tried to strike the right life-work balance, insisting the prosecutors and others in his office did the same.

"Okay, Bill, I think that's a good position to take until we get the toxicology results back. Keep me posted," Behrenfeld said before hanging up the phone and turning his attention to Amy.

"So, what have we got, Amy? Your email said Stephens wants to plea."

"They want second degree, sentence of at least sixteen years but no more than twenty with Stephens to serve the mandatory 85%, which means his best case is just over thirteen years and worst case is the full twenty." Amy responded.

"And if you re-try, do you think you get better than that?"

"The evidence is strong against him, but Carl did a good job of painting an alternative theory – he obviously was able to convince at least one juror. If convicted of first-degree murder, he would get twenty-five to life, no possibility of parole. But if he is convicted of second-degree murder, the mandatory minimum is sixteen and three-quarters. Based on the defense Carl presented, with a few tweaks, he can likely convince a jury there was no premeditation, so second-degree murder is definitely on the table for the jury to consider," Amy said, going through the same mental exercise she did in her office over the past hour.

"Do you think Judge Washington will accept that plea and proposed sentence?"

"Yes, I do. Stephens is in his late-fifties so if he takes the plea, he gets out, best case scenario, in his mid-seventies, and worst case, in his early eighties. If he was younger, I would be pushing to go to trial. But given his age, I think Judge Washington will accept it, knowing this might be best for all involved, especially Naomi Banks' family."

"I agree. Write up the plea and let's put this case behind us. Despite that wacky juror, Amy, you did a great job on this case. We're happy to have you back."

"Thanks, my wife doesn't exactly share your happiness at my return, but she's coming around," the petite redhead laughed as she left Behrenfeld's office to write up the plea agreement to present to Creepy Carl.

CHAPTER THIRTY-FOUR

Detective Garcia was just finishing up with Justin, the boyfriend who reported Sheada Lawson missing, when the Chief came into the interview room.

"Detective, can I speak with you a minute?"

They stepped out of the room, leaving Justin inside the soundproof interview room.

"What's up, Chief?"

"An officer responding to a call in Tampa Heights found the girl in a vacant house."

"Is she alive?"

"Barely, lost a lot of blood. She's at Tampa General now. What's the story with the boyfriend?"

"He's freaking out and feels guilty because they got into a fight on Thursday night, and he hasn't spoken to her since then. He thought she was just being stubborn not texting or calling him, so he didn't reach out to her either. They work in the same office so he figured they would make up today, but she didn't come into work or call in, which he said is not like her at all. So, he went over to her house and found the door unlocked, her car gone, and what he thought might be blood on her bedroom door. He came straight here to file a missing person report."

"After they found her, they found her black Honda Civic parked down the street in front of a vacant lot. Any reason to suspect the boyfriend?"

"No, I don't think so. This kid seems genuinely freaked out and worried about his girlfriend. But let's see how he reacts when we tell him she's been found and is in the hospital."

They stepped back into the interview room to find Justin pacing and repeatedly checking his phone.

"Justin, please have a seat," the Chief said gently.

Justin sat down, placing his phone with the screen facing up on the table in front of him.

"In case she texts or calls, I don't want to miss her," he explained.

"Justin, one of our officers found Sheada a little while ago."

"Is she okay? Where is she? Can I see her?" Justin blurted out as he got up, ready to bolt out of the room.

"She's been hurt, Justin. She's in surgery at Tampa General right now."

"Oh my God, oh no," Justin said as his eyes filled with tears and he sat back down, seemingly in shock.

"Was she in a car accident? What happened? Is she going to be okay?" the sad, young man pleaded, trying to make sense of what he had just heard.

"No, it wasn't a car accident. It appears someone attacked her. Do you have any idea who could have done this to her?"

"Oh my God, oh my God, Sheada, shit, I'm so sorry, I should have called her. Who did this? Did you say surgery? What the fuck? What happened to her?" he rambled, rubbing his temples while looking at the Chief and Detective Garcia, his eyes pleading for some type of explanation that he could understand.

"We don't know anything yet, Justin, but you can help us narrow down the timeline. When is the last time you spoke to her?"

"Um, it was Thursday night. I had been out with my buddies. That's why we got in a fight."

"What time was that?"

"I don't know. Wait, let me look on my phone. It'll be in my call history."

With shaky hands, Justin scrolled through his phone, until he found the call he was looking for. "It was Thursday night just after 1:00 a.m., 1:07 a.m. to be exact. And we were on the phone for sixteen minutes."

"And you didn't hear from her after that at all? No calls, no texts, no emails?"

"No, nothing."

"And you didn't try calling or texting her until today, correct?"

"Yeah," he responded, barely audible, as he looked down in shame at the phone on the table in front of him. He looked up at the Chief, "She's going to be okay, right?"

"From everything I have heard so far, it sounds like our officer found her in time. I'm sure the doctors at Tampa General are doing everything they can to help her."

"Can I go now? I want to be there when she gets out of surgery."

"Yes, you may go. That's all we need for now. We'll be in touch if we need anything else from you."

Detective Garcia escorted Justin out to the front of the precinct before returning to the Chief's office to discuss the next steps in the investigation.

"McCrink is done taking the home invasion victim's statement. We sent the victim home but told her we might have more questions as the investigation proceeds. She's pretty tough, but we felt she had been through enough for one day. Go find McCrink and get the story. I need you as the lead on this one, Garcia."

"You got it, Chief."

Marcelo found McCrink at her desk in the squad room. She gave him the summary of what Veronica told her, including how her alarm was off when she came home and that she was attacked from behind as she tried to run out the door. She remembers being stabbed and being sexually assaulted in her bed, but she only has vague memories of what he did to her, either from her blood loss or shock or both. She lost consciousness at some point and woke up in her tub, her cellphone plugged in, and her stab wounds bandaged. She never saw his face but says she would recognize his voice if she ever heard it again. For the time being, she is staying at her sister's house in Westchase.

"Thanks, Tracy, you did a good job with her. When we speak to her again, I'll want you to come along with me."

"Of course. This guy is bad news. Ms. Hill felt strongly that he's done this before, and he'll do it again. She said he was extremely calm and very organized."

"Anything else?"

"Yeah, one more thing. When she went back to the house after she got out of the hospital to get some clothes and things before going to her sister's place, she noticed the bed was made exactly how she always made it. She said she was on the bed, on top of her white comforter, when he stabbed her, she's positive. So, this guy had to have known what her comforter looked like and brought a replacement with him. It's the only possible explanation. The report from forensics says the room appeared to have been vacuumed as well."

"If that's true, about the comforter, he had to have been in her house before. You said she has an alarm?"

"That's what she said, but it was off when she came home from work that night. She thought she forgot to set it when she left for work in the morning. But obviously, this guy had the code or was able to disable it. We subpoenaed the alarm company to get her alarm history and anything else they can give us, including any videos recorded and stored on their server. I'll send those over to you as soon as we get them in."

"Okay, thanks. I'm going to head over to Tampa General now to see how our new victim is doing. As soon as she wakes up, I want to see what she remembers."

"Yeah, I just heard about that. Campbell found her, right?"

"Yeah, apparently responding to some calls from neighbors who heard a woman screaming. He noticed the front door of a home open that was supposed to be vacant, so he went to check it out. He found her in a back bedroom. Another few hours and she would have bled out."

"Wow, that's amazing. Thank God he saw that open door. Do you think the two cases are related?"

"No, it doesn't seem like the same guy. The only similarity is the brutality of the attacks but everything else is different. First one was attacked in her home, very little forensic evidence was left behind, and the guy patched her up himself so that she wouldn't bleed out. From what I heard, the scene where the second vic was found was straight out of a horror film. There seem to be too many differences for it to be the same guy."

Marcelo promised to keep Tracy updated, grabbed his backpack and keys from his desk, and headed to the back elevator that would take him to the parking garage. He checked his phone and saw it was 4:15. He had time to stop by Tampa General to check on Sheada before meeting Hallie at Hooch & Hive at 5:30. He knew Hallie would understand if he had to cancel, but he wasn't expecting

Sheada to be awake or in any condition to give him a statement. She had been through enough trauma, from the initial reports relayed to him, and he didn't want to add to her suffering.

He got in his car, sent a quick text to Hallie to confirm he would see her at 5:30, and headed out to Tampa General. Two brutal attacks on two women in a two-week period: Marcelo didn't believe in coincidences, but he hoped his gut was wrong this time.

CHAPTER THIRTY-FIVE

Hallie sat at the bar at Hooch & Hive on Cass Street, located just on the outskirts of downtown, sipping on the organic red wine the bartender-owner recommended. Later in the evening the bar would be filled with University of Tampa students, but at this time of day, the only patrons consisted of lawyers from the law firm across the street and other young professionals who didn't want to deal with the downtown parking situation. Hallie sat there listening to the music playing in the background as she waited for Marcelo.

Sheryl Crow's raspy voice emitted out of the speakers above her, the emotion-packed lyrics imploring her lover to lie to her as long as he didn't leave her. While Hallie loved the song and Sheryl Crow's delivery, she disagreed with the sentiment, having been in that position the previous year. She believed she was strong enough to be alone for the rest of her life, but she never wanted anyone to lie to her like David had lied to her.

She took a drink of her wine, thinking about the last time she saw Detective Garcia. She was looking forward to seeing him again. He seemed like an honest man, which was the most important quality she was looking for after her divorce from David. She checked her phone and saw it was 5:20, having intentionally arrived early.

"Hey Hallie, long time no see," came a woman's voice to her right.

Hallie turned to see a young, beautiful woman, dressed in a blue suit, with long, dark hair approaching her.

"Kim Hamill, look at you," Hallie said, smiling, as the two women embraced, "how have you been? You look amazing, as usual."

"Oh my God, thank you. You look amazing too. How are you?"

"Good, really good. I merged my firm with Remington Greenlee earlier this year, which has been great but I'm busier than I've ever been. How about you?"

"Same old, same old. Work is crazy, I'm planning my wedding for this fall, and Max and I just bought an old house in St. Pete, which we're renovating and might cause us to call the whole thing off," Kim laughed easily.

"You guys? Not possible," Hallie replied, as she took a sip of her wine.

"Nah, I'm kidding, we'll be fine. It's just stressful. Speaking of stressful, have you been following the Judge Stephens murder trial?"

"Yes, I actually attended most of it," Hallie said.

"Oh wow, that must have been interesting. Did you ever appear before him?"

"No, but he was the managing partner of the first firm I started with out of law school. He was a creep back then, too. So, I guess you heard about the mistrial," Hallie said, trying to divert the conversation away from her personal interest in the Judge Stephens trial.

"Yes, I did. A friend of mine in the State Attorney's office also told me that he took a plea. I'm sure that had to be a relief to Naomi Banks' husband and family, sparing them from reliving the horrible details of her murder again. Did you know her?"

"I knew of her, but I didn't know her personally. We had mutual friends. Did you?"

"No, but it's just so sad."

"I agree. I'm glad it's over for her family's sake. But I hope he rots in prison," Hallie said, unable to hide her scorn and hatred for the man.

Kim gave Hallie a puzzled look, before changing the subject, "By the way, I heard about you and David. I'm so sorry. Are you doing okay?"

"Yes, never better. I'm actually meeting someone here for a drink in a few minutes, so we'll see how this goes," Hallie said, embarrassed with herself for implying that she was meeting a date.

"Good for you! I'll get out of your way before he gets here, but let's have lunch soon. It's been too long."

"Yes, it has. I'll email you and we'll get some dates on the calendar."

The two women embraced again just as Marcelo walked up. Hallie introduced them and Kim quickly left to meet her friends at one of the tables inside. As she walked away, out of Marcelo's view, she gave Hallie a thumbs up to signify her approval of the hot detective. Hallie smiled and blushed, hoping Marcelo didn't notice.

"Detective," Hallie said, still smiling.

"Counselor," Marcelo replied, winking as he came in for a friendly hug.

Hallie loved the smell of his cologne. It reminded her of the musk her father used to wear on special occasions. Whenever she smelled a similar cologne, it always triggered one of her favorite memories of her father, dressed in a tuxedo, waiting for her mother at the bottom of the stairs so they could leave for an event they were attending. Her father was about 5'10", with wavy blonde hair, like hers, and light blue eyes, and by all accounts, a very good-looking man. To this day, in her head she could hear the adoration in her father's voice when her mother finally came down the stairs in a red evening gown, "Well, what in my lucky stars have I done to deserve this? Mrs. Robinson, you are a vision," followed by her mother's giggle, and response, "Oh Charlie," while glowing from the compliment. Her father grabbed her mother's hand, and twirled her around, dancing with her while humming a tune the significance of which only they understood. And in that moment, no one else existed in their world but the two of them. Hallie was about sixteen at the time, and because her best friend was spending the night, she pretended to be embarrassed by her parents' display of affection and silliness, but inside all she could think to herself was, that's the kind of love I want one day. Her unfulfilled wish had not changed since then.

Hallie and Marcelo sat down just as the bartender came over to take their order. Hallie ordered another glass of the organic red wine while Marcelo ordered an IPA craft beer.

"So how have you been?" Hallie asked.

"Busy but good. Thank you for meeting me tonight."

"Thank you for asking me," Hallie said, just as the bartender returned with their drinks.

Hallie was thankful for the wine in front of her. Marcelo had a way of looking into her eyes so directly, it unnerved her.

"So, how was your weekend? Do anything fun?" Marcelo asked her.

"Actually, it was very productive. I did a lot of research on Vincent Martino and Ben Young and found some very interesting things."

"Really? What did you find out?"

Hallie summarized the most important and interesting things she had learned about Vincent Martino and his relationship with Ben Young, including the allegations that resulted in Ben's conviction. She also explained how Vincent and Tommy Martino were cousins, and how their fathers, who were brothers, were both allegedly soldiers in the Trafficante crime family.

"Very interesting. What are you going to do next?"

"I've got to go visit Ben Young at Raiford to see what he wants to tell me. I'm also going to visit Tommy's wife, Nina Martino, my father's client, to see what she has to say. Tommy died in 1991, but Nina, who was eight or nine years younger than Tommy, is still alive."

"I'm impressed. Maybe I should be calling you 'detective' from now on instead of 'counselor'," Marcelo teased, smiling at Hallie.

Hallie picked up her glass and took a sip of her wine, which had started to do its job of calming her nerves. Although she had gone to the Keys with Tom after her divorce, in her mind, he was an old friend and someone she had known, or thought she knew, for over thirty years. This was technically her first date since her divorce, and she felt awkward and not as confident as she normally did. There was something about Marcelo that made her feel exposed, like she couldn't bullshit him, and he knew exactly what she was feeling.

"What are you thinking about, Hallie?" Marcelo asked.

"I'm thinking that I don't know what I'm doing," Hallie answered honestly before she had a chance to edit her answer.

She picked up her wine glass again and took another sip. Before Marcelo could speak, she laughed and with a wave of her hand quickly followed with, "Please disregard my last nonsensical answer. I think what I meant to say is, I'm having a very nice time and I was just thinking about what Ben Young and Nina Martino might tell me."

"It's okay, Hallie," Marcelo said calmly, without taking his eyes off her.

"What's okay?" she asked, looking down to avoid his gaze.

"To be vulnerable. It's okay that you don't know what you're doing. None of us really does, do we? But I like you. I think you're crazy smart, funny, and incredibly sexy. So, what I would like to do is get to know you better. That's what I'm doing. And by the way, I think your ex was not only a predator but a fucking idiot for what he did to you."

Hallie sat there speechless for a moment, stunned by his honesty and directness. She picked up her glass of wine and took another large sip before finding her voice.

"Thank you for saying that," she started, "and also for your directness. It's actually refreshing. And thank you for the nice things you said. It's been a long time since anyone, other than my mother, gave me compliments like that. And she doesn't sound like you when she says them, so I have to give you points for the delivery as well," she said, pausing to take another sip of wine. "Also, I would very much like to get to know you too. So, I'm glad that's what we're doing."

Marcelo smiled, "Good. I'm glad we cleared that up. So, when do we get to have sex?"

Before Hallie could answer, Marcelo held both hands up in a show of surrender and followed with, "I'm kidding, counselor. But I am glad you agreed to meet me for a drink tonight. I look forward to seeing you again and getting to know you better."

He picked up his almost empty beer and held it out towards her in a toast and said, "To new beginnings and new friendships."

Hallie picked up her wine glass, clinking it to his, and said, "And to sex," as she winked.

CHAPTER THIRTY-SIX

Mr. Sadist enjoyed his time with Sheada so much he almost took it too far. He realized he needed to slow down, or he was going to make a mistake. It was also time to reach out to Ronald again, the pathetic loser who had inadvertently given him access to Veronica, Sheada, Michele, and Hallie. He was saving Hallie for last. He opened the box where he kept the things he stole from their houses. He found Hallie's underwear and sniffed them, taking in the aroma of her lavender laundry detergent. Oh Hallie, he got hard thinking about what he was going to do to her. He sniffed the underwear one last time before he placed everything back in the box and put it back in the safe on the floor of his closet.

He opened his bank app on his phone and logged into his bank account. The regular monthly deposit had gone in, just like clockwork.

Next, he opened the local news app on his phone to see if there was anything about Sheada being found. He was confident the nosy neighbor who walked his stupid little yappy dog past the house each day would eventually notice the front door he left open. He wondered if the man had heard or seen anything when he brought Sheada into the house in the middle of the night. He noticed him looking towards the house on his walk the following morning but then switched his attention to the house across the street where the cute blonde lady lived, apparently oblivious to what was going on inside.

He thought about how he had pulled onto the quiet Tampa Heights street, turned off the headlights and drove Sheada's car past the vacant house. There were no lights on in the other homes he passed, nor did he see the flickering lights of televisions in any of the windows. He turned around at the dead-end, pulled into the driveway, and killed the ignition while listening to the stillness outside of the window. The nearest streetlight was at the end of the block, far enough from the empty rental to allow him to carry Sheada from the car into the home under the cloak of darkness. The ominous oaks lining the street, planted a lifetime ago before air-conditioning was invented, offered the only shade from the blistering sun during the day while the canopy of thick branches impeded the moon's ability to penetrate the blackness of the street at night. The moonlight would occasionally sneak through when a gust of warm air disrupted the stillness allowing shadows to dance across the sidewalks. He felt confident that he had gotten Sheada into the house without anyone seeing them. He had then moved Sheada's car down the street, leaving it in front of one of the overgrown, empty lots towards the dead-end.

Tampa Heights, an urban community close to downtown, had become a popular and much-sought-after area for young professionals tired of commuting from the suburbs. The mixed-use zoning provided an eclectic, affordable neighborhood on the edge of revitalization. Lee's Grocery was on the corner of Central Avenue and Frances Street, nestled among the bungalows and old houses that had been converted into apartments. A few blocks down Central, an abandoned, partially fire-damaged Methodist church built in 1910 was transformed into loft apartments aptly named The Sanctuary, the original stained-glass windows a reminder of the building's history.

When Mr. Sadist was scouring the house rentals on Zillow, he knew the home on Frances would be perfect for his plans with Sheada. He intentionally found one listed by the property owners so he could deal directly with them rather than a management company. He called the number listed on Zillow to find out when it would be safe to bring Sheada there. It was amazing how much information people were willing to give to a complete stranger.

"I was hoping to see the place this weekend," Mr. Sadist said to see how they responded.

"Oh, sorry, we can't show it this weekend because my wife and I have to head over to the East coast for our son's soccer tournament. I don't know if you have kids, but if you do and they're into sports, you know how these tournaments take over your life," Brad, the owner, joked.

"Oh, yes, I know all about those soccer tournaments for the little ones," he chuckled, "believe me, I'll never forget those days. But as much as a pain in the ass they are, trust me, brother, cherish those times. Those darn kids grow up so fast," Mr. Sadist lied, trying to develop a rapport with Brad.

After a few more minutes of small talk about youth soccer and raising children in this day and age, they had agreed they would meet at the property the following Tuesday so he could show him the house on Frances. He knew that meant no one would be in the house the whole upcoming weekend.

After he finished his call with Brad, he drove over to Lee's and found a table outside in the courtyard facing Frances Street. While enjoying a slice of cheese pizza and a few beers, he watched the activity around the rental home and concluded no one in the sleepy neighborhood would pay any attention to him. And he was right.

Thinking back on it now, he knew it was a little risky, but Sheada's place was even riskier with the blonde boyfriend likely to show up any time of the day or night. Veronica never had any guests at her place in the two months he had been watching her, so he felt comfortable there, especially since he only spent a few hours with her. But he had taken his time with Sheada, probably too long, he admitted, and was a little reckless. He promised himself he wouldn't do that again.

His only regret was that Ronald could only watch him take Sheada on her alarm camera but hadn't been able to watch what he did to her in real time at the house on Frances Street. He filmed it but would have to send the video to Ronald, which would leave a trail to him, so he couldn't do that. He could save it to a jump drive, strip all of the metadata from the clip, and upload it to Ronald's computer, which should be safe but then how could he ensure Ronald would watch it? And that wasn't as much fun as knowing Ronald was watching him live in the moment. Maybe he would break into Ronald's apartment and force him to watch it, he thought, and then he could relive the experience at the same time. Hmmm, that was certainly something new he had never tried before. The thought intrigued him.

Sheada was a break from his normal routine and not one he thought he should repeat. It was too risky. And he wanted Ronald to watch what he did to the women in real time, especially Hallie, one of his next conquests. He had to figure out when Hallie would be alone with no possible visitors dropping in unexpectedly. He would take all the time he needed to figure out her schedule and habits. Most people had consistent routines, whether they realized it themselves or not. And Hallie, he knew, would be worth the wait and meticulous planning.

CHAPTER THIRTY-SEVEN

The darkness of the bar contrasted sharply with the blinding Miami sun outside. The cool air was a welcome relief from the sweltering afternoon heat, although not enough to overcome the lingering smell of desperation, sour beer, and smoke, which hit you as soon as you were a foot in the door. It took a minute for Tom's eyes to adjust as he scanned the room until he spotted the man he was there to meet sitting alone in the last booth at the back of the worn-out bar, the watering hole of choice for those who wanted or needed to get drunk without anyone bothering them or giving a fuck. Not far from the Little Havana dive were the trendy and popular bars on Miami Beach, but they didn't offer what El Gato Rojo offered: privacy and an uncanny ability of the staff to forget their patrons' names and faces. It was the perfect spot for a clandestine meeting.

"Nice place," the well-dressed man with the goatee said sarcastically as Tom sat down.

"It serves its purpose," Tom responded.

The dark-haired bartender was wearing a black tank top, inscribed with the name of the bar across a silhouette of a red cat, a short denim mini skirt, and black Doc

Martins on her feet. She was curvy, with thick hips and full breasts, and had a pretty, heart-shaped face that reminded Tom of a more rugged version of Scarlett Johansson and Zooey Deschanel, combined. She put her cigarette out in an ashtray on the bar before coming over to their booth.

"What'll it be, Papi?" she asked, looking only at Tom while puckering her ruby, red-painted lips. The other man had an untouched drink sweating onto the table in front of him.

"I'll have Havana Club on the rocks."

"7 Años or Seleccion de Maestro?"

"7 Años," Tom replied, watching her generous ass as she walked away.

The bartender returned, placed the tumbler of dark rum in front of Tom and smiled seductively at him, adding, "My name is Esperanza, if you need anything else," before returning to her place behind the bar. He might have to explore that later when his business was done, Tom thought to himself.

The other man picked up his drink, raised it towards Tom, and said, "Salud" before taking a sip.

"Salud," Tom replied as he did the same. "So, what is the latest with our friend? Has he met with Hallie yet?"

"No, not yet. I met with Kane to let him know we might be in need of his services to eradicate this problem. I don't think he's going to give us any trouble."

"Kane?" Tom asked.

"Christian Kane, CK. He was Monica's ex before we set him up to get him away from her. In prison, they call him the Broker."

"Man, I wish Hallie had just left all of this the fuck alone," Tom said, shaking his head and draining the contents of his glass in one swallow.

"We always knew this day could come. Vincent, the stupid drunk, told Young too much. You know this. We learned from one of our informants that Young was running his mouth about shortening his sentence by trading information about an old murder while getting even with the family at the same time. The informant heard that he had contacted the daughter of the victim who happened to now be a lawyer. We knew he was talking about Hallie Miller."

"Yes, but if Uncle Vincent had kept his fucking mouth shut, maybe I wouldn't have been brought into this . . . again." Tom said in disgust, picking up his glass only to realize it was empty. He motioned to Esperanza to bring him another, "And if I wasn't born into this fucked up family, I wouldn't have been involved thirty years ago and I wouldn't be involved now. But here we are."

"I understand your frustration, but you have also reaped many benefits and opportunities from being a part of this family, so you need to consider that," the man with the goatee said, finally taking a small sip of his drink.

"Oh, I know. I've been reminded of that my entire life. But before then, I was just a student, without a care in the world, with a friend named Hallie Robinson, who I really liked and wanted to date. Hell, I thought I was falling in love with her. Then one night I get a call from Uncle Tommy, who needed a favor. I did everything that was expected of me, as you know. After that, there was no way I could have a relationship with Hallie. Not after that night, so I took off to Miami to start a new life for myself."

"Yes, and if I recall, Tommy helped you start that nice life in Miami, opening many doors for you, as did I after his unfortunate accident."

"I just don't understand why I had to reconnect with her after all these years. Even if Young knew the truth and told her what he knew, how could anyone prove anything today? There is no evidence."

"While that may be true, we don't like surprises or people interfering with the family. We had to find out what he told her. You were the only person who could get close enough to her to find out. We had to protect the family."

"Right, our trip to the Keys. She doesn't deserve any of this. She didn't do anything," Tom said, exasperated. "I really liked her; I still do. Who knows what could have happened between us," Tom said, looking down, forgetting all about Esperanza for the moment.

"Well, family comes first. You know that," the older man said, motioning to the bartender to bring them another round.

"Yes, I know. That's been ingrained in me since I was a kid. I just wish . . . aw, hell, never mind, I don't know what I wish. It was an impossible situation. I guess I would rather her hate me for ghosting her than to hate me for my involvement thirty years ago. And now."

"Yes, an impossible situation from the start," the man with the goatee agreed as he took another sip of the drink in front of him, without a hint of empathy whatsoever.

Esperanza placed their drinks down in front of them, slipping Tom her number on a napkin before walking away.

"So, what do we do next, Uncle Nicolas?"

"When the time is right, I will pay another visit to the Broker. It's time he knows the truth as well. He will take care of our problem."

CHAPTER THIRTY-EIGHT

Moni saw her mother, Nina, sitting at her usual table underneath the atrium in the iconic Columbia restaurant. She had her regular gin martini in front of her, two olives, on the rocks. Moni automatically and unconsciously pulled up the neckline of her dress while simultaneously pulling down on the hemline to make sure neither was too revealing. Nina saw her as she adjusted herself coming towards the table.

"Why are you always fidgeting, Monica? If you wear something ladylike, you won't have to always be pulling at both ends to make sure your business is properly covered. Your father, may he rest in peace, would be horrified," Nina said, taking another sip of her gin martini while watching her daughter.

"Hello, Mother. As usual, you know how to set the tone before I even sit down," Moni said as she rolled her eyes.

"Don't start, Monica. I haven't seen you in a month and I don't want any unpleasantries. You know, you could come over to the house in between our regular luncheons. You know that, right? I swear if we didn't have our standing lunch dates, I would never see you."

"Yes, Mother. I know but I've just been really busy. I'm trying to get my new business off the ground and get some of my art displayed in the local galleries in Gulfport."

"Oh Monica, galleries? Really? We're using that term a little loosely now, aren't we?" Nina mocked, taking another sip of her gin martini. "Let's not pretend that these so-called galleries in Gulfport are going to catapult you into a successful art career," her mother said callously, the edge in her voice as biting as the icy gin in her glass.

Moni bowed her head, playing with the fruit on her plate, wishing she had put some whiskey in her espresso or at least smoked a bowl before she got there. Her mother was too much for her to deal with sober. The waiter came over just then and Moni ordered a Bloody Mary while her mother ordered another gin martini, while flirting with the young waiter.

"Ernesto, you have to enjoy these mother daughter moments whenever you can," she laughed, as if this was a whimsical, loving lunch between the two of them.

"Si', Mrs. Martino, always a pleasure to have you and your daughter," he said, as he awkwardly looked at Moni and then retreated to get their drinks.

"Have you talked to Pietro?"

"No. You know he doesn't return my calls, Mother."

"Well, you need to keep trying. I'll arrange something at the house. Brunch next Sunday? We need to get this resolved before Thanksgiving. I will not have my holidays ruined with the two of you being so ridiculous. You? You're just like your father – so stubborn, oh my God, Moni – and my grandson, well, he's just a typical Martino male," her mother said, laughing, while waving off some imaginary annoyance.

The fact that she called Monica by her endearing nickname was not lost on Moni. That meant the martini she had just ordered from Ernesto was more likely her third rather than her second as Moni had assumed.

"Um, I think I already have plans next Sunday, Mother," Moni stammered.

"Cancel them. Whatever your plans are, reconciling with your son before the holidays is more important. Be at the house at 11:30," her mother said, without the possibility of any further discussion.

Her mother had a habit of referring to Moni's childhood home on Davis Islands as "the house." "The house" was a 6,300 square foot mansion on the water at the very end of the island. After that issue was settled, not that Moni had a choice, her mother immediately started chattering on about the family, as she always did, leaving no detail out, including who got drunk at this cousin's wedding or who was getting a divorce, which was a long time coming because he was a lazy no-good slob. Moni could only imagine what her mother's counterparts in the family said about her. And so went the rest of the afternoon, her mom gossiping about everyone in the family and sipping gin martinis, the stories getting more colorful as she emptied her drinks, while continuing to flirt with poor Ernesto.

Moni had always been daddy's little girl and had never been close to her cold and judgmental mother. Her mother was often cruel, especially when she was drunk, while her father was everything her mother wasn't. Not being close to her mother or having a sister or girlfriend to confide in when she was younger, Moni had started keeping a diary when she was a teenager. Her first diary, a gift from her father, became her salvation and in which she recorded all her thoughts, dreams, fears, hopes – all of the things she didn't feel she could share with anyone else. When Moni was nineteen, Nina found out about her relationship with Christian Kane, a man ten years older than her, by reading her diary, which Moni had accidentally left under her bed the last time she was home.

Moni remembered her excitement and fear, but also joy, as she wrote in her diary, "Oh my God, I can't believe I'm writing these words, but I'm pregnant! I think I'm about 6 weeks along. I'm scared but excited. Christian will be an amazing father, just like Daddy is. And I will be the mother my mother never was. I will love this baby with all my heart."

That, of course, is how Nina also found out she was pregnant. When her mother confronted her, Moni begged her not to tell her father. She wanted to be the one to tell him and to convince him that Christian was a good man.

But her mother ignored her, taking pleasure in her father's disappointment in her. When Tommy Martino found out his only daughter was pregnant, he became enraged. He forbade Moni from seeing Christian again and threatened to disown her if she went behind his back. She had never seen her father so angry. He also vowed revenge against him, which terrified Moni. Tommy Martino never said anything he didn't mean. She wanted to protect Christian, so she stayed away, hoping over time she could persuade her father to give him a chance. But things never worked out the way Moni wanted, especially that year.

A few months after her father found out about him, Christian Kane was involved in a shootout with some Mexican drug smugglers at the Port of Tampa and went away to prison. Moni knew that was her fault – her father had made good on his threat, as she knew he would, and Christian paid the ultimate price. She never had the chance to tell him she was pregnant and never wanted him to know that she had ruined his life. She couldn't bear for him to hate her. So, she stayed away and never saw him again. When her father fell to his death later that same year, Moni was devastated. In one year, she had lost the only two men she had ever loved. And she felt responsible for both of their fates.

By the time she gave birth to Pietro, she was not the same person she was just nine months before. Or maybe she was. Maybe she was bad inside, like her mother, and that's why she didn't deserve Christian or her father in her life. She tried to love her son, and somewhere deep down she did, but she also resented him, blamed him for her broken heart, just like her mother probably blamed her for hers. After that horrible year, she never wanted to feel the pain of loving or losing anyone ever again.

And so began her toxic relationship with drugs, alcohol, and bad men. She sometimes wondered how her life would have turned out if she hadn't gotten pregnant and her father hadn't died so young. But whenever those thoughts creeped into her mind, she would wash them away with tequila or pills or whatever else she had on hand as effortlessly as the ocean washed away footprints on the beach.

CHAPTER THIRTY-NINE

Ronald paced around the small apartment trying to figure out what to do about Mr. Sadist. Judas Priest played from his free Spotify account through the monitor speakers, the heavy guitars and screaming lyrics empowering him. He knew it was his fault that the psycho he brought into their lives had attacked Veronica and Sheada. Now he was worried about his other ladies, especially Hallie, who was his first. He had started watching her the year before. He got the idea after installing her alarm and interior cameras. He had only been with the alarm company for a few months when he met her, but she was so pretty and so nice to him. And she was with that dickhead, creepy husband. At least she had gotten rid of him, he thought, often fantasizing that one day he could be with her.

He wanted to warn her but how could he do that without implicating himself? He decided to send her an anonymous message. Mr. Sadist had somehow gotten into his system, he realized, but Ronald had since made changes to it to make it more secure and almost impossible to hack into. He downloaded the Tor browser, which was developed to prevent anyone from learning a user's location or tracking a user's browsing habits by bouncing internet traffic through 'relays' run by thousands of volunteers around the world, making it extremely difficult for anyone to identify the source of the information or the location of the user. The Tor browser combined with the rolling VPNs he used allowed him to surf the dark web anonymously. He also set up a temporary email account on guerillamail.com. Emails sent or received only lasted an hour and were automatically deleted from the server. There was no registration required, allowing him to send a one-time, anonymous, untraceable email to Hallie to warn her. He would be virtually invisible, just as he was in his everyday life.

He sat down in front of his computer and opened a word document. He had to figure out what to say before he created the email account. He got up, paced the wooden floor again, the curry from the Indian restaurant downstairs overpowering the smell of body odor and dirty socks that had previously permeated the room. He went to the small fridge and retrieved a PBR, thankful there were still three left in there. He popped the tab on top and took a large sip as he sat down in front of his monitor again. As he got situated, he let out a large burp, regurgitating a little of the acidic beer, which dripped onto his chin. He wiped his mouth with the bottom of his ketchup-stained t-shirt, exposing his pasty-white, flabby belly underneath.

He looked at his phone: 9:23 p.m. From outside his window, he could hear police sirens racing down 7th Avenue towards him until they turned off a few blocks before reaching his building and headed away into the night. It was early for the police. Usually, they didn't get active until after midnight. Ronald took another large sip of his PBR and drafted his email to Hallie.

Ronald drafted and redrafted the email in the Word document until he felt it was perfect. He pulled up the anonymous email application and cut and pasted the message into the anonymous platform. He read it again. And then hit send, sending it across hundreds of networks and IP addresses before it would arrive in Hallie's inbox.

CHAPTER FORTY

Hallie filled out and submitted the visitor application form via email to Raiford Prison to visit Ben Young. She learned it could take up to thirty days for her application to be approved, so in the meantime, she created an account on JPay, a web-based platform that allowed people to connect with incarcerated inmates in correction facilities throughout the United States by emailing them and sending them photos or videos, even money. After she set up her JPay account, she emailed Ben to let him know she would be visiting as soon as her application was approved. Next, she found Nina Martino's home address on Davis Islands. She didn't want to just show up at her house, so she searched and found Nina on Facebook to see if they had any mutual friends.

She was busy scrolling through their mutual friends and completely fixated on her computer screen when she heard a voice in her office doorway, "What are you doing here so late, Hallie?"

"Oh my God, you scared the shit out of me," Hallie said, holding her hand over her pounding heart.

"I'm so sorry. I didn't mean to startle you. We're doing an update tonight, so I have to make sure everyone is logged off by 8:00 p.m. Didn't you get the email?"

"What time is it?" Hallie asked, looking at her phone. "Wow, I didn't realize it was that late. I'll just be five more minutes and then I'll log off."

"No problem, you've got time. It's only 7:40," the head of the firm's IT department responded.

"Do you have a second to answer a quick question? About technology?"

"Of course, how can I help?"

"I have a client who thinks her ex may have opened her phone right before they broke up. Is there any way to see what he accessed or to see if he took anything off her phone?"

"What do you mean, took anything off her phone? Do you mean is there a way to see if he transferred data, such as pictures or messages, off her phone to his email or some other device via airdrop or something like that?"

"Yeah, I guess, for starters. How would you check that?"

"Well, obviously, your client can check her sent folder on her email accounts. But if he was smart enough to delete it or send it by airdrop, then you would need someone more sophisticated to look in the deleted and temporary storage sections of the phone or on the cloud to see if he left a trail."

"Is this something that you know how to do?" Hallie asked.

"Yeah, I have some skills in that area. If you want to bring your client's phone in, I can take a look at it for you, especially if she knows the dates when the data may have been transferred. That makes it a little easier to search."

"Thanks, Peter. I'll talk to her and let you know."

"No problem. Happy to help."

Hallie was too embarrassed to admit to him that she was talking about her own phone, but knowing it could be done, maybe she could find someone else to see what, if anything, Tom had taken off her phone when they were in the Keys. Maybe Bridget was right; maybe he was just looking to see if she was texting someone else. But then he ghosted her, so who knows.

She printed a copy of her Raiford visitor application and the email she had sent to Ben Young and put them in a manila folder. She took out her black sharpie and wrote on the label, "Charlie Robinson," her father's name. She found her yellow legal pad on her desk where she was keeping various notes about her father's murder, including the information she had learned about the Martinos in the last few weeks. She placed the legal pad containing her notes into the folder with the other documents, closed out the open programs on her computer, and logged out. She slipped the manila folder into her large black leather bag that she brought with her each day, picked up her purse, her phone, and finally left her office after her long day. As she walked down the hallway on her way to the elevator, she saw a light on in one of the offices farther down the hall. She popped her head in as she walked by.

"Hey, Marty, you're here late."

"Hey, Hallie, yeah, so are you."

"Yes, but I'm leaving now. How about you, getting out of here soon?"

"Yeah, I just have to download this brief I have to file by tomorrow onto this jump drive since they're making us log out of the system. Then I can go home to continue working on it while my kids torment me and my wife berates me for working too many hours and not helping with the kids. Hashtag living the dream."

"Well, that sounds awful. Shouldn't the kids be going to bed soon?

"Only if there's a God," Marty replied.

Hallie laughed, "You're hilarious, Marty. Want me to wait for you?"

"No, that's okay, I'm going to take my time to make the IT guys nervous as pay back for every time the system crashes and they don't respond to my desperate pleas for help, which will also prolong going home to my family. It's a win-win."

"Oh my God, you're too much," Hallie laughed as she said goodnight and headed towards the elevator.

Hallie took the elevator down to the lobby and walked through the building to the parking garage elevators, her heels clicking and echoing off the marble floor as she passed the retail shops that had all closed at 6:00 p.m. She took the garage elevator to the fourth floor where she, thankfully, had a reserved parking space. The firm paid for parking in the garage for the attorneys, but if you wanted a reserved spot, you had to pay for that yourself. It was worth the $100 a month, in Hallie's opinion, because before she splurged for her own space, she could never remember where she had parked. Also, if she got into the office after 9:00 a.m., which she inevitably did, the only available spots were on the roof, which would turn her black BMW into a broiling oven. With her reserved space, it didn't matter what time she got there or left – she always knew where her car was, it wasn't unbearably hot, and she never got caught in the rain.

She stepped off the elevator into the deserted parking garage. There were no other cars left on her level as everyone had left hours before. The overhead light closest to her car was out, which added to the eeriness of the garage and Hallie's uneasiness.

"Get a grip," she said to herself, chalking it up to the research she had been doing on visiting and contacting inmates in the Florida prison system and the possible connections to her father's murder. The ghosts were haunting her tonight, she thought.

She started walking towards her car, which was on the far end of the garage. Her heels clickety-clicked on the concrete floor, the sound ricocheting off the walls of the vacant garage, accelerating in tandem to her heart rate.

She felt her cellphone vibrate in her hand and stopped for a moment to check to see who it was from. A text from Bridget. She could wait until she got into her car to respond to her. And then she heard footsteps. She looked around her and listened. Nothing. She kept going, picking up her pace, when she heard something again, although with the acoustics of the open garage, the cars passing on the street below, and her nerves, she couldn't trust anything she was hearing. She stopped again and listened, looking around the barren garage, holding her cellphone in her hand. Again, nothing, no other cars or people in sight.

There was a stairwell through an exit door just past her car that led to the street below. Although you could always get out of the garage, the door was supposed to be locked at the street level to keep people from getting into the garage after hours without a key card. Unfortunately, people were always propping it open so they could get back to their cars after happy hour or events at Amalie Arena. Hallie looked behind her and down the ramp adjacent to her as she passed. There was no one around and the only sounds she heard were from the floor above her, where she heard the door to the stairwell open and then slam shut. The sound was almost comforting because it was not imagined and far enough away not to be dangerous to her.

She was about seven feet from her car when a large man came out of the shadows just beyond her car. Hallie screamed and ran to the door of her car, dropping her cellphone on the way, while she frantically opened the car door and threw her stuff onto the passenger seat.

"Ms. Miller, Ms. Miller, it's okay, it's me, it's just me, Walter," the familiar security guard said while stopping in his tracks and holding his hands up to show he was no threat, "I'm so sorry, Ms. Miller, I didn't mean to scare you."

Hallie leaned up against her car for a minute to catch her breath, her adrenaline racing. When she could finally speak, she said, "Oh my God, Walter, that's the second time tonight someone has scared the crap out of me."

"I'm so sorry I scared you, ma'am."

"It's not your fault, Walter, I'm just a little edgy tonight, and I let this dark, deserted garage get the best of me."

Hallie walked around to the passenger side of her car to straighten out the stuff she threw in, picking up her phone on the way, happy to see the screen had not cracked from its impact with the garage floor.

"What are you doing over here in the dark, anyway?"

"I needed to take pictures of the broken lights so the day crew can replace them. Second time this week someone has deliberately knocked 'em out. Kids, I tell ya,"

"Were they knocked out on any other floors or just this floor?" Hallie asked, her gut telling her it would be only this floor before he even answered.

"Just this floor, Ms. Miller. Kids riding around downtown on those death scooters probably came up the stairwell and did it, you know, as a prank. Don't worry, we'll get it fixed and we're going to make sure that door on the first floor stays locked."

"Thanks, Walter. You have a good night," Hallie said as she got into her car.

"You, too, Ms. Miller. And you be careful out there tonight. Get home safely – it's a dangerous world out there," the security guard said right before Hallie closed her door and drove down the ramp of the garage.

* * *

He watched as she got out of her black BMW, retrieved her leather bag she usually carried with her out of the passenger side of her car, and headed quickly towards the front of her house. Watching her, he could tell she was nervous or anxious about something. She looked around a couple of times as she walked up her front porch steps before entering the quaint, yellow bungalow. He heard Juno bark as she came to the door, likely more in excitement than as a warning to any potential visitors. He knew this firsthand. He parked a few blocks down from her house and was confident she couldn't see him with dusk setting in and the neighboring hedges blocking the view from her front porch. He had checked the angle himself numerous times. If he had time, he would sit there for hours, possibly peaking in her windows to get a closer glimpse of her while she relaxed with a glass of wine on her couch. But he didn't have the time tonight and it was still too soon to visit her. But her time was coming. He had to plan it just right. And he couldn't wait.

CHAPTER FORTY-ONE

Hallie pulled up Nina Martino's Facebook page and clicked on her friends list, pleased to see they had seven mutual friends in common. Tampa could still be a very small town despite the sprawling city it had become. She read the names of the mutual friends and found that her friend, Kim Hamill, the attorney she ran into at Hooch & Hive was friends with Nina Martino. She pulled up her phone and sent a text to Kim about getting together for lunch or a drink. Moments later, Kim replied and gave her some dates when she was available the following week. They agreed on a date, time, and place and then Hallie sent her one more text:

"By the way, I noticed on Facebook that you're friends with Nina Martino. How well do you know her?"

"Pretty well. She's a friend of my mom's. They were both on the board of the Tampa History Center a few years ago and became good friends then. Why?"

"I need an introduction to her," Hallie texted back, trying to decide how much to tell Kim.

"Okay, I can do that. But why? If this is a fundraising solicitation, she'll want to know which organization it's for before I connect the two of you."

Hallie thought quickly. Fundraising would be an excellent ruse without having to explain to Kim or Nina the real reason she wanted to meet with her. She felt bad for lying to her friend but getting to Nina to ask her about the divorce case her father was handling for her right before he was murdered was more important and she didn't want to tip her off ahead of time.

"Of course, I understand. I'm on the board of the Spring. We're raising money for our annual gala and collecting things for our silent auction," Hallie responded.

She wasn't completely lying. She was on the board of the Spring of Tampa Bay, one of the largest domestic violence shelters and crisis centers in the State, and, as the chair of the gala committee, Hallie was supposed to be doing that.

"Okay, I'll reach out to her and if she's cool with it, I'll connect you."

"Thanks so much, you're the best!" Hallie responded.

"Anytime! Looking forward to seeing you next week."

"Me too," Hallie responded, and added the happy face surrounded by hearts emoji.

* * *

The next day, Hallie received a text from Kim telling her that she had passed Hallie's contact information on to Nina Martino, and she would be hearing from her soon. Within an hour, Hallie received a call from a local, unknown number.

Hallie answered, "Hallie Miller," and waited for the person on the other end to speak or the recording to tell her about her car warranty that was about to expire.

"Hello, this is Nina Martino. Kim Hamill, Shelly's daughter, reached out to me about supporting the Spring's annual gala and asked me to call you."

Hallie hesitated a moment, caught off guard, "Yes, hello, Mrs. Martino, thank you for calling. If you have some time, I would love to meet with you to discuss all the ways our donors can support the organization and especially our annual gala."

"Please, call me Nina. Are you available today for lunch? I can get us a table at the Columbia in Ybor at noon."

Hallie was impressed with her no-nonsense assertiveness. She quickly looked at her calendar and said, "Yes, actually, I am."

"Perfect, I'll see you at noon. I'll be at a table in the Atrium. Ask for Ernesto. He'll show you the way."

And that was that. Hallie realized that this was a woman who commanded respect, took charge, and called the shots. The person she had just experienced over the phone was very different from the allegedly abused woman Hallie had envisioned and created in her mind from reading her father's case file notes.

Hallie quickly saved the number into her phone under her contacts and sent an email to her assistant that she had a lunch meeting and would be in after lunch. She needed the morning to prepare for her meeting with Nina. She needed to know what to ask the woman who was potentially one of the last people to see her father alive.

She sat down at her desk in the office of her Hyde Park bungalow. She looked out the front window at the large oak shading her property, longing to see the fat gray tabby who she knew would not appear. Juno, ever faithful, took her spot on her bed next to Hallie's antique mahogany desk. The squirrels, thankful the gray tabby had been relocated last year, were fuller and multiplying. Hallie enjoyed seeing them too.

She pulled the manila folder labeled "Charlie Robinson" out of her black leather bag, emptying the contents onto her desk. She reviewed her own handwritten notes on the yellow legal pad first. Before opening and reviewing the Martino divorce file, she took out a fresh legal pad and took the cap off of one of the many blue rollerball pens she kept on her desk. At the top of the page, out of habit, she put the date. Then she drew a line down the middle of the page and in the heading on the left, she listed "Facts" and on the right she wrote, "Questions." And she started filling in the information from her own notes, her father's notes, and the rest of his file.

For the first time she realized how similar her own handwriting had been to her father's. The thought made her happy and sad at the same time. If only he hadn't been murdered, what could they have accomplished together? Would she be a better lawyer? A better mother? A better person? She felt she would be all of the above if her father's life hadn't been cut short and he had lived to guide her. Just as she was having these self-deprecating thoughts, she could hear her best friend, Bridget, in her head from a recent conversation they had on the same subject: "Shut the fuck up, bitch, what are you talking about? Look, we all have baggage, but despite what you went through, you were able to overcome that shit and be a really good wife – not that either of those fuckers deserved you – an amazing mom, and a pretty badass lawyer. So, I'm done talking about this. Enough of this sad-sack bullshit that I don't want to hear about again."

Hallie couldn't help but smile. Bridget, just like all her close friends, always had her back but she also didn't sugarcoat things. Bridget always told Hallie what she thought, whether she wanted to hear it or not.

She finished her list of facts and questions and went upstairs to get ready for her meeting with Nina Martino. She hadn't been nervous until her brief phone call with the woman a few hours before. She wondered if she should start out with the Spring pitch, which was her ruse, or just come clean right off the bat. She decided that Nina Martino was not someone who could be bullshitted so she was better off just coming clean as soon as she sat down. Feeling better about her plan, she got in the shower to get ready for her meeting, completely oblivious to the cameras filming her every move.

She finished getting ready, put on a black skirt, pink shell, and lightweight, black sweater on top. Because of the unbearable heat, no one wore suits anymore unless they were in fact going to court, which she rarely did. Attending a hearing didn't even require a formal suit these days. But she wanted to appear professional when she presented herself to Nina Martino, and she felt her conservative outfit was more appropriate for a lunchtime meeting at the Columbia.

She sat down at her desk to gather what she needed for her meeting as well as what she might need for the rest of the day at the office. She quickly realized she had been so engrossed with thinking about her father's case and her meeting with Nina Martino that she hadn't checked her email. She opened her work email and quickly reviewed and responded to the various conflict check emails sent by the file clerk to the attorneys in the office and to the scheduling questions posed by her assistant. She was skimming through the rest of the emails, knowing what could wait until later, when she saw an email from an unknown address that caught her eye:

To: HMiller@GRLaw.com

From: x24somf333$%#12foeu90ur09ewujklnlkads@guerillamail.com

Subject: Warning from a friend

Dear Hallie,

You don't know me. But I am a friend, I promise you. There is a very bad man out there who is hurting women. Veronica and Sheada didn't deserve what he did to them. I never meant for any of this to happen. You might be next. Or maybe Michele or Laura. Or all of you. I don't know. But I wanted to warn you so you can take precautions and protect yourself. He's very evil. That's all I can tell you about him. Please be careful and warn the others. Your friend, R.

"What the . . .?" Hallie said aloud, causing Juno to raise her head and look at Hallie for a moment. She looked at the sender's email address and decided it was some type of spam email, because the address did not look legitimate. That made her feel slightly better, and she didn't have time to deal with it then anyway. Something about the email was still nagging at her, but she was unable to put her finger on it. Whatever it was, it would have to wait until she got to the office after lunch. She logged out of her work remote access, threw the rest of her files into her black leather bag, leaned down to scratch Juno behind her ears, and went out the door to meet Nina Martino at the Columbia in Ybor.

* * *

Hallie handed her keys to the valet, thankful for the service on this ridiculously hot day when she was wearing all black.

As she smoothed her skirt and looked down at her open-toed, cute heels, she was also grateful that the professional world, at least in Florida, had finally done away with the requirement of wearing panty hose. It was just too hot for stockings in Florida. She walked into the restaurant and told the hostess her name and who she was meeting.

The uninterested hostess immediately became alert at the mention of Nina's name, and quickly said, "We've been expecting you, Ms. Miller, right this way."

Hallie was escorted to a table in the center of the iconic restaurant, under the atrium, where an attractive older woman with straight, shoulder-length platinum hair was already seated, sipping a martini.

Hallie sat down and said, nodding towards Nina's drink, "Gin or vodka?"

"Gin, of course, love, I'm not a heathen," Nina Martino said, winking at Hallie.

Ernesto appeared out of nowhere just after Hallie sat down.

"Hello, Miss, welcome, what can I get for you?"

Hallie never lost eye contact with Nina, and responded, "Aviation Gin martini, on the rocks, with olives."

Nina smiled approvingly as Ernesto quickly left to get Hallie's drink.

"Thank you for meeting with me, Mrs. Martino."

"If we're going to be friends, you must call me Nina," she responded while taking a sip out of her martini glass.

"Thank you, Nina. I appreciate you taking the time to meet with me today."

"Of course, dear, any friend of the Hamills is a friend of mine," she said as Ernesto placed Hallie's drink down in front of her.

Hallie lifted her glass towards Nina, "Here's to new friendships."

The women clinked glasses, and each took a sip, sizing each other up. Based on the Petition for Dissolution of Marriage in her father's file, Nina was seventy-three years old, but she didn't look a day over sixty. Her white hair was soft and longer than most women her age, but it suited her. She was elegant in a way from another era, both in looks and in demeanor. She reminded Hallie of Lauren Bacall, an actress from classic Hollywood cinema in the days of Ingrid Bergman, Irene Dunne, and others. Lauren married Humphrey Bogart in 1945 after meeting him on the set of *To Have and Have Not*, her first Hollywood film that catapulted her to fame and the Hollywood elite.

"Nina, I have to confess that I have another more personal reason for wanting to meet with you other than fundraising for the Spring's annual gala," Hallie began.

"Yes, we'll get to all of that in due time. Let's enjoy our drinks and get to know each other a bit first," Nina said, winking again at Hallie as she lifted her drink to her lips, pausing right before she took a sip to say, "I do see a lot of your father in you, especially your eyes. He was a very kind man."

CHAPTER FORTY-TWO

"Hey, you got a visitor," the guard yelled, surprising the Broker. It was Saturday morning, just after breakfast, and it had been three weeks since the last time he had heard those words.

"I'm busy" the Broker responded angrily.

"Not today, you're not. Get the fuck up," the guard barked, suggesting the guard was on the same payroll as the visitor coming to see him.

The Broker went through the same drill as the last time he had a visitor. Just as before, when he finally arrived at the visitor's room, the man with the crooked nose, steel blue eyes, and gray goatee was waiting for him at a table. This time, the Broker walked over to the table and sat down in front of the visitor, nodding as he sat down.

"Hello, Mr. Kane," the man said.

"What's up?"

"It's time. We need your services."

"Yeah? What do you need and who's 'we'? I like to know who I'm working for."

"You're working for me. But trust me, there are much more powerful people who are going to be evaluating your performance."

"Oh yeah? What if I tell you and your powerful people to go fuck yourselves? I'm in for life and I got nothing to lose, including my goddamn life, so bring it the fuck on. I ain't scared."

The man in the very expensive suit didn't react, said nothing although he smiled slightly, and slid a picture across the table at the Broker, never losing eye contact and never taking his finger off the photo.

"We all make choices, Mr. Kane, and we always have something to lose."

The Broker looked down at the photo, trying not to show any emotion, while his heart rate increased at the sight of her. The man sitting across from him remained quiet. The picture triggered the same old questions for which he still did not have answers. It also triggered more emotions than he was ready to feel. The guard looked over, pretending not to notice that there was a picture on the table, which was forbidden. He had obviously been paid off to look the other way. Visitors were not allowed to bring anything in with them unless it was cleared in advance by the warden. The Broker looked down at the picture again, oblivious to everything around him in the moment, and studied the old photo: a young, dark-haired boy with fair skin, playing on the beach while a beautiful woman with the same dark hair as the child watched over him, smiling, the photographer capturing a sweet moment between the two. He tried not to react to the photo, but seeing Moni, from what seemed like a thousand years ago, ignited his most primal instinct and desires he had tried to bury when he knew he would never get out to see her again. He wanted to kill the man sitting across the table from him with his bare hands.

Sensing he had hit a nerve, the man said, "Mr. Kane, I am not your enemy. You do this job for us, and we will get you what you want. The picture I showed you is simply a reminder that we all have things we cherish that may be more precarious than we think."

"Are you fucking kidding me? I lost her a long time ago," the Broker growled, slamming his fist down on the metal table, angrier than he expected he would get."

The burly guard who had brought him in looked over at him, ready to restrain him if necessary. The Broker held his hands up and nodded at the guard to acknowledge he would behave.

"Don't you want to know who the child in the picture is?"

"He ain't mine, I know that," the Broker responded, "what the fuck do you want from me?"

"What if I told you he was your son?"

"I would call you a goddamn liar. Moni wouldn't have kept that from me, not then," the Broker said, starting to sweat and hating the man before him even more than he had five minutes earlier.

The man continued calmly, "I understand your skepticism, but there are certain things to which you have not been privy, including why your paternity was kept from you and the boy, who is now a man, and which may now be revealed. But those matters are for another day and will be discussed after you accomplish the task at hand. As I mentioned on our previous visit, there are very important people behind this request. You would be surprised at what they can accomplish with the right motivation."

The Broker shook his head in disbelief and asked through gritted teeth, unable to process everything the man had just told him, "What's the fucking job?"

FORTY-THREE

Hallie left her lunch with Nina, dumfounded and a little buzzed from the gin martinis. She had been prepared to question Nina about her father's notes, including the possible restraining order and withdrawal from the case. But she didn't get to ask any of those questions. Nina controlled every aspect of the conversation and would divert Hallie whenever she got too close to the circumstances of her father's representation of her. Normally Hallie would be annoyed and frustrated, asserting herself to take control, but she was captivated by Nina and the stories she was telling and all she could do was listen. It was clear to Hallie that Nina had always been a firecracker and she wondered what her husband had done to drive her to file for divorce and, more importantly, what he had done to stop her from going through with it. She wished she would have asked something, anything, that might have given her a clue to her father's murder. Maybe she would have better luck with Ben Young. After all, he had reached out to her.

She arrived at the office at a little past two, pulled into the parking garage and into her spot on the fourth floor of the garage. She gathered her things and went up to her office. A few minutes later, Paige stuck her head in.

"Hey, hon, busy?"

Hallie looked up, "Oh, hey, um, no, just got here."

Paige took one look at her and said, "Um, do you want to explain why you were enjoying an obvious drinking lunch without me and who you were with? I thought we had a pact."

"That obvious?" Hallie asked, feeling the heat blushing her cheeks.

"Well, maybe not to most but I know you better, so, to me, yes."

"Hey, come in, shut the door," Hallie commanded.

Paige came in, shut the door, and sat in one of the chairs facing Hallie's desk, "What's going on?"

"So, remember I told you about the boxes of my father's case files my mother gave me years ago?"

"Yes, of course. Don't tell me you're rummaging through those old relics again, chasing ghosts," Paige said, concern in her voice, shaking her head.

"I think I found something. A connection."

"Really, Hallie?" Paige asked. "Tell me what you've found."

Hallie told Paige about her review of the files, including the Nina and Tommy Martino file and what her father's notes probably meant, her research of the Martino family, and the strange email from Ben Young, a prisoner at

Raiford who used to be partners with Vincent Martino before Young was convicted for trying to kill him.

When she finished, Paige said, "I think you've been reading too many Michael Connelly novels, Hallie," trying not to be too pessimistic but not wanting to encourage another wild goose chase either.

"No, it's different this time. Let's not forget, my father was in fact murdered, the police destroyed or conveniently lost the case file, and Nina Martino was one of the last people to see my father alive, which brings me to my three-gin martini lunch," Hallie said.

"Three? Oh, that explains a lot," Paige laughed, rolling her eyes.

"Yes, so I had lunch with Nina Martino, and she is fascinating, but something tells me she has a darker side well hidden behind the glamourous façade. She looks like Lauren Bacall; remember that actress? Anyway, she likes gin martinis."

"Who, Lauren Bacall?"

"No, Nina Martino. She's not wrong about those, by the way."

"But did you get any answers or information from her about your father's murder?"

"No, not yet; I didn't want to spook her. But I'm going to have lunch with her again. And then I'm going to ask her the tough questions."

"Oh, okay, Perry Mason. You let me know how that works out," Paige teased.

"I will. Next time. She threw me off right from the start when she told me I reminded her of my father. I didn't think she even knew who I was."

"Well, that explains the three gin martinis."

"Yeah, it kinda does. She has a daughter, Monica Martino, who's about my age. I'm going to try to find her next to see if she'll talk to me. When I brought Monica up to Nina, she quickly changed the subject. So maybe they're not on the best of terms, which means maybe she'll tell me what her mother wouldn't. I don't know, but it's worth a shot."

"Okay, but be careful, Hallie. If Tommy Martino did kill your father, both mother and daughter may still want to protect his legacy and the family name."

"I know, but I have to do this. This is the closest I've ever been to finding out the truth."

Paige looked down at her phone, noticing the time, "Shit, I have to go prepare for my mediation tomorrow. Are you okay?"

"I'm fine. This is the first lead I've had in years, and I want to see where it goes. Unfortunately, I haven't billed a single minute today so that sucks."

"Don't worry, you'll make up the time. I know how important this is to you."

"Yeah, it is. I'll keep you posted. Dinner and drinks Thursday night?"

"Absolutely. Until then, stay safe, Perry," Paige teased as she walked out of her office.

Hallie checked her email and saw the weird email she had received that morning, which she had forgotten about, likely thanks to the three gin martinis. She read it again:

To: HMiller@GRLaw.com
From: x24somf333$%#12foeu90ur09ewujklnlkads@guerillamail.com
Subject: Warning from a friend

Dear Hallie,

You don't know me. But I am a friend, I promise you. There is a very bad man out there who is hurting women. Veronica and Sheada didn't deserve what he did to them. I never meant for any of this to happen. You might be next. Or maybe Michele or Laura. Or all of you. I don't know. But I wanted to warn you so you can take precautions and protect yourself. He's very evil. That's all I can tell you about him. Please be careful and warn the others. Your friend, R.

She picked up her cellphone and called Marcelo.

"Hey, are you busy? I got another weird email. Can I send it to you?"

"Of course. Is it from the same prisoner?"

"No, nothing like that one. I'm hoping this one is some type of scam email like those calls from the alleged grandchild who is stuck in jail in another country and you have to send money right away. But I don't know. The email address it came from looks like a scam. The sender doesn't ask for anything but says enough that it seems personal. It's definitely strange. Maybe just a prank."

"Forward it to me. I'll take a look. Am I going to get to see you later?"

Hallie blushed and smiled at the last question, "If you would like to. Want to come over for dinner?"

"I thought you would never ask. What time?"

"6:30 or 7?"

"7 is perfect. I'll see you then. Forward the email."

"Just did. See you at 7," Hallie responded, feeling the familiar butterflies whenever she spoke to or thought about Marcelo.

CHAPTER FORTY-FOUR

Marcelo read the email Hallie had forwarded to him. He grabbed the files off his desk, even though their names were already committed to memory, and confirmed: Veronica Hill, the victim from the home invasion, and Sheada Lawson, the second victim taken from her home and left for dead in the vacant home in Tampa Heights.

"Holy shit," he said, while reading the email Hallie had sent him one more time:

To: HMiller@GRLaw.com
From: x24somf333$%#12foeu90ur09ewujklnlkads@guerillamail.com
Subject: Warning from a friend

Dear Hallie,

You don't know me. But I am a friend, I promise you. There is a very bad man out there who is hurting women. Veronica and Sheada didn't deserve what he did to them. I never meant for any of this to happen. You might be next. Or maybe Michele or Laura. Or all of you. I don't know. But I wanted to warn you so you can take precautions and protect yourself. He's very evil. That's all I can tell you about him. Please be careful and warn the others. Your friend, R.

Marcelo immediately picked up his phone and called Hallie. It went straight to voicemail. He left a quick message, "Hallie, call me as soon as you get this," and then sent her a text that said, "Call me."

He read the email again, trying to figure out how someone would know the victims' names, which had not been released to the public due to Marsy's Law, a Florida victims rights law adopted in 2019 that prohibits law enforcement from releasing the identity of crime victims' names without their or their family's consent. While he waited for Hallie to call him back, he did a quick internet search to see if their names or stories about their attacks had been published. He found nothing.

Just as he was getting ready to look up Hallie's office phone number, his cellphone rang.

"Hey, sorry, I was on the phone with a client. What's up?"

"Hallie, where are you?"

"In my office, what's going on? You sound stressed."

"Okay, good," Marcelo said, exhaling for the first time in the last few minutes. "Stay there until you hear from me again. Don't go home yet, okay?"

"You're scaring me. What's going on? Oh my God, this is about that email, isn't it? Is it legit? Do I have something to be worried about?"

"I don't know yet but two women in the area have been brutally attacked recently, and their first names are Veronica and Sheada."

"Are you kidding? What the . . .? When? How? Are they okay?"

"Physically, they will both recover, but the attacks were bad. I need to get my technology department involved to see if we can trace this email. Based on the sender's email address, which is from a temporary email account platform, I doubt we will. But don't delete the email from your inbox, okay? And let me know if you receive any more emails from this guy."

"Should I notify my IT department?"

"No, not yet. Let me see what we can find out first before we get your firm involved. I'll call you back soon. And please, just stay put. I'll come by when you're ready to leave the office and I'll follow you home. And hopefully I'll know more then so we can figure out whether you are in any danger."

"You're freaking me out, Marcelo."

"Don't worry, I'll keep you safe, but I want to take this seriously until we can determine otherwise. Okay?"

"Okay. I had planned to leave here at about 5:30 to stop at Publix on my way home. Dinner, remember?" she asked hesitantly.

"Why don't we pick something up on the way to your house instead? I'll come to your office about 6:30 or 7. I'll text you when I'm downstairs."

"Sounds like a plan," Hallie said, the butterflies replaced by fear and anxiety.

Marcelo hung up and printed the email out on his desktop printer. He gathered the files on Veronica Hill and Sheada Lawson and went straight to the Chief's office, trying not to let his worry for Hallie cloud his judgment, as he whispered into the universe, "If you touch her, mother fucker, I'm coming for you."

And he meant it.

CHAPTER FORTY-FIVE

The Broker settled back onto the flimsy cot in his cell, waiting for the guards to do their final check of the night. He heard them making their way down the concrete walkway that ran the length of the cells, occasionally clanging their nightsticks on the bars for reasons unbeknownst to the Broker. He had waited until Frankie, the heavyset Italian guard who made sure everyone knew he was from Brooklyn, was on night duty before he decided to carry out the job. Frankie came to his cell, stopped, and bent down to tie his shoe while discretely picking up and slipping the five, crisp, folded up, one hundred-dollar bills left near the cell door into his sock. Frankie continued down the walkway leaving the Broker's cell unlocked. Unbeknownst to the target, his cell was left unlocked too.

The lights in Cell Block J went out after the final cell was checked. The Broker knew he had exactly twenty-seven minutes to get the job done before the guards would do their next round on the Block. He stood up onto his cot to retrieve the razor-sharp shank he had stored on the ledge of the only window in his cell. The window, if you could call it that, was a twelve-by-twelve-inch industrial-strength plexiglass, covered by steel bars, and was situated about four feet above his bed and about seven feet off the floor. It didn't open and barely allowed the sun or any other light to penetrate, but it was more than what most prisoners at Raiford had. He was thankful for the slight reminder of the outside world that the small window offered him. He grabbed the shank that was tucked up underneath the sill where it couldn't be seen by anyone standing in the cell below, not that the guards ever checked his cell after what he paid them on a regular basis.

He hid the shank in his left hand and looked out of his cell before quietly sliding the door open to exit. The block was quiet, other than the usual nightly cries, moans, and other sounds made by the desperate and the hopeless, which most of the lifers had gotten used to, if not blocked out or caused. He knew that if any of his neighbors in the nearby cells saw him, they would not make a sound nor would they admit to seeing him. It was the unspoken rule. He had developed a reputation that no matter what group or gang an inmate was associated with, the Broker could penetrate it. And if you fucked with the Broker, you would pay, often fatally. He had associates in every group and there was no such thing as a secret. It had been a long time since the Broker had gotten his hands dirty, but the man with the goatee had insisted he had to personally carry out this task himself, the significance of which was not lost on him.

The Broker crept down the walkway, counting the cells as he went, until he arrived at the target's cell. Ben Young was sitting up, wide awake.

"Do come in, Mr. Kane. Or is that inappropriate, should I only call you the Broker?"

"Shut the fuck up," the Broker whispered as he slipped into the unlocked cell, not surprised that the target was awake and waiting for him.

"To what do I owe this midnight rendezvous? Can I offer you a nightcap? Oh wait, that's right, we're in prison, I don't have any nightcaps," Ben quipped.

"I told you to shut the fuck up. We can do this the easy way or the hard way but either way, it's the end of the road for you," the Broker growled, mindful of the ticking clock. Twenty-three minutes left.

"So, is it my choice? Because if I get to choose, I'm going with the hard way, if that gives me a fighting chance to fight you off or trigger the guards to come save me, ignoring the fact for the moment that at least one of them is on your payroll," Ben responded, ready to fight back.

The Broker had had enough of the arrogant fuck's continued talking and was about to lunge at him to slit his throat when Ben spoke again, "Hey, here's another idea, if you're interested. How about you don't kill me, and we go to someone, maybe the D.A. or my lawyer or your lawyer and try to negotiate something for both of us to get out of this hellhole. Obviously, I know something someone doesn't want me to divulge, and you know who those people are who paid you to keep me from divulging it. I think we could get ourselves a pretty sweet little deal, if you ask me."

"Stop talking. Seriously, shut the fuck up. I need a minute."

"Take all the time you need. I have five to ten years to spare while you think," Ben said, chuckling at his own joke, while hoping he actually had any time left at all.

CHAPTER FORTY-SIX

Moni rolled over, trying to bury her head under her pillow, aggravated at the sound of the lawn crew downstairs, weed whacking and leaf blowing, as if everyone was up at 7:45 in the morning. Moni most surely was not. Especially after her night down the street at O'Maddy's, the local bar on the water in Gulfport. She remembered listening and dancing to the amazing band, Motel Funk, headed by Janie Richards, the singer who had the raspy but powerful voice of Aretha Franklin and Janis Joplin combined into one. She was not only amazing but one of the most beautiful people, inside and out, Moni had ever met. She always wanted to be the person who Janie saw through her kind, brown eyes, but she knew she never could be. Not after all she had done, especially abandoning her son. Moni was too flawed and broken. But Janie was one of those rare creatures on this earth who saw only the good in people and forgave them for all their sins. Her voice matched her heart.

As most nights, Moni didn't remember walking home last night. The last thing she remembered was dancing to Janie belting out "Me and Bobby McGee," one of her absolute favorites, but at least she didn't wake up with a strange man in her bed this morning. She sat up, her head pounding, regretting the bourbons she couldn't say no to last night. Her mouth tasted like the bottom of a shoe after its wearer had walked twelve miles in the desert. She needed a Gatorade and a burrito supreme from Taco Bell, maybe two of them, depending on how bad she felt. Nina would be horrified. But this was her tried and true hangover cure, which Moni had mastered many years before.

She cautiously got out of bed and found her way to the bathroom. She scrubbed her face to remove the makeup that had settled deep into her pores while she was passed out and brushed her teeth in the small bathroom, the inadequate counter cluttered with her hair products, brushes, eyeliners, and lipsticks in various shades of red. She padded out to the kitchenette in her bare feet to brew her strong Italian caffe, noticing her platform heels discarded haphazardly on the terrazzo tile floor near the door, her blouse and bra draped over the arm of the sofa and her denim skirt crumpled on the floor nearby, probably right where she had let it slip off her bony hips, not that she remembered undressing much less anything after dancing to "Me and Bobby McGee." She tossed three Tylenols into the back of her mouth and chased them down with a glass of warm tap water. The throbbing in her head should subside in a few minutes.

She picked her clothes up off the floor and couch while her coffee started to brew and was hit with an overwhelming scent of Victoria Secret Angel perfume and last night's smoke from the countless cigarettes she had undoubtedly smoked with her bourbon. The combination almost made her wretch. She placed the acrid clothing in her laundry hamper and tossed her heels into her closet before returning to the kitchen where the aromatic coffee beans percolating on the small stove had converted the drab kitchen into an Italian café. She poured the dark elixir into a Lenox demitasse, one of four Nina had given to her a few Christmases ago, one of her most prized possessions. It truly was one of the most, if not the only, thoughtful gifts her mother had given her over the years and Moni cherished each dainty cup in the set.

She grabbed her smokes on her way to the balcony, hoping to beat the impending rain she knew was coming from the thunder she heard rumbling in the distance. She lit her cigarette, enjoying the first, long drag of the day, and followed it with a sip of the strong coffee she had come to rely on to start her day, especially after a hard night at O'Maddy's. She picked up her phone to peruse her social media and news of the day when she noticed she had received a text from a familiar number in the middle of the night.

"Old ghosts are stirring"

Reading the words on the screen before her, she knew exactly what the cryptic message was about. She picked up the demitasse, taking another sip of her caffe, and smoked the rest of her cigarette, refusing to look down at her phone again. If anyone had been sitting with her that morning, they probably would not have noticed the slight tremor in her hand as she lifted her cup up to her permanently stained scarlet lips, the outer rim around her mouth wrinkled from years of smoking – unless, of course, the person who sent the text was sitting across from her. He, most assuredly, would have noticed and would have known why she was afraid. She looked down and read the message again:

"Old ghosts are stirring"

The dark clouds overhead became more ominous and the large palms lining the street started to sway as a tumultuous, no-named storm swept in from the Gulf. Within minutes, the sky turned black, the wind picked up, and lightening lit up the sky over the Gulf as thunder boomed around her. Moni felt the first drops of warm rain pelt her face. She put the Marlboro out in the ashtray and quickly retreated inside the garage apartment just before the downpour erupted, the storm no doubt a warning of what was to come.

She looked down at her phone again, hoping she had imagined it, but she knew better than that. But there they were, the words, or the implication of them, that she had been dreading for the last thirty years:

"Old ghosts are stirring"

Each time she read the text she grew more anxious, but she knew running from it would be pointless. She had nowhere to go.

CHAPTER FORTY-SEVEN

Hallie waited in her office for Marcelo to text her when he arrived at her building. She was confused about what was going on, but she trusted him. She looked out of the floor-to-ceiling window in her high-rise office, down at the Bay twenty-three floors below. From her stance, there wasn't a ripple across the surface of the dark water, suggesting a tranquility that Hallie knew firsthand was only a façade. She crossed and uncrossed her arms, pacing her office until checking her phone again to see if Marcelo had texted her. No text. She sat down at her desk and opened her email, trying to pass the time while she waited for Marcelo.

She read through the latest work-related emails she had received from clients and various senders from inside the firm. One of the first of twenty emails she had received that day notified her it was Desereah Washington's birthday, which was lovely except the original email was sent to "all," which meant she also received a barrage of emails from the usual "reply all" offenders in the firm who also wished Desereah a happy birthday. Worse than the "reply all" offenders were the ones who required a "read receipt" on every email, such as the infamous cat lady, one of the paralegals who was stationed in a cubicle just outside of Hallie's office. In addition to requiring the read receipts, throughout the day, Hallie would hear her delightfully exclaim, "would someone please come look at these babies?" while giggling and watching the live streaming cameras she had apparently set up in her home to film her many feline friends throughout the workday. No one ever came to look, not that cat lady or her cats noticed or cared. The cats brought her all the joy she apparently needed in life, a fact which almost made Hallie jealous. And then she remembered they were cats. On camera. And suddenly Hallie felt a little bit better about her life.

As she skimmed through the rest of the emails, deleting the birthday wishes as she went, she stopped on one from the Florida Department of Corrections:

To: HMiller@GRLaw.com
From: 1249078@FDOC.com
Subject: Visitor Application

Hello again, Ms. Miller,

Thank you for submitting your application to visit me at Raiford, my humble abode for the foreseeable albeit possibly limited future. I'm afraid the slow wheels of justice and red tape of our fine Florida prison system may prevent me from making your acquaintance in person, so in case we do not get that opportunity, I wanted to let you know that your father helped someone once who was not worthy of his compassion and good nature. Based on certain interactions I have had of late with some of my fellow cell block mates (and I use that term in the loosest sense possible), which I cannot go into, I know you are on the right track with whatever you are doing on the outside. However, be forewarned: there is evil in that bloodline – I know this firsthand, and it seems to get worse and more sociopathic with each generation. I've already said too much. I hope to see you when your visitor application gets approved if I am fortunate enough to still be among the living. Please be careful, Ms. Miller. These are not nice people.

Yours truly,
Ben Young

Hallie printed out a copy of the email so she could show it to Marcelo when he came to pick her up. She was excited and intrigued at the mention of her father and suggestion that she was on the right track. She felt in her gut that Tommy Martino was responsible for her father's death, and now Ben Young's email was one step closer to confirming that suspicion. She read the email again. Why did she need to be afraid, she wondered? She realized the family would want to protect his name, the family name, but Tommy Martino was dead, which meant he couldn't hurt her. Also, there was nothing Hallie could do, legally, because you can't arrest a dead man and she couldn't go after the family because the civil wrongful death statute of limitations had run a long time ago. But by finding out the truth, she might get some closure for her mother and herself. She didn't trust Ben Young and knew he was probably trying to use whatever information he might have to his advantage, especially if he thought she could do anything to help him get out of prison early. But Hallie didn't care. If she could prove Tommy Martino killed her father, maybe she and her mother could finally put her father's murder behind them . . . just maybe. She checked her phone again. No text. It was now 7:23 p.m.

Hallie's cellphone rang just as she set it back down on her desk. She picked it up automatically, assuming it was Marcelo to let her know he was there.

"Hey, are you downstairs?" Hallie asked.

"Mom? Um, hello?"

"Katie? I'm sorry, I thought you were someone else. I mean, I was expecting someone else to be calling . . .. Um, never mind, how are you, love?" Hallie said, trying not to sound flustered.

"I'm okay, but how are you? You sound funny. And who's waiting for you downstairs? Are you still at the office? Why are you working so late?"

"Whoa, so many questions," Hallie laughed easily, actually delighted and calmed by the sound of her daughter's voice. She hadn't realized how on edge and tense she was until she could hear it through her daughter's voice reacting to her own.

"Honey, I'm sorry I answered the phone like I did, but I'm fine. Just waiting for a friend to pick me up to go for a drink. Yes, I'm still at the office because I'm swamped with three deals that need to close and I can focus better here. Enough about me, how are you? How are classes so far?" Hallie asked, trying desperately to sound calm and to change the subject.

"Yeah, classes are good so far, but I hate one of my professors, so I'm going to try to drop his class. He's a total asshole, completely misogynistic and full of himself. There's another class I want to take on art history if I can get into it. We'll see."

"Well, he won't be the first misogynistic asshole you'll face in your life, so if you can't get out of his class, just try not to be too disrespectful. It will give you good practice for the rest of your life."

"Well, maybe if my generation of women are more disrespectful and we stop letting these assholes get away with their misogynistic behavior, maybe they'll stop thinking it's okay to treat women that way."

"You have a point, my beautiful and smart daughter," Hallie laughed, as she saw Marcelo's text come through that he was downstairs.

"Honey, my friend is here now so I have to go. Were you just calling to chat? Can we talk later?"

"Sure, Mom, I was just calling to chat. I can call you later. By the way, is there any way you can Venmo me like fifty dollars? I need to go to CVS for a bunch of stuff for my dorm room, including toiletries and shower shoes. I'm afraid I'm going to catch something in the community shower if I don't get some shower shoes soon," Katie said.

"Okay, but I swear I've already sent you money for shower shoes, more than once. But fine. I'll send you money now, but we need to set up some type of budget and allowance going forward. You're bleeding me dry, Katie."

"I know, I'm sorry. I'm going to try to find a part-time job soon."

"Let's talk about this later. I have to run. I love you," Hallie said.

"Love you too, Mom. Thank you and I'll call you later."

Hallie ended her call with Katie and gathered her stuff including the latest email she had printed out from Ben Young. She was anxious to hear what Marcelo had found out about the other email she had received, hoping it was just some kind of joke. But as Hallie knew from experience, the likelihood of receiving an email mentioning the names of two women who were recently attacked was neither funny nor random.

She quickly responded to Marcelo's text, "I'll be right down, headed out now."

Most of the offices were empty as she walked towards the elevators, except for Marty's office, whose light was still on as usual.

"Jeez, Marty," Hallie said, looking in and waving as she walked by, "do you ever go home?"

"Not if I don't have to," he replied in his usual, dry delivery.

Hallie knew how much Marty, the quintessential family guy, loved his family. Their photos adorned his office, showing fishing trips, summer vacations at the beach, and winter vacations in Park City. Although he liked to pretend otherwise, Hallie knew he spent the long hours at the office to keep his kids in private schools and the family in a nice house in Palma Ceia on the golf course.

"Go home, Marty," Hallie teased, "your family isn't going to recognize you soon."

"That's the goal, Ms. Miller," Hallie heard from behind her as she continued towards the elevators to meet Marcelo.

CHAPTER FORTY-EIGHT

He stood over Michele's bed watching her sleep, listening to her breathing – not quite a snore but a sweet, gentle little hum. He imagined holding one of his large hands over her mouth and nose while gripping her tiny neck with the other one and watching her struggle as the life drained out of her. He could do it quickly, he knew, and she wouldn't be able to make a sound. Her eyes would open, wide and terror-stricken, unable to fully comprehend the import of what was happening – at first – but then as she looked into his dark, hateful eyes, she would know. At that moment, the synapses in her brain would ignite and she would realize she was about to die . . . or worse. He felt himself hardening in his black jeans as he fantasized about her terrified, coffee-colored eyes looking up at him while he stood over her as she slept, admiring her beautiful face and bare, breakable neck.

"Patience," he whispered to himself, as he backed out of the bedroom, almost tripping over the annoying white cat on his way. He grabbed onto the door frame as he tripped, which miraculously kept him from falling. He paused and looked back at Michele to see if she was stirring. Nothing. Only that same cute little hum he had been listening to before.

The previous times he had visited Michele's place, he waited until she left for work before he went in to explore. Like all the others, he would memorize where things were, including furniture and hallways and doors, so he could find his way around in the dark without making a sound or turning on a light. And like most single women, Michele kept a spare house key where it was easily found, which in her case was on a keychain labeled "Michele" in sparkly pink letters on a hook in her kitchen. She probably gave the key to a friend whenever she went out of town so the friend could feed her cat and water her plants. Women would be so much safer if they weren't so goddamn predictable, he thought to himself. He had taken the key with him on a previous visit, made a copy, and returned the original to its place on the hook before she ever returned from work that day. Now he could let himself in and out whenever he wanted, which he did on a regular basis. And of course, since he had Ronald's email and password to her alarm system, he would disarm the alarm and reset it. That fucking, stupid Ronald. What a Godsend finding him in that chat room, demented little weirdo, Mr. Sadist chuckled to himself.

He would visit Michele again soon, for one final visit, before moving onto Hallie. Hallie was the main attraction, the entrée, if you will, because Hallie was personal. The thought exhilarated him, and he couldn't fucking wait. The other women, including Michele, were mere appetizers and practice runs for the grand finale. The only thing he had to decide next, besides what night he wanted to return, was whether he would kill that damn cat before or after he tortured and raped Michele. Before. Definitely before – so he could make her watch. He smiled, adjusting his pants from his current arousal, and started to drive away from her townhouse, thinking about their next rendezvous, noticing her bedroom light come on in the reflection of his rearview mirror.

* * *

Michele woke up anxious with the feeling that someone was in her bedroom, watching her. She instinctively reached for her phone on her nightstand to check to see that the security alarm was set, a reaction she often had since her ex-husband had moved out of the house, especially when she woke up in the middle of the night.
Only this time, the alarm was not set.

She jolted upright, her adrenaline surging, as the shadows from the large palms swaying in the rainy, night air danced across her walls. Her eyes adjusted to the darkness, and she prepared herself to fight or flee. Just then, something appeared out of nowhere and pounced onto her bed, towards her. Michele inhaled so deeply, she almost choked on her own saliva, and couldn't even manage a scream.

"Jesus, Bella, oh my God," Michele exclaimed when she finally caught her breath while the oblivious white cat rubbed up against her, purring, and making it clear she was ready to be scratched.

As Michele's heartrate started to return to normal, she finally had the courage to turn on her light. No one was in her bedroom. She waited and listened. She heard nothing but the sound of a light rain hitting her roof and an occasional car driving through the puddles that had accumulated on the street out front. She got out of bed, the wooden floor cool on the bottom of her bare feet, and cautiously tiptoed out of her bedroom to inspect the rest of her small townhouse. Thankfully, no one was there, and all the doors were locked. She convinced herself she had just forgotten to set her alarm, while admonishing herself for the two or three Irish whiskeys she drank the night before. It was the three-month anniversary of the day Paul had moved out, and she was feeling sad and alone. Most of the time, she was happier alone than she had been with Paul during the past few years, but the nights could be hard at times, especially when she was feeling vulnerable. Last night was one of those nights, but whiskey, as her slightly throbbing head reminded her, was not the answer. She would not make that mistake again, she told herself.

Michele looked down at her phone, the keypad still displaying 9-1-1, ready to call at the push of the green send button. She carefully deleted the numbers and swiped up on the screen to close the keypad. The time on her phone read 5:41 a.m. – too late to go back to sleep, not that she could if she tried at this point. She made herself a cup of Earl Gray tea, grabbed her CBD pen, and retreated to the balcony to listen to the sounds of the rain and water below and to watch the sun burn off the dreary, gray sky.

The waters in the Bay below her balcony were calmer than usual, which was often the case the morning after one of Florida's summer afternoon thunderstorms that continued into the night. The same could not be said for her nerves. A seagull cawed nearby while the sound of a motor revved in the distance from a boat starting up in the nearby marina, someone undoubtedly taking advantage of the break in the rain and the sun trying to peek out behind the clouds. She hit her CBD pen while looking for dolphins or manatees swimming by in the channel below, trying to convince herself that she was only being paranoid from a bad dream, and sipped on her Earl Gray tea.

CHAPTER FORTY-NINE

The Broker lay in the dark, waiting for the guards to do their final sweep. It had been a week since he had gone to Ben Young's cell and learned the horrible secrets that the Martino family had been hiding for over thirty years, if they were even true. He was still having a hard time believing what Ben told him, in addition to the veiled threats from the man with the goatee. But why would they lie? Well, Ben would lie to save his ass, of course. It worked the other night, hadn't it? He was still breathing.

Seeing that picture of Monica, his Monica, with the little boy who might be his own flesh and blood had his mind reeling. He had asked Ben about him, but Ben didn't seem to know anything about the boy. Maybe it was all bullshit, he thought. He was so confused about what he had learned in the last week. None of it made any sense, yet it explained so much. Fucking Tommy Martino. He would break his neck with his bare hands if the bastard was still alive.

He felt the vibration from his contraband phone, which was lying on his chest under the flimsy but coarse, prison-issued blanket, alerting him to a text from a blocked number.

"Is there a problem?" was all it read but the Broker knew who it was from and why they were asking.

He wrote back, "No."

"Get it done," was the only and final response.

The Broker knew what he had to do. He had no other choice now. He slipped the phone into the slit in his mattress, silently slipped off his cot and made his way over to his cell door. As he suspected, the unlocked cell door slid open easily. He peaked out, looking up and down the block, and saw the path to Ben Young's cell was clear. He was hoping Loopy Larry, his neighbor two cells down, was asleep. If he wasn't, he would yell out to him, as he always did, or anyone else walking by his cell. Everyone knew Larry should be in a mental institution, but he was a lifer who got convicted before anyone ever considered someone's mental status as a mitigating factor for their crime. And Larry, now in his seventies, never had anyone on the outside who gave a shit whether he ever got out, much less how he was treated while he was on the inside. As much as the Broker felt sorry for him, he would slice his throat too if he had too. He cupped the self-made, razor-sharp shank down by his side and crept down the prison walkway towards his destination.

* * *

The next morning, the prisoners in Cell Block J lined up outside their cells for routine inspection before being escorted to the cafeteria for breakfast.

"Rodriguez," the burly guard yelled, "let's go, out of your cell," while looking down at his clipboard and down the walkway, counting prisoners.

"You too, Clark," as he continued to scan the men standing outside of their cells and back at his clipboard.

A mean-looking Hispanic sauntered out of the cell next to Loopy Larry and took his place in the line of prisoners. Loopy Larry started laughing for no particular reason, earning an angry leer from Rodriguez.

"Clark and Young, let's go," the guard barked, "out of your cells, now!"

Clark, the short, fat prisoner with the pudgy face, scarred from an adolescence of acne and bad choices, allegedly in for killing his parents after they took his video games away at the age of twenty-seven, sluggishly came out of his cell, taking his place on the railing.

The guard checked his clipboard and counted the prisoners again.

"Young! Get the fuck out of your cell, now. If I have to come pull your sorry ass out of bed, your privileges are getting yanked," the guard yelled down the walkway.

After Young didn't come out, the agitated guard handed his clipboard to one of the other guards and headed towards Young's cell. He stepped into the cell and came back out moments later.

"Everyone, back in your cells, now!" the guard's voice boomed, followed by an immediate groan in unison, except for Loopy Larry who started to laugh again, while the guard signaled to the two guards at the front and back of the line of prisoners. He took out his walkie talkie and immediately conveyed the situation to whoever was on the other end, which triggered an alarm resonating throughout the block.

The Broker returned to his cell, just as all the other prisoners did, and waited. But unlike the other prisoners of Cell Block J, the Broker was intimately aware of what the guard found when he entered Ben Young's cell.

CHAPTER FIFTY

Hallie walked into the dark garage, noticing the overhead lights at the far end had been knocked out again. The outdoor streetlights reflecting off her black BMW provided some light as she walked towards her car. Her heels echoed off the concrete in the empty garage, the sound reminding her of how alone and vulnerable she was in the moment. She pulled her phone out of her purse and called Marcelo.

"Hey, I'm out front," Marcelo said as he answered.

"Yes, I know, I got your text. I'm walking to my car in the garage, but someone knocked the lights out again so it's pretty dark. Stay on the phone with me?" Hallie asked, trying not to sound as anxious as she felt for some reason.

"Absolutely. And what do you mean, 'again'? Does this happen often?"

"Well, recently it seems to be happening a lot. And always near my parking spot."

"Let's talk about this when we get to your house. For now, let me know when you're in your car, and make sure you look in the back seat before you get in."

"Jeez, don't make me more nervous than I already am."

"Sorry, just let me know when you're in."

A few seconds later, Hallie was safely in her car. She locked the doors and turned on the ignition, looking around as she backed out of her parking space. Thankfully, she saw nothing, and breathed a sigh of relief as she said to Marcelo, "Okay, safe and sound, heading out of the garage now towards you."

"Good, I'm here. I'll follow you as soon as you come out."

"I can't remember, are we stopping at Publix or are we picking something up?"

"Let's pick up a pizza. Sally O'Neal's okay with you? I'll call it in, and we can stop there to pick it up on our way to your place."

"Perfect, Sally O'Neal's is the best. And I have wine. I need a glass. Or two."

"What do you like on your pizza? Please tell me you're not one of those pineapple freaks," Marcelo teased.

"Good God no! Fruit does not belong on pizza. I love plain cheese, you know, the classic, but I can also do pepperoni or tomatoes or onions or any combination of the above."

"I knew there was a reason I liked you, Counselor. I'll meet you there, but I'll take care of the ordering."

Hallie blushed as they hung up, her uneasiness from the afternoon and dark parking garage experience slowly dissipating. Marcelo had a way of making her feel safe. She headed towards Sally O'Neal's on Howard Avenue, with

Marcelo following behind in his black Ford F-150. She was anxious to hear what he had learned about the strange email she had received, especially about the women mentioned in the email who were attacked.

She pulled into Sally O'Neal's parking lot, Marcelo's truck right behind her. He got out and signaled to her to stay in her car as he went into the restaurant to pick up their pizza. Hallie was so used to being the one who took care of everything, it was nice being with someone who took charge for a change. She could get used to this, she thought. As she waited for Marcelo to come out with the pizza, she checked her face in the vanity mirror and reapplied her lipstick.

Unfortunately, she didn't notice the silver Audi Q7 that had been following them since they left downtown and had just completed its second loop around the block.

* * *

Marcelo and Hallie sat at her kitchen counter, enjoying their pizza and the wine. Hallie had opened a bottle of Faust cabernet for them, one of her favorites and usually reserved for special occasions. In some ways, she felt having Marcelo over was a special occasion. She hadn't dated anyone since her brief rendezvous with Tom Egan in the Keys, which, of course, went nowhere. She felt a connection with Marcelo that she hoped wasn't all in her head — after all, she felt a connection to Tom, too. Was this a date, she wondered? Or was he just there because of the emails and the possible connection to the latest cases he was working on?

"Hey Counselor, why so quiet? What are you thinking about?" Marcelo asked, interrupting her thoughts, as he reached out and touched her knee.

"Um, I don't know," she lied, trying not to stutter, "I just blanked out for a second," while her body tingled from his touch.

"Hmmm, okay, Counselor," he smiled, "if you say so."

God damnit, why did she turn into an insecure schoolgirl whenever she was around him? She was normally so in control, rarely flustered by anyone or anything. But him? He rendered her a bumbling idiot. "Get it together, Hallie," she silently chastised herself, while he just looked at her, smiling.

"What?" she asked, defensively, trying to regain her composure.

"You're adorable. And I want to kiss you," Marcelo said, so matter-of-factly, that, it, too, threw Hallie off.

"Oh, well, um, okay, um, thank you?" Hallie said, not sure what to do, feeling herself starting to sweat.

Without another word, Marcelo leaned over and kissed Hallie. She felt his five o'clock shadow against the soft skin of her face and could taste the wine from his kiss on her tongue, exciting her and causing her to lean further into him. He stood up, gently encircling her smooth neck with his large, rough hands while he continued to kiss her and back her up against the counter. She automatically arched her back as her body responded to his touch, holding onto the sides of the barstool she was sitting on as he pressed his body into her. His mouth moved from her lips, down her neck, until he was nestled in her cleavage. He lifted her in one move onto the counter while continuing to kiss her. She instinctively wrapped her legs around him, kissing him back, and felt herself begin to throb, yearning for him.

Marcelo responded in turn – both of them frantically undressing each other, moving the pizza box, wine glasses, and candles Hallie had lit to the side – while Marcelo climbed up onto the counter, his knees on each side of Hallie, as he hovered over her. He had one hand beneath the small of her back, lifting her up into him, as they continued to kiss, with the other hand on her now bare breasts, her nipples hard to his touch. Hallie let out a high-pitched moan as he finally entered her and they rode in rhythm until they both came, collapsing in a heap of sweat on Hallie's counter. It was simultaneously the most uncomfortable place Hallie had ever had sex and the best she had ever had.

"Any chance we can move to your bedroom now, Counselor?"

Hallie collapsed onto the counter and started to laugh, ridiculously happy for the first time in a long time. After they recovered, they climbed off the counter, both awkwardly getting dressed.

As Hallie sprayed the counter with Clorox kitchen spray and wiped it down, she said, "Well, that was a first," trying to hide her embarrassment and to minimize what had just happened.

Marcelo came over to her, embracing her from behind, "Oh baby, it won't be the last. How I have wanted you," he said, his directness and honesty always causing Hallie to feel uncomfortable and good at the same time. She turned into him, and he kissed her again.

"I've wanted you, too," Hallie whispered.

"I know," he said, as a fact and without any of the cockiness it suggested.

They made their way to Hallie's living room. Juno, who was lying on her bed next to the couch, looked up at them, happy to see them join her, seemingly oblivious to whatever had just happened in the kitchen. Hallie rubbed Juno's head and behind her ears as she sat down on the couch, causing Juno to wag her tail.

"Such a good baby," Hallie cooed as she rubbed the sweet, loyal pup.

"How old is she?" Marcelo asked.

"She's about ten or eleven. I don't know exactly because she was a rescue. She's my absolute love, you know? Completely unconditional, for both of us."

"Yeah, I get it. I have always loved dogs and always had a dog until the last few years when I was afraid my job would keep me away from them longer than they deserved. I gave my last dog to my mom so I can still visit him but so he's not lonely. I felt terrible giving him up."

"That's actually very responsible of you. And that makes you an animal lover because you put his needs before your own. I'm sorry, I get on my soapbox when it comes to animals. What great after-sex talk, right?" Hallie laughed, nervously again.

"Hallie, you don't have to apologize for anything. I like whatever you want to talk about. If you haven't figured it out by now, I like you. Period. I just like you."

"Um, yeah, that's the part I can't figure out," Hallie joked, as she did whenever she was nervous.

"I get it, you're nervous. But it's okay. Unless you tell me you're not interested in me, we'll get comfortable, and we'll figure it out. Are you not interested in me?" he asked, point blank.

"Yes, I mean, no, I'm not not interested you – see, these double negatives confuse people. Yes, I am interested in you. I think I just expressed that on my kitchen counter, in case you don't remember that," Hallie responded.

"Oh, trust me, I do remember. That is not a moment I will forget for a long time."

"So, before we get sidetracked, well, I mean, okay, we've been sidetracked, but before we forget, what did you find out about that email?"

"Okay, let's have a glass of wine and talk about these emails you've received."

Hallie brought the bottle of wine from the kitchen, refilled their glasses, and sat across from Marcelo in the living room, Juno at her feet.

"Tell me about the women who were attacked. Are they the same women referenced in the email to me?" Hallie began.

"Yes, we believe they are. They both lived but the second one, barely. If this cop who lived in Seminole Heights wasn't familiar with the area and super vigilant, I don't think we would have found the second woman alive," Marcelo said.

"Seminole Heights? What's the cop's name?"

"I guess I can tell you because it was in the paper. Officer Jay Campbell. Solid police work there. He was following up on a couple of call-ins and noticed the front door to a supposedly vacant house slightly ajar. And that's where he found the second victim, Sheada Lawson. Barely alive, but alive. He saved her life."

"Wow, are you kidding me? Jay was the officer who found her? That's my best friend's husband. This is like those six degrees of separation, except everything is somehow connected to me," Hallie said, as she bolted up and started to pace, picking up her phone to call Bridget.

"Hallie, it's okay," Marcelo said as he reached out to try to take her hand, "As much as I don't believe in coincidences, I think in this case, it really is just a coincidence. I mean, Officer Campbell lives near there, was on shift when the call came in, and answered it. And thankfully he did, because he's a good cop and he found that girl while she was still alive."

"Oh my God, you're right, you're right. I'm just freaking out. I just don't understand why someone would send me an email mentioning these two women who I don't even know. This is all hitting too close to home – again," Hallie said as she paced, trying to catch her breath.

Marcelo got up and took Hallie's hands into his, forcing her to stop pacing.

"Baby, it's okay. You're okay. Veronica and Sheada are okay. So, we just need to figure out your connection to them and who sent you this email. And then we'll get this son of a bitch."

"I'm scared," Hallie admitted, looking up at Marcelo.

"I'm here. I'll protect you."

"Can you stay with me tonight?" Hallie asked, regretting her vulnerability as soon as it came out of her mouth.

"I planned to, even if it meant sitting out in my car and watching your house. But it will be a lot more comfortable in your bed, unless you want me to stay on the couch," Marcelo offered.

"No, I want you next to me," Hallie said, without hesitation.

"That's exactly where I want to be."

* * *

"Wow, fucking whore!" Mr. Sadist exclaimed as he watched from the street as Hallie and Marcelo seemed to disappear up the stairs.

He was excited and furious at the same time. He couldn't believe she had fucked him on the kitchen counter, which he had watched via the camera in the kitchen that he initiated through the alarm app on his phone. He thought she was different from other women, classier, but now he realized she was just a cheap slut, no different than his mother. She had fooled him but now he saw the real Hallie.

He normally could read people better than that, the only positive skill he may have gotten from his grandmother. Man, he hated his grandmother. He wasn't too fond of his mother either. Seeing Hallie on that counter reminded him of his childhood, being locked in the closet, peeking out the slats as his mother rode on top of some guy or sucked him off. It made him feel uncomfortable and he didn't like it. When they got rough with her, it scared him too. She would make him sit in the closet – "*Quiet as a mouse*," she would tell him – while she whored herself out in the apartment's only bed with strange men not two feet away from where he hid. He never saw the same man twice, at least from his vantage point through the slats of the closet doors, and sometimes she forgot about him, and he would fall asleep in the pile of laundry on the closet floor trying to forget the sounds coming from the bedroom.

But that was before his mother dumped him on his grandmother's doorstep one day, and never looked back. He could forgive his mother for being a whore, but he would never forgive her for abandoning him with that cold bitch of a grandmother. To the outside world, Grandma Nina appeared the doting and caring grandmother, taking in her only grandson because his train-wreck of a mother couldn't – or wouldn't – take care of him, but in private, whenever she was drunk, she was mean and always demanding perfection. And she was always drunk: a family trait, apparently.

"When is my mom coming back to get me?" he would ask.

"She's not coming back to get you, you little bastard. You know what a bastard is, don't you? It's a child who doesn't have a father and even his own mother doesn't want him. You need to stop whining about her and be grateful you have me and all the opportunities I will give to you that you would never have with her."

He would start to cry, not out of sadness but anger. Hot, angry tears, that he couldn't hold back. Before he was forced to hide in the closet and before she made him live with his grandmother, his mom was nice to him and they had fun. That was the only time he felt loved. And then it all went away one day and he realized she never really loved him. If she did, she never would have left him with his horrible grandmother.

"Aw, is the baby crying now? You better toughen up. You don't want to be a little bitch your whole life, living like a sad, pathetic, weak loser. Do you want women to think you're a loser with a tiny little dick?" she would chastise.

"Leave the boy alone, Nina," his great uncle Nicolas, who always seemed to be around, would finally yell from the den.

"I'm just trying to make a man out of him. Believe me, he's going to thank me one day."

"Are you sure about that? Just let the boy be, Nina."

And so it would go, day in and day out, and the months and years wore on, and his mother never came to get him. She would visit, of course, telling him about the jobs she was getting and houses she was setting up for them, which were always followed by excuses and preposterous explanations for the delays. By the time he was fourteen, they all stopped pretending that she would ever get her shit together and behave like a mother. In some ways, letting that go eased his burden and allowed him to focus on doing well in school so he could go away to college to get out of his grandmother's home. He would always resent Monica, but it hurt less when he was no longer hopeful or expecting anything from her. His mother wasn't cruel, just broken and incapable of being a good mother, probably because she didn't have a good example herself. Grandma Nina was a cold, cruel bitch who got off on intimidating and emasculating the men around her, especially him.

One day, he would slit his grandmother's throat and revel in her pain as he watched the life drain out of her. Would she cry when he sliced through her paper-thin skin, he wondered, like the little bitch she always accused him of being? Unlike Veronica, one of his favorite experiences so far, he wouldn't sew up Nina's wounds or stop the bleeding. No, he would watch until the last drop of blood left her wrinkled, heartless, bony body. He might enjoy doing the same to Monica for leaving him with that cunt, but with her slutty lifestyle and blackout drinking habits, someone would probably beat him to it. But Grandma Nina, her day would come, and he would make her suffer more than any of the others. She deserved it more than any of them.

Hallie reminded him of a much younger version of his grandmother, although Hallie didn't seem cruel. But her smile and the way she threw her head back when she laughed, there was something familiar. He had seen pictures of his grandmother when she was in her twenties – before he was born, before his grandfather had died – smiling, laughing, a different person than the one who raised him.

He realized that was the reason he probably chose Hallie in the first place. And now seeing her getting fucked on her kitchen counter, he knew he had made the right decision.

CHAPTER FIFTY-ONE

Marcelo arrived at the precinct early the next morning, eager to figure out the connection between Veronica Hill, Sheada Lawson, and Hallie. For the next several hours, he read through every detail of the case files on Veronica again. Starting with Veronica's file, he recalled there was no sign of forced entry into her home. How did her attacker get in, Marcelo wondered? He pulled out the transcript from Veronica's interview after she got out of the hospital and read through it, making notes on his yellow legal pad of key points or follow up questions he wanted to ask her. He read through it again, picking up on something he hadn't the first time.

Veronica: "No, the only other people who have a key to my house are my mother and my son. And I checked with both of them after the attack and neither of them have lost or misplaced their keys to my place."

Detective: "What about an ex-boyfriend? Any chance you gave a key to someone you forgot about?"

Veronica: "No, absolutely not. I don't make a habit of giving my keys out, detective."

Detective: "Of course, but we have to ask. We saw you have an alarm system. Do you set it on a regular basis?"

Veronica: "Yes, I set it every day. But it wasn't armed when I got home from work that day. I was working on a big deal that week and I remember racing out that morning, worried I was going to be late for one of my meetings. So, when I got home and it wasn't on, I thought I must have forgotten to set it when I left for work that morning."

Detective: "Do you think you forgot to set it that day?"

Veronica: "I just don't know. I can't remember. I just know it wasn't on when I got home that day. But a few minutes later when I noticed my pillows were out of place on my bed, I knew someone had been in -- or was still in -- the house. By then it was too late. I never made it out the front door."

Marcelo pulled out Sheada's file. They had not gotten an in-depth interview with Sheada yet because she was still in the hospital. A note in the file indicated that Tracy McCrink was scheduled to interview her as soon as her doctor gave her the green light. He reviewed all the other notes in the file, including the forensic report from the investigation of her home and the transcript from the interview with Sheada's boyfriend, Justin. Like Veronica's home, there was no evidence of forced entry. Marcelo was almost done reading the interview transcript when a comment made by the boyfriend jumped out at him.

Justin: "I told her she should set her alarm, but she laughed at me, told me I was being too paranoid. She would say, 'Justin, this is Hyde Park, not the south side of Boston,' which is where

I grew up. I tried to tell her there were sickos everywhere, even in Hyde Park, but she never listened."

Marcelo thought about the alarm system that each woman had. Veronica said she was vigilant about setting it each day, although she couldn't remember if she set it the day of the attack; Sheada seemed less likely to set it regularly, according to the boyfriend's statement. He sent Tracy a text telling her to ask Sheada about her alarm system when she interviewed her. She sent him back the thumbs up emoji, followed by a quick text that said, "Talking to her tomorrow."

He scanned the files again looking for information about the alarm systems. If a victim of a home invasion had an alarm system, the forensic team would usually note it in their report and request copies of any video that may have been captured directly from the alarm companies. As long as the homeowner consented, the alarm companies would produce what they had, although sometimes it could take a few weeks. It didn't appear that they had received any video yet from either request, but Marcelo noted that both women had the same home security system from SmartDefense.

"Interesting," he thought, "but probably just a coincidence."

SmartDefense was a popular yet relatively new system in the area, which provided the latest technology, cameras, and ability to login and do virtually everything from your smart phone.

He sent a quick text to Hallie, "Hey babe, dinner tonight? Also, what's your alarm company?"

Within a few minutes, Hallie wrote back, "Hi, yes, dinner sounds great. My alarm company is SmartDefense. Why?"

"Just checking out a few hunches, nothing to worry about. I'll let you know if I find anything. 7?"

"7 is perfect. My place?"

"Yes, see you there."

Marcelo felt the familiar adrenaline rush when he was onto something, believing this was more than just a coincidence. Someone familiar with the attacks sent an email to Hallie, attempting to warn her, and the only connection he had found so far between Hallie and the two victims was their alarm system. All three homes also had electronic keypad openings, which were also tied to the alarms. If someone had the codes to shut the alarms off, it would also explain how there was no evidence of forced entry at Veronica or Sheada's homes.

Before alerting Hallie or his Chief, he had to find out everything he could about the company including who owned it, who worked for the company, and who had installed all three women's security systems. He started on Sunbiz.org, the Secretary of State database of companies registered to do business in Florida, and looked up SmartDefense. He found three local entities, surprisingly, all of which seemed to be related: SmartDefense Holding

Company, LLC, SmartDefense Management, LLC, and SmartDefense, Inc. All three companies listed the same P.O. box for the mailing address, a physical address in care of a law firm in downtown Tampa, and a lawyer named Robert S. Bolt as the registered agent of all three companies. Marcelo thought his name sounded familiar but couldn't remember where their paths may have crossed. He jotted down the name of the law firm, lawyer, and address in his notebook. He would ask Hallie that night at dinner if she knew him. All three companies listed a Delaware corporation, Yamamoto Enterprises, Inc., as the officer or manager, and listed the same P.O Box address.

* * *

Hallie finished revising the Asset Purchase Agreement she was working on, ran a comparison to generate a redlined version to show opposing counsel the changes she made to his last version, and emailed both versions to opposing counsel with her additional comments. She answered a few more emails and quickly recorded her time spent on the files she worked on over the last few hours into the firm's billing management system. Keeping track of her entire day in six-minute increments was Hallie's least favorite part of being a lawyer but it was how clients were billed. Because of that constant clock running in the back of her brain while she was working, Hallie decided that when she wasn't working, she would try to live in the moment, forgetting about the clock or the time. But it was hard to shut that part of her brain off, especially during the week. She looked down at the time and saw it was 5:43. If she left now, she could get home in time to take a shower and unwind a little before Marcelo came over. She shut down her computer, grabbed her purse, leather briefcase, and her phone, and left her office.

Arriving in the garage, she was thankful that the overhead light near her car had finally been replaced. She got in her car and started the ignition, the dashboard display coming to life. Before backing out, the display flashed a red warning light, indicating that her back right tire pressure was low. She got out and walked around to the passenger side of her car, noticing the tire was completely flat.

"Shit," Hallie said, aggravated, and thinking, there goes my time to take a shower and unwind. She turned off her car, grabbed her purse, briefcase, and phone, locked her car and started to head back into the office building to call Triple-A and Marcelo. No use hanging out in the garage when it was likely going to take them awhile to get there, she thought. As she walked towards the elevators, a silver Audi Q7 was coming down the ramp from one of the floors above.

"Everything okay, Ms. Miller?" the man in the Audi asked as he slowed down next to Hallie.

Turning and seeing the familiar face of her IT director, she answered, "Oh, hi, Peter, yeah, I'm fine but my car has a flat. Like completely flat. I don't know, I must have run over a nail or something and didn't realize it."

"Can I help? Do you have a spare?"

"Oh, that's okay, I'm sure you want to get home. I'm just going to call Triple-A," Hallie said as she resumed her walk towards the elevators while trying to pull the app up on her phone.

"Don't be silly. I can change it for you in a few minutes. Let's take a look," Peter said, not taking no for an answer, as he pulled into the parking space right next to Hallie's car.

Hallie turned and walked back to her car, popping the trunk on her car from her key fob, as she said, "You know, I don't even know if I have a spare. I've never had a flat on this car before."

"Well, I guess we'll find out," Peter said as he got out of his car and walked towards Hallie's open trunk, stopping on the way to open his own trunk, saying, "I have some tools back here if we need them."

Hallie was leaning over, inspecting her trunk to see if she had a spare under the lining, when something slammed into the back of her head, sending her into complete darkness.

CHAPTER FIFTY-TWO

The summer storm had finally retreated back out to the sea, while the flooded, potholed-filled streets and tree limb-covered sidewalks were a reminder of its power and recent fury. Moni knew firsthand her storm would always return, angrier and more unforgiving than before. Her childhood had taught her that. She had the cherished family moments – always short-lived but filled with laughter and hope that this time would be different – contradicted by the tumultuous, often violent, waves of anger, jealousy and irrational accusations of her mother. Her father tried to placate Nina, tried to convince her that her suspicions were unfounded, that he loved her. But she wouldn't listen, not when she was in one of her "states," as her father called them.

That fateful night, over thirty years before, Moni had come home from the University of Florida for the weekend. She had just gotten home, neither of her parents realizing she was there, sitting at the top of the stairs, listening to them fight in the living room below. Nina was drunk, as she often was at that time of the night, spewing wild accusations of infidelity and other horrific misdeeds at her father. His patience was waning, understandably so, and he started to yell back. This fight was worse than any she had witnessed before, and she was scared. Nina was going too far this time.

"You think you're so smart, above reproach, you and your fucking family," Nina screamed, "Well I've got news for you," she slurred, pausing to take another gulp of her martini, "I told my attorney everything. You hear that? Every-fucking-thing. He said he's going to the D.A. tomorrow. You and your brother are going to spend the rest of your miserable lives in prison for all the shit you've done in this town, and I'll end up with everything."

"Nina, what are you talking about? What did you tell your attorney?" she heard her father ask.

"Oh, I told him everything. I told him about the politicians you've bought and the fraudulent deals you've made. You're going to rot in prison, and I'm going to divorce you and get everything. And I'm going to make sure you never see your precious Moni again. Charlie Robinson is going to see to that, he told me."

Monica felt sick. What was her mother talking about? She had heard the stories about her grandfather's connections to the mafia, but her father was not like him. He was a good, honest businessman. Nina was mean and crazy, had been all of Monica's life, and Monica wanted to protect her father. He was all she had. When she was younger, after another one of their horrific fights, she asked her father why he stayed with her.

Her father answered without any hesitation, "because I love her. I have from the day I met her. And when she's good, she's funny and loving, and there's no one I would rather be with."

"She's not fun, Daddy. Or good. She's just mean."

"She doesn't mean to be. She loves you so much and she loves me. But sometimes her emotions take over her and she doesn't know how to handle them."

"She doesn't love me, Daddy."

"Yes, she does, in her own way. You have to take the good with the bad, pumpkin, and I don't ever want to live without her, even if all the days aren't perfect."

Monica never forgot that conversation. As she sat at the top of the stairs listening to the vitriol spewing out of her mother's foul mouth, surely her father couldn't feel the same way anymore. But maybe he did. Maybe he would forever subject himself to and excuse Nina's abuse, as he always had. And in that moment, she realized that her father would never stand up to Nina, never protect himself from her, and would continue to be abused by her, apparently with the help of her attorney, Charlie Robinson.

Moni knew who Charlie Robinson was. She had gone to high school with his daughter, Hallie. His office was right next to her dance studio downtown, and she had passed by the sign on his door a thousand times. She would not let him go to the D.A. and ruin her family's life. She just had to explain to him that her mother made it all up – whatever craziness she told him – to hurt her father. If he was still at his office, she had a chance to stop him, she thought. He would have to listen to her.

Monica crept down the stairs and into her father's office while her parents continued to fight in the living room. She heard glass shattering on the marble floor, apparently from Nina dropping or throwing her martini glass, further distracting her parents from any sounds Moni made in the adjacent office. She found the key to the gun cabinet in her father's unlocked top desk drawer where she knew he always kept it. She opened the gun cabinet and ran her fingers down the cold steel of a few guns in the cabinet before selecting her favorite, a .38 caliber revolver, the first gun her father had ever taught her to shoot. She checked to make sure it was loaded, grabbed another box of ammunition from the cabinet, and slipped both into her pink backpack she had slung over her shoulder. As she snuck out the backdoor, she heard her mother screaming something incomprehensible while her father yelled back, "Nina, please stop. I can't do this anymore!"

Moni retrieved her ten-speed bike from the side of the garage where she had left it, hopped on it and rode down her street and off the island to Bayshore Boulevard. From there, she rode the winding road along the Tampa Bay and over the Brorein Street Bridge and into downtown, following the same path she had taken all those years to dance class. She easily found Robinson's office, and then circled back, parking her bike in the alley next to the old brick building. She walked out front and sat on a bench across the street facing the entrance to his office. Alongside his name, the logo on his front door read: *"Here When You Need Us Most."*

Moni reached into the pink backpack that she had brought home from UF, which still contained her notebooks and psychology textbook she had planned to catch up on while she was home. She retrieved the .38 and checked the chamber again, making sure it was loaded, not sure exactly why she had brought it. She just knew that one way or another she would convince Charlie Robinson not to contact the D.A. and to leave her family alone.

* * *

Forcing her thoughts back to the present, Moni looked at the text again.

"Old ghosts are stirring"

She took a long drag from her Marlboro before finally responding, *"When and where?"*

Within moments, she received a response: *"Tonight, 6:30, Malio's, at the bar."*

She didn't respond, knowing it was not necessary. She would meet her cousin, Tom, at the bar at Malio's in a few hours, and they would talk about the night Charlie Robinson was murdered.

CHAPTER FIFTY-THREE

Marcelo tried Hallie's cellphone again, both calling and texting her. His calls went straight to voicemail and his texts went through as SMS messages, which meant her phone was probably dead or turned off. That wasn't like her, and he was getting worried. He drove to her house and saw that her car wasn't there. He went to her office, which was locked up for the night. He pulled his car into the temporary drop-off circular out front and saw there was a guard on duty. An older gentleman came out, making sure the heavy glass door closed behind him.

"Can I help you sir?" the guard with the nametag that read "Walter" asked.

"Hello, sir, I am Detective Marcelo Garcia. I'm wondering if Hallie Miller is still in the building," Marcelo said as he showed Walter his badge.

"Well, hello, Detective." Happy to have someone to tell, he continued, "You know, before I retired because of a busted back caused on the job, I was on the force, CI division. Always nice to assist a fellow officer. Why are you asking about Ms. Miller?"

"Criminal Investigations, huh? So, you were in the big leagues, huh?" Marcelo responded, trying to develop a rapport with the older man so he would let him into the parking garage, at the very least.

Walter laughed lightly, obviously happy at the respect, "Oh, those were many days ago, son, many days ago. I left the big leagues too many years ago to remember."

"Once on the force, always on the force, right, brother?" Marcelo said, sincerely.

"True that, my brother. Now what can I do for you and your inquiry as to Ms. Miller? She's one of the good ones around here," Walter said, eying Marcelo guardedly.

It was obvious to Marcelo that Walter liked Hallie and would protect her, even above any loyalty he may have to the force. He decided to level with him.

"I was supposed to meet up with her, but she's not answering her cell or office phone. Also, she's been getting some disturbing emails lately, and she mentioned some issues with lights being smashed in the parking garage near her car, so I just want to make sure she's okay."

"Oh, I reported those incidents with the lights, Detective. I know all about that, but I think that's just kids or drunks up to no good. I watch out for her, you know," Walter said, defensively.

"I am sure you do, and I didn't mean to imply otherwise. But do you know if her car is still here? Can we check? Maybe she's stuck in a late meeting but, like I said, there are some things going on that are making me a little nervous and I just want to make sure she's okay."

"Okay, Detective, let's go take a look, professional courtesy, shall we say? I like Ms. Miller. Again, she's one of the good ones," the old security guard repeated as he used his pass key to unlock the electronic door that would lead them into the building and out to the garage.

Walter pushed the button for the fourth floor, knowing exactly on which floor Hallie parked. They rode up in the small elevator in silence. The elevator arrived at its destination and the old guard sauntered off in front of Marcelo without the same sense of urgency Marcelo felt. He opened the door to the garage and there at the end of the empty parking lot was Hallie's black BMW.

Marcelo quickly walked past Walter, somewhat comforted by the fact that the overhead light over Hallie's car had been replaced. But any relief he felt quickly dissipated when that same light illuminated the droplets of fresh blood on the concrete floor at the back of Hallie's car.

* * *

Hallie's head was throbbing. As she fought to wake up, she tried to shake the fog from her brain to figure out where she was. She didn't recognize her surroundings. It was dark and cold. She was shivering and the room smelled like lilies, a smell Hallie had associated with death ever since her father's funeral. She hated the smell of lilies. She sat up, which sent her head spinning as she grabbed onto the sides of the leather couch underneath her to steady herself. In the darkness, she saw a shadow and someone moving.

"Hello Hallie."

The voice was familiar. Yet she couldn't place it. It was deeper, darker, yet familiar somehow.

"Who are you? Where am I?" Hallie managed to ask, her mouth unbearably dry as she craved water.

"Oh, you know me, Hallie, don't hurt my feelings by pretending that you don't."

"I think I've been in an accident," Hallie said, trying to remember anything about how she had gotten there, reaching up to check the bump, clotted with dried blood, on the back of her head.

"No, it wasn't an accident, Hallie. I hit you in the back of the head with a tire iron on purpose. And here we are, so we can have this nice little party. Just you and me, together at last. I have been looking forward to this moment for quite a while."

The words didn't make sense to Hallie, yet the mention of the word "tire iron" brought her last conscious memories rushing back into her head. She was leaving work, saw she had a flat tire, was on her way back inside when her IT director stopped by her car. And offered to help. And then her world went dark.

"Peter?" she asked, hesitantly. Her body started to shake uncontrollably, and she wanted to run. But as her eyes adjusted to the lighting in the small, windowless room, she didn't see a way out, further terrifying her.

"Oh good, you do remember."

"Why are you doing this?" Hallie asked, trying to make sense of what was happening to her.

"Because I can."

CHAPTER FIFTY-FOUR

After Walter and Marcelo quicky confirmed that Hallie was not in her office, Marcelo called in a team to investigate the parking garage. Walter, feeling like he was a part of the force again, took his position very seriously, only letting in authorized, credentialed personnel and directing all others to the front of the building where he would bring their cars to them. The team found Hallie's cellphone in her trunk together with her purse and black leather bag, and more blood. The discovery hit Walter hard, not to mention Marcelo, who was able to maintain his composure and professionalism only slightly better than Walter.

After confirming Hallie was not at her house and everything appeared secure, Marcelo returned to the precinct, determined to find the connection between the attacks on Veronica and Sheada and the strange email warning Hallie had received recently. The only connection he had found so far was that all three women had the same alarm system, SmartDefense, which was owned by a company called Yamamoto Enterprises. Marcelo didn't believe in coincidences and all three women having the same alarm company, statistically, had to be something.

Also, Hallie suspected Tommy Martino was responsible for her father's murder and was asking questions when she went missing. Was she getting closer to the truth? There did not seem to be any connection with Yamamoto Enterprises and the Martinos, but his gut was telling him they were connected.

"But how could the recent attacks be connected to a murder that happened over thirty years ago," Marcelo wondered out loud.

Maybe Hallie's disappearance was only related to her investigation of her father's death and completely unrelated to the attacks on Veronica and Sheada. But then again, the anonymous email sent to Hallie mentioned them and connected all three women together. Marcelo was missing something, and he couldn't figure out what it was.

He texted McCrink: "Hey, can you find out what you can on a company registered in Delaware called Yamamoto Enterprises, stat? It may be nothing, but I need to check. Let me know if you can find out who owns it and anything else you can find out about it. The works."

"You got it. Heard about Miller on the APB and the BOLO. Everyone is looking for her."

"Thanks partner," Marcelo responded, slightly comforted that the 'Be On the Look Out' warning had gone out on the police All Points Bulletin.

He decided to call Raiford to see what this Benjamin Young wanted to tell Hallie. Maybe that would give him a clue as to who had taken her. He called his Chief on her cell, explained what was going on, and enlisted her assistance in reaching someone who knew the warden to get him access to Young.

He was reviewing the case files again, including the notes and emails Hallie had sent to him, when his Chief called him back.

"Garcia, I've got some bad news."

"What?"

"Young is dead. Murdered in his cell two nights ago."

"What the fuck? This cannot be a coincidence. Do they know who killed him?"

"No, the only one talking is a prisoner named Loopy Larry, who keeps saying '*The middleman comes out at night*' or some shit like that, but no one knows who or what he's talking about. He's mentally ill and probably has dementia according to the warden."

"So, they have nothing? No cameras? Nothing?"

"No, nothing yet, but he assured me, '*We are conducting a full investigation into the incident*'," the Chief said, imitating the warden's good ole' boy southern accent. Marcelo understood this was the Chief's way of conveying that neither the warden nor anyone else at Raiford cared about Ben Young's fate or who caused it and wouldn't be investigating anything.

"I'm going to go talk to Nina Martino. Hallie started getting the weird emails around the same time she reached out to Nina Martino, I think. The only connection that I can find between Hallie and the other victims, Veronica Hill and Sheada Lawson, are their alarm systems – all three have SmartDefense, which is owned or managed by a company called Yamamoto Enterprises. I've got McCrink looking into the company. But in the meantime, I'm going to go see what I can get out of the matriarch of this family."

"Okay, Garcia. Be careful. Keep me apprised and check in on the hour."

"You got it, Chief."

"Hey, Marcelo, don't worry, we'll find her. We've got everyone on this."

"Thanks, Chief."

* * *

Ronald woke up in his usual t-shirt and sweatpants. He was shivering, his head hurt, and his tongue – thick and sour from drinking the night before – felt like one of the dirty blankets he used to wrap around himself in the foster homes where he grew up. But it was something more than a hangover. He never blacked out and his tongue tasted metallic. He knew he had been drugged and brought to this strange place. His surroundings came into focus as his eyes adjusted to the poor lighting in the windowless room. He had no idea where he was.

There was a single lightbulb hanging on a wire in the middle of the small, cold room. The concrete floor beneath him was hard, as was the cinderblock wall he was leaning up against. In the center of the freezing room were giant black electronic boxes, which Ronald recognized as large computer servers. At the other end of the room was a metal desk with a computer monitor and keyboard on top of it. Next to the desk was a small, brown leather couch. And on top of the couch appeared the silhouette of a woman's lifeless body.

CHAPTER FIFTY-FIVE

Marcelo looked at his phone, 8:02 p.m., as he drove onto Davis Islands from Bayshore Boulevard, passing Tampa General Hospital on the left, and on the right, the quaint bars and restaurants supported mostly by locals who lived on the island. He hadn't been to the infamous Corner Bar in years but was not surprised to see it was packed. He headed down Davis Islands Boulevard until he got to Martinique, one of the prettiest streets on the island. Having looked up Nina Martino's address in the DMV records before he left the precinct, he knew exactly where he was going.

He checked his phone; still nothing from McCrink. He arrived at the address he had put into his GPS and pulled into the driveway of the impressive Mediterranean style mansion, with the red brick roof and beige stucco structure. There was a balcony facing the street next to a giant palm with other natural tropical fauna, which, no doubt, was meticulously cared for by an expensive landscaping crew. He could only imagine what the back of the house facing the Tampa Bay looked like. He turned off his car, grabbed his phone, sent a quick text to the Chief – *'arrived at Martino home'* – and walked to the front of the house where he was happy to see some interior lights still on.

He rang the doorbell, imagining the sound had to be startling at that time of night if you were not expecting anyone. He had to wait only a few seconds before the large, glass-paned door opened, revealing a beautiful, thin older woman with shoulder length, perfectly straight white hair, wearing a black tunic top over black leggings and black sandals, while holding a martini glass filled with a clear liquid. The woman was attractive and commanding in her presence.

"What can I do for you?" the woman asked, apparently expecting someone else, yet seemingly unfazed by a stranger appearing at her door, while she looked past him at his car parked on the street.

"Mrs. Martino? Nina Martino?"

"Who's asking?"

"I'm Detective Marcelo Garcia, and I just need to ask you a few questions."

"About what? What has my daughter done now?" the woman asked, the first noticeable crack in her so-called charming demeanor.

"Nothing, as far as I know. I'm here about Hallie Miller."

"Who?"

"Hallie Miller, I believe you had lunch with her recently," Marcelo prodded.

"Oh, yes, Ms. Miller. I did have lunch with her recently. She wants me to donate to the Spring's annual gala. Has something happened? This can't be about that."

"Hallie Miller has gone missing under suspicious circumstances. Her car was found at her downtown office building with her purse and cellphone found in her trunk."

"Oh no, that's terrible," Nina said, sounding genuinely surprised, "but I don't know how I can possibly help you. We had one lunch meeting over a week ago."

"Did you talk about anything else during your lunch, besides the Spring gala, Mrs. Martino?"

"We talked about many different things, Detective, as women tend to do. Are you asking whether we talked about her father's murder? Is that what you really want to know?" she asked, raising her martini glass to her lips and taking a sip.

"Interesting that you bring that up. What can you tell me about that?"

"Not much, Detective. Hallie's father, Charlie Robinson, was my lawyer when my husband, may he rest in peace, and I contemplated getting a divorce before we worked out our differences and reconciled. They didn't have counseling back in those days, you know? You had to work it out on your own. And we did. And we were happily married until his death, God rest his soul."

"How did your husband die, Mrs. Martino? Wasn't it only a short time after Charlie Robinson's death?"

"I don't know what you're implying, Detective, but my husband died from a tragic accident at one of his construction sites. The two deaths, while both tragic, are completely unrelated."

"And what about Charlie Robinson's murder? Do you know anything about what happened to him the night he was killed?" Marcelo asked, amazed at how cool and unflustered Nina Martino appeared.

"Nothing more than what was in the papers at the time. And frankly, this is ancient history. I don't remember the details any longer. Look Detective, I knew the Spring gala fundraising was just a ruse. Poor girl is still chasing her father's ghosts. But I didn't know anything then and I don't know anything now," Nina replied. "I can't help her or you," she said as she started to shut the door.

"One more question, Mrs. Martino. Have you seen Hallie since the day you had lunch?"

"No, I haven't seen or heard from her since," Nina responded quickly, as a black Cadillac Escalade pulled into the driveway. "If that's all, Detective Garcia, I have company," she continued, apparent that she wanted to end the meeting.

By now the driver had gotten out of the Cadillac and was walking up the brick walkway towards them. An attractive, thin, dark-haired woman climbed awkwardly out of the passenger side of the Escalade. She was wearing four-inch, red heels and a short black dress, which barely contained her large, enhanced breasts. As she came into the lighting of the front patio, her ruby red lips were striking against her olive complexion and straight black hair, while her face wore the scars of a hard-lived life. When she looked at Marcelo, for a moment her eyes reflected a wariness and sadness in contrast to the aloof, edgy person she attempted to exhibit to the world. She could not have been more different from the well-maintained woman at the front door, yet the family resemblance was undeniable. Marcelo could see that at one time both women must have been stunning.

"Who is this hottie?" the dark-haired woman asked seductively, sizing up Marcelo.

"Monica, I see you didn't restrain yourself tonight, as usual," Nina admonished, "this is Detective Marcelo Garcia. He is here inquiring about the possible disappearance of a woman named Hallie Miller."

Marcelo noticed Monica's mouth drop slightly open while her eyes darted to the driver of the Cadillac at the mention of Hallie's name. She recovered quickly, but not before Marcelo saw her reaction. The Cadillac driver avoided Marcelo's eyes, pretending to be distracted by something on his phone. There was something unsettling about the pair's intentional aloofness.

"Hello, Monica Martino, is it?" Marcelo asked, extending his hand out towards her as she approached the doorway.

Ignoring Marcelo's outstretched hand, Moni turned back to the Cadillac driver, "I need a drink, Tom. Come fix me one of your famous martinis. Hello, Mother," Monica said, pressing past Marcelo as if he wasn't there and air-kissing Nina's cheek as she walked into the house.

Tom followed close behind her into the house without looking at Marcelo as he passed, while he continued to focus on his phone.

"Detective, if that's all, you'll have to excuse me. It's getting late and I need to tend to my guests."

Before Marcelo could respond or ask another question, Nina Martino retreated into the house, closing the heavy door behind her. He walked towards his car, passing the Escalade on the way, and took a picture of the license plate with his phone. When he got in his car, he texted the photo to McCrink, with the text, *"need this run stat,"* and headed back towards the precinct.

After a few minutes, Marcelo's cellphone rang, and he saw it was the main number of the department.

"Garcia," he answered.

"Hey, it's Tracy. I got the info you asked me to run on the Escalade."

"Whatta ya got?" Marcelo asked, anxious for some type of break.

"Black Escalade is registered to a Thomas Egan of Miami, Florida. I did some additional background searches on him and found out he was born and raised in Tampa, Florida. His mother, Gianina Martino Egan, was married to a Mickey Egan, and they had one son, Thomas Egan.

Gianina was Tommy Martino's sister, which makes Thomas Egan Nina and Tommy Martino's nephew and Monica Martino's cousin."

"Anything else?"

"He went to U.S.F., but he left in September of 1990, when he relocated to Miami. Like his uncle, Tommy, he got into real estate development in Miami, and owns a few properties down there, including a condo on Fisher Island. Nothing more than a few speeding tickets on his record. Seems clean."

"Anything else?"

"One more thing, he may be friends with Hallie Miller, at least according to Facebook."

"When was Hallie's father, Charlie Robinson, murdered? Can you look that up?" Marcelo's heart was beating fast, the way it did whenever he knew he was close to putting the pieces of a puzzle together.

"Um, let me see," McCrink responded as Marcelo heard her tapping away on her keyboard. "Okay, got it. Charlie Robinson was gunned down outside of his downtown office on Friday, September 7, 1990. Holy shit, well isn't that a coincidence?"

"You know there's no such thing as a coincidence, McCrink, no such thing," Marcelo quickly responded, his adrenaline racing as he pressed down harder on the accelerator.

CHAPTER FIFTY-SIX

"Hello?" Ronald said meekly from across the room.

His voice was quieter and hoarser than he expected. The body of the woman on the couch wasn't moving. Ronald was terrified that she might be dead. Was he in a room with a dead woman?

"Oh my God, please help me get out of this. I just want my life back. Please God, I'll never do anything bad again, please just help me," Ronald pleaded out loud, his hands clasped in front of him while he looked up at the cement ceiling – not that he had ever believed in God before, but he was desperate. And if there was a God, he needed him or her or it now more than ever.

At the sound of his voice, the woman started to stir. The lightbulb hanging in the center of the room offered the only light in the windowless, frigid room. After a few minutes, she tried to sit up. He could tell it was a petite woman with long blonde hair. She was wearing a black sweater, black slacks, and black heels. She immediately reached up, clasping her head in her hands, and quickly leaned back onto the couch. Ronald had done the same when he woke up, except he was on the hard floor.

He tried again, "Hello?"

The woman bolted straight up at the sound of his voice and turned to face him, her hands in front of her, her fists clenched.

"Oh, it's you," Ronald said softly, after seeing her face, "Hallie."

"Who the fuck are you and how do you know my name?"

"I'm so sorry, are you okay?"

"Do I look okay? Fuck, my head hurts. Who are you?" Hallie demanded, her fear giving way to anger as she looked around, trying to figure out where she was and what she could use as a weapon. Her memory of the parking garage was coming back to her in waves congruent with the waves of nausea washing over her, causing her hands to start trembling.

Ronald didn't answer. He looked down, unable to maintain eye contact with Hallie.

Hallie was terrified, even though the timid man on the floor in front of her didn't seem to pose as much of a threat as Peter. "Fuck, where's Peter," she thought to herself.

"Where's Peter? Do you work for him?" Hallie asked.

"No, oh my God, no, I don't even know him," Ronald rasped. "Or at least I didn't until recently. I wanted to stop him from hurting anyone else, but I couldn't," Ronald said, looking down in shame.

"What is this place? Where are we?" Hallie said, looking around the small room they were in.

"I don't know but I think it's some type of server room for computers. From the temperature in here, that would be my guess."

"What's your name?" Hallie asked, trying not to panic and to control her emotions.

"Ronald."

"How do you know my name, Ronald? And how do you know Peter?"

Ronald looked down at his hands again and didn't answer.

Hallie's mind was racing, but the more she talked, the more she started to regain her bearing. She desperately wanted to find a way out of this horror show but she also wanted to learn what Ronald knew about Peter, who, thankfully, was not in the room with them at that moment. Hallie remembered waking up the first time alone in that room with Peter. She will never forget how he looked at her, with his cold, dark eyes and evil smirk, right before he lunged at her with a syringe in hand, easily overpowering her as she screamed in terror before whatever he had injected into her knocked her out. She forced herself to shake the memory from her mind so she could focus on her current situation, knowing it wouldn't be long before Peter returned. She had to find a way out before he came back to do God knows what to her.

Trying to remain calm and convey a self-assuredness she did not feel, she started with, "You look familiar, Ronald; have we met?"

"Yes, once or twice," Ronald admitted, pleased that she recognized him.

"Where did we meet?"

"I would rather not say right now," Ronald stuttered, afraid to tell her the truth, "but I promise I would never hurt you. I'm not like Mr. Sadist."

"Mr. Sadist? What are you talking about? Who is Mr. Sadist?"

"The one you call Peter, I think. I only know him as Mr. Sadist."

"I don't understand," Hallie said, confused, her head throbbing as she tried to make sense of her situation and what this stranger was saying to her.

"It's his online name."

"His online name? I know him as Peter Martin, the head of our IT department. How do you know him, Ronald?" Hallie asked.

"We met in a chat room. Things have just gotten out of hand. I didn't know he would hurt anyone. I tried to warn you. I'm so sorry," Ronald almost whispered, once again looking down in shame.

"Oh, wait, you're the one who sent me that email, aren't you?" Hallie asked more as a statement than a question.

Ronald nodded timidly. There was something sad and pathetic about the young man cowering on the floor across from her. She believed him for some reason, or at least believed he was the lesser of the two evils.

"I, I captured a picture of you," Ronald stammered. "I uploaded it to the chat room, and he saw it. That's when he first contacted me. I had no idea he knew you. He must have planned this from the beginning. I'm so sorry."

Incredulous and aggravated at what she was hearing but not wanting to lose control of the situation, Hallie said, "Okay, Ronald, we'll get to that later. Right now, we need to get the fuck out of here before he comes back."

Ronald started to get up off the floor when he noticed the cameras in the upper corners of the room, and quickly returned to his position against the cinderblock wall.

"Don't get up, Hallie. He's watching us. We need to come up with a plan before he realizes we're both awake now. He might have already noticed when I got up earlier to try to find a way out. He could be on his way here now," Ronald said, the fear evident in his voice.

Hallie looked around, noticing the computer monitor on the desk.

"What about that computer? If it has internet, can't we use it to get help?" Hallie asked, trying to convince herself she was still in control, while looking around and realizing the severity of her situation in the windowless cinderblock room, the gray cement walls threatening to close in around her.

"Possibly, but it's probably password protected with multiple security features that would take me too long to bypass. He would be on to us before I could hack in."

"Right, he's in charge of IT," Hallie said, catching her breathe in her throat as she became more aware of the hopelessness of her situation. "Well, I'm not going to sit around here waiting for him to come back. I'm going to get out of here," she said, lifting herself off the brown leather couch and feeling a new wave of pain and dizziness rush to her throbbing head.

"I don't think there's a way out except that door over there, but it's locked. It has an electronic keypad lock on both sides of the door and a regular deadbolt, so we need either the code or a key. Earlier, I tried to disarm the keypad, which sometimes will trip the lock, but I couldn't do it."

"How long have we been in here?" Hallie asked, rubbing her temples and trying to keep the nausea at bay.

"I don't know for sure, but a couple of hours, at least, I think." Ronald said.

"Well, then, he'll probably be coming back soon. If we can't get out, we need to barricade the door so he can't get in before someone finds us. Someone will find us," Hallie said, trying to convince herself more than Ronald, trusting that Marcelo was out there looking for her.

"We have to keep him out," Ronald said with more conviction than Hallie had witnessed from the fragile man. "I've seen what he does to women. He's a very bad man. Maybe we can block the door with the servers or the furniture. I'll do whatever I can to keep him from hurting you, Hallie," Ronald said genuinely.

Hallie inspected the door for herself, fearing that Peter was going to push through it at any moment. She anxiously looked through the desk and everywhere else in the room where someone might hide a key, but with no luck. While Hallie looked for the key, Ronald stood on the desk and repositioned the cameras to face the walls instead of the room's unwilling occupants. Hallie quickly came to the same conclusion as Ronald: barricading the door was their only option until they could figure out what to do next. At least it would keep Peter out.

"The servers are the heaviest things in the room. Let's try to move those first," Ronald said.

They quickly discovered the heavy servers were bolted to the concrete floor and immovable. But they were able to move the couch and wedge it in between the door and the servers leaving only about an inch or two to spare making it impossible for anyone from the outside to open the door, which thankfully opened inward.

"Now that the door is barricaded, it gives me more time," Ronald said hopefully. "If I can hack into that computer, maybe we can contact the police."

"But we don't know where we are," Hallie said, losing her composure for the moment. "Even if we get through to someone, how will they find us?" she asked in a higher pitched voice than she intended.

"Every computer has its own IP address, which is traceable to your location unless you use a rolling

VPN," Ronald explained shyly, with a hint of pride in his voice.

"What's a rolling VPN?"

"A rolling VPN is a virtual private network that hides your location by changing your IP address every fifteen seconds or so, bouncing it around the world through different networks."

"What if that's already installed on that computer?"

"If I can get in, I can reconfigure it so that our IP address is discoverable."

Ronald sat in front of the computer and moved the mouse to bring the screen to life. Hallie sat down on the couch, her head pounding from her head injury, being drugged, and previous exertion, while Ronald started tapping away on the keyboard.

He had been working at it for about thirty minutes when they heard the chime of the keypad from the other side of the door. Someone was outside and trying to unlock the door.

Hallie froze and thought she might throw up. She involuntarily started to tremble imagining Peter on the other side of the door.

CHAPTER FIFTY-SEVEN

"Why the fuck was that detective here?" Monica asked as soon as her mother came into the living room.

"Really, Monica, don't use such crass language. It's very unbecoming," Nina calmly admonished as she walked to the wet bar to fix herself another martini.

"Let me do that for you, Aunt Nina," Tom said, taking the glass from Nina's hand.

"Thanks, Tom, you've always been such a doll."

"So, what was that detective saying about Hallie Miller missing? Since when?" Tom asked, his personal interest not lost on Nina or Moni.

"All he said is that she's missing. Maybe she just ran off with some guy for the weekend and didn't tell anyone," Nina replied dismissively, "who the hell knows."

"But why would the police be here asking *you* about her, Aunt Nina?" Tom asked, remembering when Hallie ran off to the Keys to meet him for the weekend, confused by her apparent jab. Did his aunt know about that?

"I don't have the slightest idea. I had lunch with the woman one time, for God's sake."

"What? What do you mean you had lunch with her? When did you have lunch with her, Mother?" Moni asked, surprised.

"About a week ago, I guess. She's on the board of the Spring and used their annual gala as a pretense to ask me questions about her father."

"What did you tell her, Mother?" Moni asked, incredulous, her eyes darting to Tom.

"Nothing, of course. What could I tell her? I don't know anything about what happened to her father. And frankly, I'm bored with this subject. It's ancient history and needs to stay dead and buried, just like her father. Tom, be a love and add a little ice to this martini," Nina said, indicating the conversation about Hallie Miller and Charlie Robinson was over.

* * *

The year was 1990. Monica Martino sat on the bench with her pink backpack on her lap, the night breeze offering a brief respite from the stagnant humidity that permeated that warm September day. Moni pulled her long black hair into a ponytail and wiped the sweat from the back of her neck and onto her denim miniskirt. And she waited. She had left her house on Davis Islands at about a quarter to seven and arrived about fifteen minutes later in front of Charlie Robinson's downtown office, happy to see the light still on in his first-floor window. As the sun set, the streetlights around her came on, and she looked up and down the deserted sidewalk in front of the building she was watching. With no restaurants or bars around at that time, downtown Tampa became a virtual ghost town after 6 p.m., except for the occasional homeless person perusing the area garbage bins.

She thought about what she would say to Charlie Robinson. She had practiced over and over in her head. She had seen him before. She was confident she would recognize him when she saw him, having gone to high school with his daughter, Hallie, although they weren't friends. Hallie Robinson: so straight, so smart, always the teacher's pet, surrounded by so many friends, from a perfect family, so unlike Moni. She couldn't stand her, not that Hallie had ever done anything to her personally, but they were different, from very different worlds.

Over the years, Moni had heard the rumors herself about her family's mafia connections, but she knew her father wasn't in that world, so she ignored them. Monica had friends – lots of friends – until the middle of seventh grade when that son-of-a-bitch, Robbie Thompson, brought in her grandfather's mug shot and that damn newspaper article that told all about the underworld of Tampa, which, of course, included stories about her grandfather, Nico Martino, and his brother, Sal. One by one, the friends distanced themselves from her, and everyone treated her differently after that. It was enough to keep her from being invited to the popular girls' sleepovers and birthday parties, and Moni kept mostly to herself after that. She never believed her father was in the mafia, despite the stories about her grandfather, but now her mother, in a drunken rage, had all but confirmed it. Moni didn't care. Her father was all that mattered to her, and she would not let her bitch of a mother or her mother's lawyer hurt their family.

She had no intention of using the gun – she just needed Charlie Robinson to listen to her. After about fifteen minutes of waiting on the bench, the light in his office went out. Moments later, a man appeared under the streetlight and locked his office door. There was a weariness about him as he slipped his keys into his pants pocket and then switched the hard, rectangular briefcase he was carrying into his other hand. She watched the man – the same man who was threatening to destroy her family – casually walk down the street, presumably to go home to his happy family who was waiting for him for dinner. The thought enraged her, and she had to let him know what he was doing to her family before he took it any further.

She slung the pink backpack over her left shoulder, letting it rest by her side, and unzipped the outside pocket to grip the gun with her right hand. She would only take it out if he wouldn't listen to her, just to scare him, stop him. That's all she wanted to do, she swore to herself, just get his attention and make him stop to listen to her.

"Mr. Robinson," her voice quivered, as she came up behind him after crossing Madison Avenue over to his side of the desolate street.

He glanced over his shoulder, not seeing her at first, and without responding, kept walking.

"Mr. Robinson, I need to talk to you," she said louder, more forcefully, the anger rising inside of her.

This time he stopped and turned around, "I'm sorry, do I know you? I'm in a bit of a hurry," he said, obviously taken aback by the unknown young woman approaching him.

"I'm Tommy Martino's daughter," Moni said, knowing her father's name would get his attention, while she kept the gun hidden behind her.

Charlie Robinson looked at her then, his confused expression softening as he said, "Ms. Martino . . . Monica, right? Please go home. I can't talk to you. You should go home and talk to your parents."

"Oh, my parents are talking right now, if you call screaming at each other 'talking.' And I blame you!! It's all your fault!" Moni yelled, the hot tears unintendingly streaming down her face. "I heard what my mother told my father about you – I won't let you destroy him."

"I don't know what you're talking about, but I see you're upset. Please go home and talk to your parents. I can't talk to you about their case, but I'm sure it will all work out," Charlie said gently as he turned and started to walk away from her, his pace quicker than before.

She heard the ear-shattering explosion of the gun before she realized that the gun was in her hand or that she had pulled the trigger. Her ears were ringing. She had no idea how many shots she had fired. Charlie Robinson was face down on the sidewalk in front of her and the gun was still in her trembling hand. He wasn't moving. She dropped to the sidewalk onto her knees, placed the gun down next to her, and started to sob.

CHAPTER FIFTY-EIGHT

Nicolas Martino was the most dangerous of the Martino boys, having followed in his father, Nico's, footsteps. Like his father, he earned his place among Tampa's mafia through violence and intimidation and by adhering to their strict codes. He never raised his voice and was always calm, which unnerved even the most formidable of his adversaries. He had a long, angular face, scarred from his early years of fighting his way up the ranks, and an unsightly bent nose that had been broken one too many times. His gray-blue eyes never blinked, like a shark cutting through the dark waters stalking its prey, and he was calculating and cunning.

He smoothed his gray goatee, instinctively feeling the scar that ran from his chin to underneath his jawline, a permanent reminder of the first time he killed a man. He was twenty-two at the time and was supplying drugs to a number of smalltime dealers throughout Tampa for a twenty-five percent cut of street value, paid up front. He was doing well financially while also making a name for himself within the organization when one of the dealers got greedy. Nicolas arrived at the drop spot: a tiny park in Old Seminole

Heights next to the Hillsborough River. The unnamed city park was set back in a residential neighborhood, and seldom used except by a few neighborhood kids who liked to fish off its bank. At night, the quiet park was dark and empty and secluded by heavy brush and overhanging trees.

Nicolas had arrived early that night, as he always did, and watched as the dealer pulled up in a black Z-28. The dealer was not alone, which was a violation of the rules Nicolas had set. As the dealer approached, the streetlight reflected off the blade cupped in the dealer's hand. Nicolas sat still, not saying a word, when the dealer lunged for his neck. Nicolas easily deflected the attack, but the blade caught him on the chin once, leaving a sizable gash, before Nicolas adeptly removed the knife from the dealer's hand and slit the dealer's throat with his own blade. The dealer's driver quickly sped away and Nicolas dumped the body and the knife into the river, the proximity of which was another reason why he had selected the tiny park as the meeting place. By the time the body would be found, if the alligators hadn't gotten to him first, Nicolas would be gone, and no one would care about a small-time thug washing up downstream on the shore of the Hillsborough River.

Over the years, Nicolas earned a reputation for being a sociopathic killer. He was emotionless and would kill without provocation. It was rumored that he preferred knives over guns but would use whatever he had on hand as needed. He allegedly killed one double-crosser by strangling him with his own necktie. He spent a decade in Japan, where he trained in various martial arts, including Ninjutsu, one of the deadliest. Ninjutsu originated over a thousand years ago and was the martial art believed to have been practiced by ninjas. His training included tactical training in guerilla warfare, espionage, and fighting with and without weapons. When he returned, he was fluent in Japanese and purportedly maintained his overseas connections with the Yakuza, Japan's more violent version of the American mafia.

Upon his return, Nicolas invested in various legitimate businesses, including commercial real estate, restaurants, and even a strip club, the most nefarious of his investments. He allowed his inept cousin, Vincent Martino, to manage the strip club for him, mainly so Nicolas could keep an eye on him. At various times in his life, Nicolas came under investigation by the Florida Department of Law Enforcement, the FBI, and other international task forces, but no one was ever able to find enough evidence against him to charge him with a crime.

With the development of the smart phone and other technological advances, he partnered with a software development group in Japan to develop a state-of-the-art home security system, which he named SmartDefense. By all accounts, it seemed like a legitimate business, as most of his businesses and investments appeared, but his ultimate goal was to sell SmartDefense to casinos, banks, and other institutions where millions of dollars were exchanged on a daily basis. He believed he could use SmartDefense to bypass the usual security features of such institutions' financial systems to access their accounts and transfer millions of dollars into an offshore account in the Caymans within seconds without detection. By controlling their security systems, the servers, and the IP addresses, he believed he could cause the funds to disappear in less than a minute without a trace. He would only do it once from multiple accounts at the same exact time and never have to do it again. Even his partners in Japan wouldn't be able to trace the transfers, although he would send them their cut from the Caymans. He would have all the money he needed to live out the rest of his life with the only woman he had ever loved, Nina Martino.

Nicolas launched SmartDefense in Tampa in 2017 to monitor it closely and work out the bugs as he and the Japanese developers continued to work on its real intended purpose. At Nina's request, he hired his great nephew, Pietro Martino, to help him set up the servers in the windowless building Nicolas had acquired on the outskirts of Ybor City to operate SmartDefense. His great nephew had a degree in information technology, but there was something off about him that concerned Nicolas. Pietro was cold and cruel in a way that reminded Nicolas of some of the Yakuzas he had encountered in Japan. Like them, Pietro had pure ice in his veins and the warmth of a sociopath. But he also had impulse control issues just like his drunk of a mother, Monica, which made him even more dangerous. Nicolas didn't want him involved in his business at all, but he couldn't say no to Nina. He asked Pietro to help with the physical installation of the servers and initial programing to get them online, but then planned to let him go.

After the servers were set up and running, Nicolas retained an independent management company to hire and manage the technicians, sales force, and customer support for the legitimate security system side of SmartDefense, none of whom had any idea what the Japanese developers were working on in the background. Nicolas was relieved when Pietro quit shortly after the installation, having landed an important job as director of IT with a prestigious law firm downtown. Nicolas assumed that's why the boy changed his name to Peter Martin, to distance himself from the infamous Martino family name.

Nicolas heard the notification on his phone and opened the app secured by his facial recognition security feature. Someone or something had tripped a button on the server. The only people who knew where the servers were maintained were Nicolas himself, Pietro, and Nicolas's most trusted soldier, Tampa Rico, who had been working for Nicolas for the past ten years. Tampa Rico did anything Nicolas told him to do. He was paid well, but he also had no conscience, so he was the perfect hired hand. His most recent job was keeping an eye on his nephew and, after learning that he was communicating with one of his security system installers, keeping an eye on him too. The installer lived above the pizza joint Pietro had started patronizing, and Nicolas knew Pietro and the installer were up to something. It was just a matter of time before he found out or confronted Pietro.

There appeared to be no interruption in service or operation, but Nicolas received a notification when anything changed on the servers, including the temperature or when a button was pushed. This time, it was the button to unlock the panel to change the filter to the cooling system, and it had been pushed at 8:32 p.m., according to the notification he had just received. As no one would be changing the filters at this time of day, he assumed it was either a rat that sometimes came in through the ceiling or a glitch in the system. To be sure, he opened the app to view the server room to make sure no one was in the room. At first, he thought the cameras were broken, but then he realized that they had been turned to face the cinderblock walls, which caused his blood pressure to quickly rise. He immediately called Tampa Rico.

"Are you in the server room?"

"No, Boss, am I supposed to be?"

"I need you to head there now. How long before you get there?"

"Fifteen minutes. On my way."

"Report when you get there. Bring a piece."

While he waited for Tampa Rico to get to the server building, he sent a text to Nina.

"Hi, my love, are you alone?"

A few minutes passed before she finally replied.

"No, I'm having cocktails with Tom and Moni, care to join us?"

"What about Pietro, is he there too?"

"Not tonight. He's not responding to my texts – you know how he goes dark sometimes."

"And how is Monica tonight? Is she behaving?" Nicolas asked, knowing that Nina's mood would be affected by Monica's.

"She seemed in good spirits until I told her why the detective was here."

"A detective? What was he asking about?" Nicolas asked calmly.

"He was asking about Hallie Miller and what I knew about her father's murder that happened thirty years ago. Apparently, Ms. Miller has now gone missing," Nina replied.

"I don't understand. Why would he be asking you about her? Do you know her?"

"I had lunch with her about a week ago. Her father was Charlie Robinson, my divorce attorney, remember? I have no idea why this detective thinks I would know anything about either situation."

"Do you recall the detective's name?"

Nina retrieved the card from her pocket and typed, "Garcia. Detective Marcelo Garcia."

"Got it. I have to see about something going on with my servers but then I'll be over. I must see you tonight, my love."

Nina responded with the heart emojis and the purple devil.

Nicolas had fallen in love with Nina the day his brother introduced him to her over fifty years before. He was two years younger than Nina, and she was the most beautiful woman he had ever seen. She was twenty at the time, stunning, full of life, and better than his older brother deserved. He knew he couldn't have her, but he couldn't help how he felt. He kept his distance over the years, seeing her at family gatherings, but his feelings had never changed. After she and Tommy had Monica, Nicolas left for Japan, not able to bear watching the happy little family together.

He returned from Japan ten years later, when his father, Nico, got sick, and Nicolas took over the remaining illegal family businesses. Within a few years, Tommy and Nina were fighting all the time, and Nina started to confide in Nicolas about her marital problems. Nicolas convinced her to file for divorce, secretly hoping they could be together one day. She hired an attorney, filed for divorce, but then had second thoughts, mostly out of the fear of losing her extravagant lifestyle that being married to Tommy afforded her. She was planning to have her attorney withdraw the divorce petition when her attorney was shot and killed.

Nina had confided in Nicolas that she believed Tommy was responsible for Charlie Robinson's death. She had her replacement attorney withdraw the divorce petition and reconciled with Tommy, believing that any man who would kill to keep her must really love her. Nicolas was outraged. His brother didn't deserve Nina. Tommy couldn't make her happy like he could. But his unsuspecting brother had also confided in him what really happened that fateful night Charlie Robinson was murdered and made him swear to protect Nina and Monica if anything ever happened to him. Tommy also charged Nicolas with protecting their nephew, Tom Egan, whose own father, Mickey, had died of a massive heart attack. Nicolas promised his brother that he would take care of the family if anything happened to Tommy, and intended to keep that promise to his death, but he couldn't bear the thought of Nina being with Tommy rather than him for the rest of their lives.

After Nina withdrew the divorce petition, she and Tommy seemed to be working hard to restore their relationship. Nicolas realized he would never have his beloved Nina as long as Tommy was alive. He tailed Tommy to one of his high-rise developments, which was in the very early stages of construction, and using the skills he had mastered in Japan, he followed him up to the tenth floor of the undeveloped high-rise undetected. No one saw Nicolas enter the building, or leave it, for that matter, and later that morning, Tommy Martino mysteriously plummeted to his death from the tenth floor, paving the way for Nicolas to be with Nina. After his brother's death was ruled a tragic accident, he was there to console Nina, playing the grieving brother and caring brother-in-law without anyone suspecting a thing, including Nina.

He had been taking care of Nina since Tommy's death, under the guise of his solemn promise to his brother, until she finally succumbed to his advances about five years ago. He didn't care who knew about their relationship but Nina, always worried about appearances, was adamant about keeping it a secret. After all, he was her dead husband's brother. But Nicolas was tired of the secrecy and was ready to run away with Nina. Everything he had ever done was for her, including killing his own brother, and it was time.

He looked down at his phone again – nothing from Tampa Rico. There would be no reason for anyone to be in the server room. He had changed the codes to the door after the servers were installed, and Tampa Rico was the only person besides himself with a key and the code to get in. He checked his phone again. Ten minutes had passed. Rico would be there soon.

Nicolas paced while he waited, vowing to kill anyone who sabotaged his servers or his plans. All he needed was one final, big score and he and Nina could run away and live on an island together for the rest of their lives. He would deal with this detective, too. He didn't need anyone poking around the past, further threatening to delay his plans with Nina.

His phone pinged.

"Almost there. I don't see anyone around, but I'll let you know when I get there."

CHAPTER FIFTY-EIGHT

Eighteen-year-old Monica Martino put the gun, still hot to her touch, in her pink backpack and ran to the alley to get her bike. Her legs felt wobbly and like they might not hold her up, but she knew she had to get out of there, fast, hopefully without anyone seeing her. She rode away from downtown, heading north on Tampa Street towards Tampa Heights. Tampa Heights, once a premier neighborhood, had been overtaken during the previous two decades by blight and crime, especially drugs and prostitution. No one in the Heights trusted the police, and if anyone noticed Moni, they probably wouldn't admit it. She stopped at the corner of Tampa Street and Columbus Avenue where she found a payphone outside the Gold Ring Café, an iconic Latin breakfast and sandwich shop. She found enough change in the front pocket of her backpack to make a phone call. She picked up the receiver with her trembling hand and tried to insert the coins into the slot without dropping them. Her fear yielded to relief at the sound of her father's voice answering the phone.

Within twenty minutes, Tommy Martino arrived at the Gold Ring Café. Moni was surprised to see her cousin, Tom, get out of the car together with her father. The dome light did not come on when they opened the doors, and the car was left running. Tom left the passenger side door open for Moni to get in. Her father took her backpack from her while Tom mounted her sky-blue bike, the tires of the girly bike registering the weight of his impact. In one quick move, her father transferred the gun and ammunition into a black bag Tom had over his shoulder, and Tom took off on the bike towards the Hillsborough River. The entire transaction was less than thirty seconds and they never spoke a word. As her father got back in the car, she noticed that her overnight bag that she had brought home for the weekend was on the back seat.

Her father didn't speak to her until they were about an hour up I-75, heading back to the University of Florida.

"Who knows that you came home to Tampa today?"

"Just this kid I got a ride with," Moni answered quietly, her voice shaky and meek.

"What's his name?"

"Mike."

"Mike what?" her father asked impatiently.

"I don't know his last name. He lives in my dorm. He put a note on the bulletin board that he was heading to Tampa this weekend if anyone wanted to split the gas expense."

"Do you still have his number?"

"Yeah, I have it here," Moni said as she looked through her backpack and retrieved a scrap of paper with a number written on it.

Her father pulled off the highway and into the nearest gas station, pulling up next to a pay phone. He opened his ashtray, retrieved a few quarters from the tray, and handed them to his daughter.

"Call him. Tell him you forgot about something you had to do in Gainesville tonight, so your parents took you back right after he dropped you off. Keep it short, no other details."

Monica got out of the car and made the call as instructed. She got back in the car, and they drove the rest of the way in silence.

When they arrived in front of her dorm, Moni started to cry, "I'm sorry, Daddy, I didn't mean to do it; I just wanted to protect you," she sobbed, tears streaming down both of her cheeks as she wiped her nose on her sleeve.

"I just don't know what you were thinking, Moni," her father said sadly, finally looking at her for the first time since he picked her up outside of the Gold Ring Café.

The streetlight streamed in offering enough light for Moni to see her father's eyes glistening from the tears he was trying to hold back. She would never forget that moment for the rest of her life, and it broke her heart.

"Now, get yourself together and get in there. Go straight to your room to put your things away first, and then I want you to walk around, visit people in the dorm. Make sure you talk to a few people and do not mention that you went home. Got it?"

"Yes, Daddy. Will you ever forgive me?" Moni asked, still crying, but trying to pull herself together.

"Moni, there's nothing to forgive. You're my baby; you'll always be my little girl."

Moni hugged her father, gathered her stuff, and got out of the car.

As she made her way to her room, she heard a party in full swing down the hall. She put her stuff in her room, removed the mascara from her tear-stained cheeks, put on fresh lipstick and made her way to the party. She made sure she was seen by many people, just as her father had instructed her to do. That was also the night she learned that if she drank enough vodka and tequila, she wouldn't have to feel anything. She became very good at both over the years.

The last thing her father said to her that night before he pulled away was, "Moni, we will never speak of this night ever again."

And they never did. Her father died in a tragic accident the following year. Moni was devastated and felt she had brought this tragedy on her family. Not only had she killed someone else's father, but she had gotten pregnant out of wedlock a few months later. She was convinced her bad behavior had karmically caused her own beloved father's death and she would never forgive herself for it.

After her father's funeral, she learned that her cousin, Tom, had gotten rid of her bike and thrown the gun off the North Boulevard Bridge into the Hillsborough River. Neither the gun nor her bike was ever found, and as far as she knew, only she and Tom knew what had happened that night. But, of course, she was wrong about that, just as she was wrong about so many things in her life.

CHAPTER FIFTY-NINE

Tampa Rico left the pool hall where Barrett Mullen, the prep-school kid turned pool shark, had beaten him for the third time. He was into the kid for sixty bucks and was happy his boss had rescued him with his phone call. He hurried along the old, abandoned railroad tracks that ran along the outskirts of Ybor City. He passed by the dilapidated casitas – tiny row houses that were built at the turn of the century for the workers who rolled cigars at the factories in Ybor – the wood rotted and disintegrating from years of neglect, the blistering sun, thunderstorms, and termite infestations. The road leading out of Ybor brandished the original red-clay bricks, a sign of an era long gone, next to overgrown and unkempt vacant lots. Eventually those bricks would be buried in asphalt, just as countless others had been in the name of progress. In the distance, he could see the cargo ships at the Port, docked next to the industrial warehouses where smoke billowed out of the adjacent silos.

He arrived at the stand-alone, windowless, concrete building that was situated at the edge of the city, far from the eclectic restaurants, bars, and vintage shops for which

Ybor City had become known. The small sign on the black door announced: *Yamamoto Enterprises*. He sent a quick text to his boss before entering the code to open the door.

"Just arrived. Stand by."

He entered the code, but it didn't work. Instead of the usual green light, the panel buzzed and flashed red. He tried it again before sending the following text to his boss:

"Did you change the code?"

"No, it's not working?"

"No. Tried it 3 times."

"Try your key."

Tampa Rico took his key out and put it in the lock. The deadbolt turned and he attempted to open the door, which was blocked by something that only allowed him to see about two inches inside the door.

He texted Nicolas Martino again, "Something is blocking the door. I can't get in. What should I do?"

After a minute, he received a response: "If anyone besides me shows up, start shooting. I'm on my way."

* * *

They both heard the deadbolt turn at the same time. Hallie looked at Ronald and ran behind the server, terrified Peter had returned. Ronald didn't move, continuing to type away on the keyboard in front of him.

"Ronald, get over here," Hallie whispered, "you're exposed. He'll be able to see you," wondering to herself why she was worried about Ronald at all.

"I'm almost through," Ronald said, never looking away from the computer, continuing to tap rapidly on the keyboard.

"Ronald," Hallie said louder, "forget it, what if he has a gun? Just come over here."

"No. I have to make things right. I told you I won't let him hurt you again. I'm almost through. I can do this," Ronald said with more determination and ambition than he had ever exhibited in his life.

Someone kept pushing on the door, trying to force it open. The couch had done its job, much to Hallie's relief, as she cowered behind the server.

"There, that's it. I did it," Ronald said, as he ran over and joined Hallie where she was crouched behind the servers. "I got a message to the TPD online tip-line. Now let's just hope someone sees it and comes."

"They have to see it. They will see it," Hallie said, trying to convince herself more than Ronald. "We will hide behind these servers until they get here. It won't be long."

Hallie felt relief knowing it would be impossible for anyone to get in with the couch barricading the door or shoot at them where they hid behind the servers. They had done all they could to protect themselves, but she prayed

Marcelo or someone at TPD would get Ronald's message and be able to find them.

"Thank you, Ronald. I think you just saved our lives," she whispered while they hid behind the server, painfully aware that her life was dependent on a creepy stranger and an old brown, leather couch she hoped would stay in place to block the door from Peter Martin.

CHAPTER SIXTY

Marcelo was back at his desk in the precinct, trying to find out whatever he could about SmartDefense and Yamamoto Enterprises. He knew in his gut it was the connection that was going to lead him to Hallie. He also reviewed the files in the Veronica Hill and Sheada Lawson cases again as well as the emails Hallie had sent to him. If there was a connection, he was going to find it.

As he scoured through everything Hallie had sent him again, he realized she had also sent him all her notes and documents related to her father's unsolved murder. He remembered Hallie mentioning that the police records from her father's case had been destroyed, but that went against cold case file retention protocol. Marcelo realized he had never checked to confirm this was true. He picked up the phone on his desk and called down to records.

"Records," a sleepy-sounding voice answered on the third ring.

"Hello, this is Detective Garcia. I'm looking for an unsolved cold case file from 1990. The victim's name is Charlie or Charles Robinson. Can you see what you have?"

"Whew, 1990, that's not digitalized yet, Detective. I'm going to have to go to the cabinets. This could take a while and my shift ends in thirty minutes," the seemingly put-out records keeper responded in a voice gruff from years of smoking.

"What's your name, Officer?" Marcelo asked.

"Officer Daniels," he answered hesitantly.

"How long have you been on the job?"

"Coming up on twenty-two, no wait, twenty-three years."

"Okay, so you probably know the filing system better than anyone down there. I need a favor here, Officer Daniels. A woman's life is at stake and there might be something in that file that helps me find her, if you can even find a file. It may have been destroyed."

"An unsolved case file destroyed? Nah, that wouldn't happen. Okay, Detective, I'll see what I've got. If we have a file, I'll find it. Give me the V's name again."

"Charlie or Charles Robinson, murdered in September 1990."

"Got it, gimme your extension, Detective. I'll call you when I find something."

Marcelo reviewed Charlie Robinson's handwritten notes from the Martino divorce case while he waited. He read the last entry written on the yellow legal pad Hallie had scanned from her father's file dated about a week before his murder:

8/28/90, t/c Nina, more issues. "Family" getting involved. RO? Withdraw? F/up next week to discuss next steps.

Lost in thought about the implications and timing of the note, he jumped when the phone on his desk rang.

"Garcia," he answered.

"Detective, I may have found what you're looking for. There's not much in it, but I did find a thin file on your victim."

Marcelo's heart picked up a beat as he rose out of his chair.

"Don't go anywhere, Officer. I'll be right down," Marcelo said hanging up before the officer could respond.

He checked out the file, thanked Officer Daniels, and raced back to his office. He sat down at his steel, government issued desk and opened the file, hoping there was something in there that would shed light on the case. The first paper in the file was the chronological record of the case, beginning with the initial notification to the primary investigator, Anthony Russo, badge #4390.

Date	Time	Case No. 90-2571
90-9-7	1932	Notified by District 3 Watch Commander of gunshot victim at 212 E. Madison Street, downtown Tampa. Unidentified white male found on sidewalk with apparent gunshot to the back, deceased on arrival. T. Russo

	1935	Notified my partner, Det. K. Walter #5473, of the murder and to meet at the scene. T. Russo
	1947	Walter and I arrive at the scene. Briefed by patrol officer on scene of incident and witness who called it in. T. Russo
	1953	Located and interviewed Witness Mike Ford, a transient walking north on Franklin Street on his way to Salvation Army when he heard gun fire. Stated as he got closer to Madison Street, he saw a young girl come from the right side of the building on a bike and head north on Tampa Street. Witness pointed to the side of the building to the east of where the victim was found. Witness described girl as white female, late teens, long, black hair tied in a ponytail, pink backpack, blue or purple bike. After she rode away, witness saw victim face down on the ground and went to pay phone on the corner of Madison and Franklin and called 9-1-1. T. Russo
	2100	Investigator C. Ketchey from Medical Examiner's office arrived at scene. Rolled prints of victim, identification in wallet identified victim as Charles Robinson, DOB 7-4-44. Crime lab tech from ME's office at scene. Completed photographs of body, scene, bullet casings, and blood spatter; recovered swabs of blood and bullet casings. T. Russo
	2155	M.E. Ketchey took possession of the body. T. Russo

The report ended abruptly, the sheet having been torn after the last entry Marcelo read. Turning to the next documents in the file, Marcelo found the grainy crime scene photos. And that was it. But there was a witness. And the witness had seen a young woman with long black hair, riding away on her bike within minutes after the witness heard gunfire. All this time, he and Hallie suspected Tommy Martino was responsible for her father's murder. Could it have been Monica Martino, he wondered?

He left the precinct and drove the ten minutes back to Davis Islands. He easily found the house and saw the black Escalade was still in the driveway. He knocked on the door. No one answered. He knocked again. This time the man he now knew as Tom Egan answered the door.

"What can I do for you, Detective?" Tom asked, his stance making it clear Marcelo would not be invited into the home.

"Sorry to bother you again, Mr. Egan, is it?"

"What do you want?"

"I just have one more question for Mrs. Martino and her daughter. Can you ask them where Monica Martino was on the night Charlie Robinson was shot?"

"I don't know what you're getting at, Detective, but this conversation is over. Don't come back unless you have a warrant," Tom said angrily and shut the door. Tom took his cellphone out of his pocket and quickly sent a text to his Uncle Nicolas.

* * *

A few hours later, Marcelo was still at the precinct intently focused on the old documents and recent case files spread out on his desk. He wasn't going to go home until he found Hallie, and he believed the answers were somewhere in front of him. His cellphone rang, breaking the deadly silence of the empty precinct.

"Garcia," he answered curtly.

"Detective, sorry to bother you so late, but we received a message through our online tip link that we think you'll want to see. We're forwarding it to your email now."

Marcelo pulled up his email, waiting for it to come through, "Okay, got it," and read the message:

"Please take this message seriously and give it to Detective Marcelo Garcia. I am with Hallie Miller and we have been kidnapped. We don't know where we are being held but you should be able to trace our IP address to find us. Please hurry. The man who kidnapped us is evil and has hurt a lot of women. We think he's going to kill us."

"Can we trace this?" he asked, desperately, reading it again, praying Hallie was okay.

"We're trying now. We saw Hallie Miller's name on the missing persons and BOLO alert that went out. Unless it's encrypted, we should have a location within the next five minutes," said the officer with the IT department who monitored incoming tips and messages on the department's website.

Marcelo grabbed his keys and ran for the exit closest to where his car was parked, and on his way yelled to the officer, "Text the address to my cell as soon as you have it and send back up."

"You got it, Detective, stand by."

* * *

Marcelo's cellphone rang and he saw it was McCrink's personal cellphone.

"McCrink, what's up?"

"Hey, I've been working on this all night, and I think I found something."

"Tell me what you found, McCrink," Marcelo demanded, sounding more impatient than he intended.

"Okay, remember how I told you SmartDefense is owned by Yamamoto Enterprises?"

"Yeah, of course. What else did you find?"

"I just learned Yamamoto Enterprises is owned by Nicolas Martino."

"I knew it!" Marcelo exclaimed. "Anything else?"

"Yes, one more thing. Yamamoto Enterprises owns a building on the outskirts of Ybor, located at 1845 E. 2nd Avenue."

Just then, Marcelo's phone indicated he had an incoming text from a number within the department.

"Hang on, McCrink," Marcelo said as he looked at the text that just came through on his phone.

"*The message to the tip-line came from an IP address located at 1845 E. 2nd Avenue in Ybor City.*"

"Send back up to that address, McCrink, STAT! And call the Chief," Marcelo yelled into the phone as he hit the accelerator and hung up.

CHAPTER SIXTY-ONE

"Hallie! Are you in there," came the familiar voice through the two inch gap in the doorway.

"Marcelo? Is that you?" Hallie asked as she started to cry, finally succumbing to her fear.

"Baby, I'm here! You're safe! What's blocking the door?"

"A couch. We'll unblock it. Hang on."

Hallie and Ronald came out from around their protective servers and started to push the brown leather couch away when they heard voices on the other side of the door.

"What are you doing, man? Get away from that door, this is private property."

"I'm Detective Marcelo Garcia and this is official police business. Do you own this building?"

"No, but I work for the dude who does. He's not going to like this," the man said reaching inside his pocket.

"Keep your fucking hands where I can see them," Marcelo barked, reaching for his government issued gun in his waistband.

"Dude, I'm just reaching for my phone. I have to call my boss."

Hallie and Ronald listened to the exchange while watching through the three-inch crevice they had created when they started to move the couch. As Marcelo kept his eyes on the man he had been arguing with, Hallie saw Peter Martin rapidly approaching from behind Marcelo.

"Marcelo, watch out," Hallie screamed, just before gunshots rang out into the night.

"Marcelo!!!" Hallie yelled.

No response.

"Marcelo!!!" she yelled again.

Nothing, no response.

Ronald looked at her helplessly, not knowing what to do.

"Mother fucker! No, he's not winning," Hallie yelled, as she started to push the couch further out of the way.

"No, wait, he's out there, he'll kill us," Ronald said, obviously afraid, trying to block her from moving the couch the rest of the way.

Hallie stopped and took a breath, "Ronald, I have to go out there. I can't sit here and do nothing while my friend may be bleeding to death on the other side of this door. You can re-barricade the door after I go out there if you want."

"No, I promised you I would keep you safe, keep him from hurting you, especially since I brought him into your world."

"He works at my office, Ronald. You didn't bring him to me. He was already there," Hallie said, remembering what

Ronald had said earlier about uploading her picture to the chat room.

"But the chat room. That's where it all started. I'm so sorry," Ronald said, starting to fall apart again.

"What are you talking about? What is this chat room? And how did you get my picture in the first place?" Hallie asked, confused.

"It's a long story. I . . . I will explain," Ronald said, tears welling up in his eyes.

Hallie gathered herself, knowing she had to get to Marcelo. "I don't have time for this right now, Ronald. You can explain later. Help me move this couch," Hallie said, more determined than before.

They opened the door, not knowing what to expect on the other side of the heavy door.

No one was there.

Ronald started to run towards 7th Avenue, "C'mon, Hallie, this way," he implored.

Hallie didn't run. She stopped and looked around, looking for Marcelo, her heart stopping as she spotted him lying motionless on the old brick road about twenty feet in front of the building. She ran to him and crouched next to his crumpled body as she heard sirens approaching in the distance. Ronald came back and knelt next to her, waiting for the police to arrive.

"Marcelo, I'm here," Hallie said, putting pressure on his wounds while trying to ignore the blood that was pooling underneath his body. "Hang on, baby, please, just hold on," she begged as the sirens got closer and closer.

CHAPTER SIXTY-TWO

The next morning, Hallie was relieved to hear from Chief Mastandrea that Marcelo had survived the surgery, the bullet having gone in and out of his shoulder. He lost a lot of blood, but he was going to be okay. She would be allowed to see him in a few hours.

The security cameras outside the building captured most of the events of the evening. Nicolas Martino, the owner of the building, provided copies to the police to confirm that he had nothing to do with Hallie and Ronald's abductions. Hallie was asked to go to the station to view the footage.

She sat in the interview room with Officer McCrink.

"Can I get you anything, a water, coffee?"

"No, I'm okay, thank you. Has Peter Martin been found yet?"

"No, not yet, but there's a warrant out for his arrest for your abduction and his attack on you. We have footage from your office parking garage identifying Peter Martin as the one who hit you on the head with a tire iron before placing you in the trunk of his car. Don't worry, we'll find him. We also need you to watch this video to see if you can identify anyone in the video who may be responsible for shooting Detective Garcia."

"Okay, I'm ready," Hallie said, as Officer McCrink hit play on the video and the screen came to life.

Hallie watched as a man arrived at the building and was captured entering a code to unlock the door. He appeared to be doing something on his phone before finally unlocking the door with a key.

"That's the man who showed up first and was arguing with Marcelo," Hallie said.

"Do you recognize him?"

"No, I've never seen him before last night," Hallie said.

"We believe he's a thug who goes by the street name Tampa Rico and works for Nicolas Martino, the owner of the building where you were kept."

"Nicolas Martino? Wait, what do the Martinos have to do with this?" Hallie asked, confused about the connection.

"We don't know yet, Ms. Miller. But we're looking into every possibility. He was picked up at a pool hall in Ybor later that night but immediately invoked his right to counsel. We didn't have enough to charge him, so we had to let him go. His lawyer is someone on the Martino payroll so we're not expecting much cooperation there. But we're watching him."

"Okay, can we continue?" Hallie asked, the exhaustion washing over her.

Officer McCrink resumed the video. The man she had identified as Tampa Rico continued to work on the lock and the door in an attempt to get in. As Hallie watched the video, she saw something startle him and he ducked behind something, out of the view of the camera.

Another man appeared on camera for a moment, heading calmly towards the door.

"Stop. That's Peter Martin," Hallie said, her adrenaline surging at the sight of him.

McCrink paused the video, rewinding it a few seconds, and then hit play again.

"Are you sure? You are identifying this man on the screen as Peter Martin?"

"Yes, I'm positive. He's the director of IT at my firm."

"And you're sure you've never seen the first man who appeared in the video?" McCrink asked, rewinding the video again and freezing on the face of the first man.

"No, I'm sure I've never seen him before."

McCrink let the video play forward.

Peter came back into view, approaching the door of the small room in which Hallie and Ronald had barricaded themselves. He had something in his hand. Was it gun? A bat? A crowbar? Hallie couldn't tell. He unlocked the door and tried to push it open when it appeared as if he heard something that caused him to abruptly turn away and retreat somewhere outside of the camera's view. Within moments, Marcelo appeared on the screen, causing Hallie's breath to catch in her throat as she watched him approach the door. He, too, tried to push the door open while calling out to Hallie. The first man, Tampa Rico, came back into view and the video captured what Hallie had seen and heard from her position on the other side of the door the night before.

Within a few minutes, as Marcelo argued with Tampa Rico, Peter appeared behind Marcelo and gunfire erupted. Tampa Rico and Peter ran in opposite directions while Marcelo staggered out of the camera's view towards the red brick street where Hallie found him. Hallie was relieved the camera did not capture the moment he crumpled to the ground.

McCrink paused the video again before saying, softly, "I know this has to be hard, but can you continue?"

Hallie's heart was pounding, but she cleared her throat, "Yes, of course. Let's continue."

McCrink played the rest of the video and then started it again, stopping it from time to time at Hallie's direction. After they had watched it numerous times, McCrink took Hallie's statement. Hallie explained in detail what she had seen in the video and what she had seen and heard from inside the room. McCrink took meticulous notes and typed up Hallie's statement for her to review and sign. It had been a grueling three hours, but if it helped convict Peter for what he did to her, and to Marcelo, Hallie knew it was worth it.

"Okay, so are we done here? I want to get to the hospital to check on Marcelo," Hallie said.

"Yes, we're done. Thank you so much for your time. We'll let you know when we find him. In the meantime, please be safe."

"Thank you, I would appreciate that."

Hallie picked up her purse and black leather bag the police had retrieved from the back of her car, which had already been processed for any evidence. Paige was waiting for her when she came out of the police station.

"You okay?" Paige asked.

"I think so. Still trying to make sense of everything that happened. You know it was Peter Martin, our IT guy, who attacked me, right?"

"Yes, I know. It's crazy. Everyone at the office is talking about it. I saw on the news that the police are investigating whether he's responsible for attacking some other women in Tampa recently."

"I heard that, too. What they've pieced together so far is that Peter was a member of a creepy voyeur chat room on the dark web and teamed up with another voyeur who also lives in Tampa. That guy worked for a local alarm company – my alarm company, by the way – and is the same guy who was locked in the server room with me. His name is Ronald. From what I understand, all the women who were attacked, including me, have the same alarm system, which were all installed by the same technician."

"Wait, let me guess, the technician is Ronald, right?" Paige asked.

"Yup, you guessed it."

"But how does Peter fit in here? Doesn't it make more sense that Ronald may have attacked those women?"

"I guess they don't think so based on whatever evidence they've found so far, including the video footage from our garage as well as the building in Ybor City. And there is no question that Peter attacked me. Ronald is not blameless, but the videos corroborate his story and he's cooperating with the police."

"Wow, it's all so scary. I'm just relieved you're okay," Paige said, the concern evident in her soft voice.

"Yeah, me too. If Marcelo didn't show up when he did, I don't know that I would be. Speaking of which, can you drive me over to Tampa General?"

"Of course. I'm glad he got there in time to save you from that psycho. How is he doing?"

"He's out of surgery and is going to make a full recovery, I understand. The bullet went straight through and didn't hit anything vital."

"Thank God, Hallie. Do they know if Peter was the one who shot him?"

"I think so. And I have no doubt he is responsible for hurting all those other women too. The moments I spent with him after I regained consciousness were terrifying. I'll never forget how he spoke to me and the pure evil in his eyes. I have no doubt he planned to hurt me the same way he hurt those other women."

"I'm glad you're okay, Hallie," said her lifelong friend who always seemed to be there for her in her darkest hours, as she placed a hand on Hallie's forearm. "If you want to stay with me until they catch him, you know Mike and I would love to have you."

"Thanks, Paige. I appreciate it. For now, I just want to see how Marcelo is doing."

They drove away from the police station and rode the rest of the way to the hospital in silence. Nothing more needed to be said.

CHAPTER SIXTY-THREE

Marcelo was sitting up in bed when Hallie walked into the room. He had an IV of fluids hooked to one arm and various tabs hooked up to monitors attached to him, but otherwise seemed lucid and on the mend.

"How are you feeling?" Hallie asked as she put her purse down in the chair and sat on the edge of the hospital bed.

"Better now that you're here," Marcelo said, smiling sleepily.

Marcelo told Hallie about how the bullet had entered his back shoulder blade and exited through the front, missing anything vital. He had lost a lot of blood, but he assured her that after his blood count was back to normal and his wound healed, he would be as good as new. He also told her that he had seen the man who shot him before he collapsed, and he was able to identify him as Peter Martin, a/k/a Pietro Martino, the son of Monica Martino and grandson of Nina Martino.

"Wait, Peter Martin is really Pietro Martino?" Hallie asked, shocked by this revelation.

"Yes, and the building you were locked in is owned by Yamamoto Enterprises, which, coincidentally, is owned by Nicolas Martino."

"I don't believe in coincidences, Detective," Hallie said, thinking about her father's murder again and how every connection and clue led her to the Martinos. "Tommy Martino must be responsible for my father's murder, I just know it. Or maybe his brother, Nicolas, or someone else in the Martino family. None of them are right. Do you think the family directed Peter to hurt me, or worse, so that I would stop asking questions?"

"I don't know. It seems that Peter had his own dark proclivities that seem to be completely unrelated to his family or your father's murder. When they searched his apartment, they found a safe that contained women's underwear, jewelry, and other personal belongings, including long strands of hair in plastic baggies. We believe they are trophies he took from his victims' homes. I know you have been through a lot, Hallie, but you may have to see if any of the items belong to you."

"I still can't get my head around all of this. Do they have any idea where Peter is?"

"No, not yet. There is some indication that he may have already fled the country, but it's not confirmed yet," Marcelo said.

"What about Ronald, the guy who was in the room with me and saved my life by getting that message to the police department?" Hallie asked.

"He's a voyeur, Hallie, a creep. He's been watching you and other women through the alarm systems he installed in your homes. He took pictures of you and the other women and then uploaded them onto a chat room on the dark web so other sick fucks could get their rocks off too. He may seem harmless compared to Peter, but those guys often progress to more predatory crimes. Don't let him fool you."

"I know you're right, but he seemed remorseful and ashamed of what he had done. And don't forget, he sent me the warning message and then risked his own life to save mine. I know he's weird and creepy, but I don't think he's evil. Peter Martin is evil. I want Ronald to get help, not prison time, if possible."

"Well, he's cooperating and, you're right, he's no Peter Martin, so he will likely get probation and some type of mandatory counseling if he pleads. But that son of bitch, Martin, if I ever find him, I'll kill him for what he did to you," Marcelo said, his eyes looking at Hallie so intently, she believed him.

"As your lawyer, Detective, I must advise you not to say such things, especially things you don't mean," Hallie said, trying to lighten the mood.

"Hallie, I mean it. I will kill him if he ever comes near you again. I promise you. I love you," he said while his eyes closed involuntarily, and his breathing settled into a sleepy cadence.

Hallie sat silent, not knowing what to say or how to react.

"Have I scared you?" he asked, opening his hazy eyes to look into hers. "I know you think these painkillers are affecting my thoughts but they're not. I love you, Hallie Miller. If you don't feel the same way, that's okay, I'll wait until you do," Marcelo said, his heavy lids closing again.

"You don't scare me," Hallie said, pausing to collect her thoughts before finally saying, "I love you, too, Marcelo. And that scares the shit out of me, but not you. You are one of the most honest men I've ever known, and I trust you," Hallie said as she leaned in and kissed him gently on the lips.

He stirred when she kissed him, and Hallie realized he must have dozed off. She wasn't sure if he had even heard her.

"Get some rest now, baby. I have to get home to Juno, but I'll be back first thing tomorrow, I promise," she said as she kissed him once more on the forehead as she got up.

"Wait, I need to tell you something else, Hallie. I found your father's case file at the precinct. I think I know who killed your father," Marcelo said sleepily, as he reached out for Hallie's hand.

"What? What did you find?" Hallie asked.

Marcelo opened his eyes briefly and whispered something almost inaudible before succumbing to the opiates in his system and drifting off into a deep sleep. Hallie picked up her bag and walked out of the room, replaying the words over in her mind that she thought she heard.

As she walked out of the hospital room and headed towards the elevator, Hallie heard the sounds of alarms going off as multiple medical personnel raced past her into Marcelo's room with crash carts and medical equipment and other things Hallie couldn't comprehend. She stood immobilized in the hallway trying to make sense of the chaos around her and trying to breathe.

In the stairwell of the west wing of the hospital, Tampa Rico texted his boss, "it's done," before dropping the syringe into a trashcan as he made his way to the exit on the first floor.

CHAPTER SIXTY-FOUR

Pedro Martinez, his newest alias, sat in the lounge chair overlooking the Caribbean Sea, sipping on his pina colada. Peter Martin, f/k/a Pietro Martino, had been on the island less than twenty-four hours but was already fitting in with the regulars. He was fluent in Spanish, thanks to his overbearing and relentless grandmother, Nina, who would only allow them to speak Spanish in the home during the summer he was turning nine. He was thankful for it now, not that he liked to give the heartless bitch credit for anything.

"Senor Martinez, puedo traerte otra pina colada?"

"Si´, Julio, gracias, uno mas" Pedro responded.

Why not have another drink, he thought. After all, he was on vacation. Permanently. He had always planned to run away one day, away from his grandmother, away from his mother, his stupid, thankless job, and all the things he hated about his life. Thankfully, he had set up new identities and accounts in various foreign countries in case he ever needed them, mainly to make sure his grandmother couldn't find him. He knew his mother would never try. But his great Uncle Nicolas had connections, and he would try to find Peter if Nina ordered him to.

He hated Nina and blamed her for all that was wrong with him, including giving birth to his whore of a mother. But he was grateful for the one thing she was faithful about. Each month, his grandmother would deposit his monthly distribution from his trust into his account, mostly to coerce him to come to Sunday dinners at her demand. Thanks to those distributions, over the years he had wired funds into multi-tiered shell company bank accounts he had opened and closed. Those funds ultimately found their way into a bank account in the Cayman Islands in the name of Pedro Martinez. Between his Cayman bank account and his duffle bag full of cash, he had managed to accumulate over nine hundred thousand dollars over the last fifteen years. He would be able to live on that for quite a while, especially in Santo Domingo, an island in the Dominican Republic.

As Peter sipped his second tropical drink, he watched every movement of a beautiful, curvy Dominican woman in a lime green bikini setting up her towel on the tan-tinted sand near the edge of the calm, aqua water of the Boca Chica beach. She placed her black leather backpack on top of her towel, checked her phone before slipping it into the side pocket, and twisted her curly, brunette hair into a ponytail on top of her head. She slipped off her flip flops and started to make her way down to the water. Noticing one of her breasts trying to escape the tiny triangles of her bikini top held together by one or two pieces of string, he could tell she was naturally endowed and did not have any tan lines.

He was instantly aroused. He looked around to see if anyone was joining her. To his delight, she appeared alone.

He headed towards the water, pretending not to notice her. The hot sand burned the bottoms of his virgin, American feet, forcing him to pick up his pace very noticeably until he practically ran into the water. He heard her laughing at him as he turned to look at her, the blood and heat rising in his face, bringing back old feelings of shame and embarrassment.

Without a hint of an accent, the stunning brunette said, "I'm so sorry, I'm not laughing at you. It's just, I did that too when I first moved here. The sand is like fire, isn't it?"

"It is," he said, "I wasn't expecting that."

"You'll build up a tolerance," she smiled easily, "the bottoms of my feet are like leather now."

"I can't imagine getting used to it. That shit is hot," Peter laughed, the initial anger giving way to excitement.

"Well, I come out here almost every day. Trust me, you will. By the way, my name is Rebecca, but everyone calls me Beck."

And with that, Peter knew he was going to like the Dominican Republic. A lot.

* * *

The Broker sat in his cell, the moonlight peeking in from the tiny window above his cot. He had carried out his job with precision and was being rewarded. A new set of lawyers, at no cost to him, were working on his case. They were confident they could get him out for time served based on some irregularities in his plea deal and a lack of full disclosure of the State's evidence to his defense attorney, neither of which the current administration wanted publicized. For the first time in a long time, the Broker was hopeful.

His phone vibrated on his chest underneath his blanket. He smiled as he looked at the two-word message: "*Dominican Republic.*"

He had a son, and he couldn't wait to meet him.

And his long overdue reunion with Monica would be next.

ACKNOWLEDGEMENTS

To my dear family and friends, thank you for your unwavering support and encouragement. You all know who you are! I appreciate your feedback, suggestions, and editorial guidance during the writing process – it is more helpful than you will ever know.

Thank you also to anyone who reads my books. I am eternally grateful to all of you.

Jen Murphy is a corporate and tax attorney in Tampa, Florida, where she lives with her two daughters and two rescue German Shepherds. She is the author of two murder mystery suspense novels, *When She Runs . . .*, her debut novel, and *When He Watches*, her second in the Hallie Miller series. When she's not practicing law, she's working on her next novel or spending time with her many friends and family. You can read more about Jen and her books on her website:

www.JenMurphyBooks.com.

www.ingramcontent.com/pod-product-compliance
Lightning Source LLC
Chambersburg PA
CBHW021407310726
48971CB00005B/1242